Mary Wings began her writing career with *She Came Too Late*, winner of the *City Limits* Best Novel of the Year Award, and first published by The Women's Press in 1986. *She Came Too Late* launched the bestselling career of intrepid detective Emma Victor, and was followed by *She Came in a Flash* (The Women's Press, 1988) and *She Came by the Book* (The Women's Press, 1995).

Mary Wings has also written the bestselling gothic detective novel, *Divine Victim* (The Women's Press, 1992), which won a Lambda Literary Award in 1993. Her books have been translated into Dutch, German, Japanese and Spanish. Mary Wings has been nominated for the Raymond Chandler Fulbright in Mystery and Spy Fiction and lives in San Francisco, California with various cats.

Also by Mary Wings from The Women's Press:

She Came in a Flash (1988)
Divine Victim (1992)
She Came by the Book (1995)

MARY WINGS
SHE CAME IN A FLASH

THE SECOND EMMA VICTOR MYSTERY

First published in Great Britain by The Women's Press 1988
A member of the Namara Group
34 Great Sutton Street, London EC1V 0DX

Reprinted 1990, 1995

British Library Cataloguing in Publication Data

Wings, Mary, *1949–*
    She came in a flash
    I. Title
    813'.54 [F]

    ISBN 0-7043-4108-5

Typeset by Boldface Typesetting and Design, London EC1
Printed and bound in Great Britain by
BPC Paperbacks Ltd
A member of
The British Printing Company Ltd

For Rita Hendriks

One

My wits and I were about to part company. And we'd just found each other again. I was coming to an unpleasant consciousness, complete with bright lights and blasting music.

'C'mon, c'mon, c'mon, hunnah do da dance to da disco BEAT!'

I was afraid to open my eyes, but I couldn't close my ears. I was more afraid of a dance floor than a mediaeval dungeon. But after opening one eyelid and then the other I saw to my relief that I was only in a basement room painted white, not in a scene from *Saturday Night Fever*. Men in polyester suits were not going to ask me to shake my thing, and postpubescent hopefuls from Los Angeles were not going to torture me to death with bad acting. The innkeepers here had other methods.

'Shugga buggy, shugga buggy . . . '

I tried to think, but the disco beat left no vacancy in my head. I could feel a tender egg growing above my cheek. Someone had tried to remodel my face, and they hadn't stuck around to see the results.

They would have done better to work on the room. Only a tiny window far above me broke the monotony of the white concrete walls. A white chair and a white table stood in the middle of the cell. The legs descended through carefully cut out squares in the high-density foam floor covering. Apparently wall-to-wall carpeting wasn't enough.

'He-ey, yow-ow, shake a tail feather – to da disco BEAT!'

But maybe my wits had deserted me long before this. I had thought that California was going to be just another sunny spot in the universe to land on for a while. I tried to ignore all the myths as I packed my suitcase, but whatever else it is, California is a fantasy place in everyone's mind. And unfortunately, I had packed that fantasy along with all my unseasonable, dark, East Coast clothing. And my unfashionable dark, East Coast attitude. The real California was sharing. Sharing a drug hangover that I didn't volunteer for, and my unexpected lodgings.

1

My swollen face pounded. Thirst engendered a headache. I closed my eyes but it didn't help. Even the thought of light was blinding. It went on and on, the sound, the light, the seamless walls. It went on for something that could have been hours. Or even days. There was no escape, physically or mentally, because there was no escape sensually. Something was very familiar about the room, but it wasn't like any hotel room I'd ever checked into before. It was the white-painted furniture that struck a note in my head, along with – 'da *DISCO BEAT!*'

Suddenly with a pop of the speakers the music stopped. In the bright white stillness part of the wall started to move. It split open and in the dark space behind a figure was revealed. The glaring lights dimmed. I could feel my pupils expanding gratefully.

I wasn't expecting to be relieved at the human intrusion. I was normally a solitary being, but this time I was ready to do anything Californian to relieve the monotony. I was ready to relate, to share, to network. My vocabulary and I had parted ways too.

I watched the legs sauntering purposefully towards me. I was inexplicably happy when I should have been suspicious. The clean hair, falling on sport-shirted shoulders, the finely shaped fingers, every human detail was appreciated. My face still hurt, and I knew I wasn't as much fun to look at.

The figure entered the room, pushing a chair on wheels and closing the door quickly. The power of purpose, the grace of movement could have moved me to tears. The wheels squeaked and clattered as they hit a crack in the matting. They stopped when the chair was positioned behind the table. The beautiful interrogator sat in the chair and looked at me. I touched the sore spot around my eye. I took my hand away from my face. I tried to look steadily back at the eyes that were gazing at me. The aquiline nose dotted with a few brown freckles. A calm presence with graceful gestures. I was invited to sit down by a manicured hand, and I was happy to oblige.

'Name, Emma Victor?' said the calm voice.

'What?'

'Your name is Emma Victor?'

'Yes.'

'Good.' A smile. A nice, friendly-neighbourhood-interrogator smile complete with capped teeth. The dental work disappeared with the next question.

'And you drive a Plymouth four-door Satellite Custom Sedan?'

'Yes.' I squirmed but the wooden chair didn't squeak a glued dowel. I looked down at the point where the chair legs descended into the mat. They were bolted to the ground.

'Your car still has Massachusetts licence plates, correct?'

'Yes'.

The interrogator frowned and read off the clipboard, 'NB2607Q?'

'Yes,' I said. I realised I didn't know the number by heart. Saying 'yes' to every question the interrogator put to me was easy. Too easy. I leaned forward and tried to put my elbows on the table but couldn't quite reach it. The interrogator leaned back in the swivel chair. The mouth that had questioned me drew back under the plateau of an upper lip into something resembling a smile. The experience was familiar: the chair that didn't move, the elbows that couldn't reach the table. It wasn't anything I'd ever experienced myself. A bell rang, but only in my head.

'Hey, let's not dick around here,' I began, but anger dissolved into sweat and ran from under my arms to my waist. 'You're asking me questions you already know the answers to.'

'Why should that bother you?'

'That's the point,' I said, trying to match the smile and ease of the questioner and failing. 'It's supposed to make your job easier.' Another rivulet of sweat made a cold trail to the waist of my blue jeans. They'd taken my belt.

'You seem to know a lot, Miss, Miss Emma Victor.'

'I used to be in public relations.'

'I see.' The interrogator leaned forward over the table at me, not bothering to look mean and powerful. That was another trick. I was remembering a seminar called Management Techniques except we used to call it Mind Manipulation One. I'd burned some midnight oil in the library researching the darker developments of psychology and it hadn't helped my opinion of the human race.

'And I love your white sale furniture.' I tried laughing but it came out wheezing and I lost a drop of urine out of my urethra. 'Did your decorator pick it out of a West German sensory

3

deprivation outlet?' I let out a breath. The interrogator laughed and said nothing.

'That's how they broke Ulrike Meinhof. She hanged herself, right?' This earned me a smile and no comment.

'You've got pretty high hopes for me, don't you think?' I said, wondering if I would get my belt back for the purpose.

'And you, Miss Victor, have much too high an opinion of yourself. You think you know a lot, but you don't know that sometimes knowledge doesn't make any difference.' The interrogator grinned and leaned back further in the chair.

'Frankly, I'm tired of sharing,' I said.

'Too bad, because we'll be continuing,' said the interrogator. My keeper got up and marched towards the door. I was right behind, ready with a kick to the back of the knees when a cosy little black revolver in the hand stopped me. Then another smile, the hand dropped and I let my keeper walk out. The door closed, with only hairline cracks left to outline its existence.

'I want some goddamn water!' I cried. It was working already. I heard a switch and then I heard – *'to da disco BEAT!'*

I lay down on the floor and curled my arms around my chest. I closed my eyes against the light, I put my fingers in my ears against the noise. It was no way to run away. The thing was to escape where no escape was possible. The thing was not to focus on the immediate. Thirst, hunger, and the hot burning need to urinate.

I tried to place myself geographically outside the walls and the disco beat. Maybe the only way was to go back to the beach.

Calling it a beach was complimentary. It was littered with old tyres, tin cans and the rubble of forgotten real estate. But it hadn't been forgotten for long. The beach had figured big in a couple of people's plans. It just hadn't figured so good for Lana Flax. What was left of her was bloated and had washed up on the shore and been hauled away by the time I made the trip out there. Lana Flax, physics whizz kid and sister of my best friend. All that was left was the imprint in the sand, and the cops and technicians sifting for evidence.

I could still see the half-inch headline in the newspaper that had told me Lana Flax was dead. It had taken a while for my heart to stop pounding and by that time, I was already driving on the clogged asphalt ribbon to Moraga City, home of the Divine Vishnu Inspiration Commune. I was firmly in control, too much in control. I had wanted to see something that would show me that Lana was dead. Something that would prove that it wasn't a mistake. Didn't all those commune kiddies look alike anyway? But when I arrived I saw only squad cars, their cherries still spinning on the roofs. A few officers paced around and looked over their shoulders at the fence that cordoned off the beach terrain. It would be there, I was sure, the answer to the numbness I was feeling. Lana was down there. I had to find her. Then the tears would come.

'This area's off limits, ma'am.' The beefy white cop had a cold, blank face, too blank for anyone who'd been a cop for long.

'I knew the deceased. I'm a close friend of the family,' I said, and a lump began to rise in my throat.

'That's what they all say.' He jerked his head towards the Inspiration Commune, the brand-new redwood shingled complex behind us.

'But they all belong to the good fairy family. I don't.'

'Yeah?' he smiled. 'Well, why don't I take you down to Lieutenant Youtoga, by the beach.' We walked to the fence and through an open gate.

The big cop lumbered next to me quietly as we walked along the bluff; I handled the twists of the bald path better in tennis shoes. His holster slapped against his thigh. The lump had melted in my oesophagus. I saw the crowd of colourless men gathered by the shoreline, hunched over, their brown and black raincoats flaring out as they stood up. Crows looking for shiny pieces of treasure.

We walked towards them through scrub and aluminium cans, passing a truck cab tyre with pampas grass growing out of it, and on through the sand down to where a couple of men stood watching and waiting. One held a big ball of twine. A photographer was busy packing his wares into a black leather case, closing shop and clearing a space for the string men. They were down on their knees starting to make a fence around a series of depressions in the ground which must have marked the place Lana Flax's body had finally washed up on shore.

I suppressed an urge to jump over the string boundary and start digging, as if Lana, and not just her imprint, were lying there. Lana was probably on her way to a sliding cooler drawer in the county morgue.

'This way, ma'am, don't walk through the sand.' I looked around at the tiny stretch of beach which didn't look like it would cough up any more clues. It had been very carefully raked in lines which a few waves had started to melt. The policeman brought me to Lieutenant Youtoga, who was more concerned with string than family friends.

'She thinks she has some information, Lieutenant.'

Youtoga turned around, sized me and found me wanting.

'I don't have any information,' I said. 'I just knew Lana.' I took a deep breath, 'And I'm a friend of the family.'

'Forgive me if I'm a little too busy for condolences at the moment,' Youtoga grumbled and turned his back on me.

'I didn't know if you knew how to reach them.'

'Yes, they've been told. Now if you don't mind – ' He nudged me over as a slouch-shouldered string man came by. 'No, don't step over *there*! Downy, if you don't get this dame away from the scene you're going to find yourself on traffic duty inhaling exhaust fumes until your retirement.'

'Yes, sir, c'mon miss.' Officer Downy tugged on my arm and I let him guide me away. I looked back at Youtoga. The detective was standing on the sand looking slowly back and forth across the beach and then out to the water. His gaze followed a few shallow waves up on to the sand as far as the imprint of the body.

'C'mon, lady,' grumbled Officer Downy and he took my elbow and started to steer me. But I was pretending to be slow on my feet. Being a pest was helping me to feel the reality of Lana's death.

My eyes followed the sand and rubble up the bluff, where a big plate glass window stared out over the scene. I didn't see anyone moving behind the glass but the window was reflecting the sky too strongly to afford a view of curious faces that might be behind it. I looked back at the men on the beach. I knew what Youtoga was thinking. The newspapers had suggested it was the work of the jogging murderer. All the elements were there. There was always a trace of the hand that did the deed.

6

'C'mon, lady, I don't want to have to twist your arm,' Downy's voice carried the anxiety of a potential traffic cop.

'Sorry, I think I twisted my ankle.'

'Great, demoted by a damsel in distress,' Downy grumbled, letting me lean on his arm. I took a good look at the cameraman who was walking by, shouldering a big black leather case. 'Whadda we got here, Joe?' But I didn't get to hear Joe Youtoga's answer; Downy was half dragging me along the beach.

I took a last look at the tiny inlet filled with scummy grey suds, like dirty dishwater. I tried to imagine Lana Flax's body in the champagne kimono on the sand in the big rubbled lot that ran down from the Vishnu Divine Inspiration Commune. I got a last glance at the plate glass window affording the faithful a view before the services began. It was a view I'd seen from the inside. I'd had a nirvana nightmare flash there myself. It had begun with red roses and ended in a bottomless pit.

'Concrete blocks,' I heard a man say as we walked by a crouching pair hunched over a grey cube with a rope attached to it. He bent forward, plucking something long and invisible with a pair of tweezers from the jute rope and putting it in a little plastic bag. He squinted into the centre of a thick knot, and applied the points of the tweezers to it again.

'Must have been another one, we found another rope on her ankle.'

'Looks like someone was a little behind on their bowline knots.'

'This one held up pretty well, what with the tide and that big dropoff,' he pointed to the knot of rope on the concrete block. They went on discussing death knots they had known and untied, buried in putrified flesh from the sea and fresh necks in gaol cells.

Suddenly it began to hit me. The ropes which must have sunk into Lana's flesh made a connection which turned my stomach and brought tears to my eyes. My breakfast was somersaulting and I did my best to hold on to it all the way back through the wasteland. Lana Flax was dead. And all that was left was the imprint in the sand and the cops and the technicians working their side of the evidence.

Downy took my address and phone number and I limped back to

7

the Plymouth and drove home. After three stoplights I had started to cry.

'Da disco BEAT!' I was back in the little white cell. My fantasy was spent, and I was invaded by light and sound. Only the tears were mine.

I looked up at the high window again. It was about nine feet from the floor. Painted black from the outside, a certain reflection of light made me think that it was wire fortified glass, but maybe it was just the refracted light of sunrise. Or sunset. I ran to the wall and crouched and sprang. But the window was too high and my hips were too heavy these days.

Hours passed, maybe. Maybe many hours. All in succession at least. The light didn't get any brighter or dimmer. This wasn't what I thought California would be like.

Finally I lay down upon the mat. Sleep was impossible. The cell wasn't equipped with blankets, but I made a warm shield around my body with my mind. I went back to the beginning, the very beginning. The reason why I'd moved to California in the first place. The story began to take hold. I could hear the hum of the freeways in my mind, mingled with the smell of eucalyptus. And a wrenching sadness in my heart.

Two

'We got problems. Two of them. You should call Roseanna to get complete notes of the meeting.' Maya leaned forward and a frown ran across her broad forehead. We were sitting on her stuffed sofa in the overfurnished living room of her chicken farm.

'I'm really getting worried,' she continued. 'Time is running out. The concert is just two days away. All this is ruining my sleep. I wouldn't mind if I wasn't in love and hoping for a phone call all evening.'

'Don't worry, she'll call.' They always did call Maya; she picked them that way. 'Now what are the problems?' I asked gently.

Maya nervously smoothed her hair, the same long brown folk-singer's hair from 1969. She had called me four months earlier, when I still lived in Boston, wanting me to do publicity for the Women's Benefit Concert they were organising. The African Band Aid Concert had been such a success a group of San Francisco Bay Area women had put together a benefit concert against domestic desperation, as we called it. Sulky male journalists who found the Band Aid concert better copy called it Menstrual Pad. After a while we called it that too.

We had twenty solid acts, lots of hard-working women, and Nebraska Storm, a superpunk superstar who was going to be our big draw. The proceeds would go to the Battered Women's Shelter, the Women's Crisis Line and a lobbying fund for daycare centres. Now Maya was coming with some potential bad news.

'Point one. A five thousand dollar cheque has bounced,' she said. 'It was written by the Women's Freedom Foundation which nobody has ever heard of. They have an account at the same branch we do, but the bank won't give us any information. We can't seem to get a handle on them. It could be a lot of things.'

'Now it's also a negative five thousand bucks.'

'Right. It's strange to get such a big donation which bounces and then we can't seem to find out about the sponsor. And I'm just worried they're using the concert, that's all. Screw the five grand, I don't want them making any disruption.'

'You're thinking it's fetus fanatics?'

'We've got booths from everything from Planned Parenthood to Bay Area Transsexuals out there. And the right wing is into acting out these days. I don't want any problems and I don't want to have to send out the ball breakers.' Maya traced a finger along the edge of a lace antimacassar on the arm of the sofa. Her T-shirt had chicken shit on it.

'I'll take care of it. Everything will be okay.'

'Yeah, you're right.' Maya looked at me with the sudden warm admiration that never failed to make me feel wise. It was the caretaker hook that made being her agent a feel good proposition.

When she sang I could almost fall in love with her. When she closed her mouth the feeling would disappear. Maya and I were employer and employee, and good friends.

'On top of all that we've got a competition for political immediacy with the Latin American Committee. Of course we're giving them some stage time but it's too bad they're playing the righteousness edge. There's talk of the CIA starting some kind of psycho warriors course in the county, you know, revamping the villagers for freedom. I just got off the phone with the Latin American Liberation Supporters. They think their phones are tapped, their donations have dried up and they would like to make me just as unhappy about it as they are.' She sighed.

'Looks like they're doing a good job.'

'Oh Emma, sometimes I miss the old days when we were together. I mean when you were together, keeping me together.'

Years ago I'd been Maya's press agent and we'd always kept in touch. Now I was doing publicity again for the big woman with the bigger voice. She'd turned out to be a good friend. She said my presence always reassured her and that I was great with details. She was probably right about the details.

'Sometimes I just can't take the infighting any more,' Maya said. 'Well, on with the show. The story is,' she continued, 'the Women's Freedom Foundation has an unlisted phone number and our own bank won't even give it to us. The cheque is signed by a Bu Mper Lee, if you can feature that for a name. She's unlisted too.' A Rhode Island Red strutted by in front of the window. 'The long and short of it is, would you find out the story on this Women's Freedom Foundation thing? Either get them out or get our five thousand bucks. I know you've got the nerve and diplomacy to do it right.'

'And what's point two on my list?'

'We haven't got our copy of the signed contract back from Nebraska Storm. I want you to get it.'

'Maya, you'll have to twist my arm.' Nebraska Storm. Our big draw, the high card of the concert. We had it on paper that the former punk princess would open her throat for two short sets, but she had the only signed copy. It was one more detail to be nervous about, but maybe it would turn out to be a choice chore. Or maybe not. I hoped Nebraska wouldn't be problematic for the concert. We had no recent photographs and no one had heard her latest tunes. The last time she'd been seen in public was a year ago and all her eight by ten glossies told why. In every portrait she wore opaque dark glasses; presumably her dilated pupils would reflect the glare of any camera flashbulb.

And then there was the Edwin Anvil affair. The gifted young percussionist had just joined Nebraska's East Coast tour when he overdosed. It seemed that Nebraska had held the needle. Concerts were cancelled and then Nebraska was acquitted.

But maybe she wasn't guilt free. Rumour had it she'd gone bonkers, her body riddled with drugs which she squirted continuously into her arms, and eventually she'd fallen apart at the perforated edges. Her career came to a complete stop. After that no one heard anything. But the rock and roll rags don't comment if a star disappears down the deep throat of some luxurious snake pit. Not until the stars become born-again anti-drug prophets.

'Good luck.' Maya wrote down something on a piece of paper and handed it to me. 'You can try reaching her at this number. I was really happy to volunteer you for this, Emma. You look like you could use a little excitement.'

'Well, I'm awfully busy moving into my villa and brushing up on my backhand,' I said.

I wasn't lying. When Maya had called me to suggest moving to California it took me about five minutes before I started wondering which closet had the suitcases. When she called back to say that she knew of a Spanish stucco bungalow set off the street with a sunny deck and low rent, I started mentally packing boxes. When she reminded me that the public tennis courts were free and cited the annual rainfall statistics for the last three years I was already folding blouses. And Maya was glad to have me in California. She enjoyed worrying about me too. When I arrived we had a big barbecue at her place. It was a nice group of co-workers who were shy, shrewd, over-confident, polished and underdressed. I had a great time.

'You look like you could use a detonator for your personal life,' she said. She leaned back and crossed one knee over the other, making little circles in the air with a shit-encrusted boot.

'My personal life is fine. And it's mine.'

'Yeah, like my personal life isn't yours? I know you well enough to see the restlessness at the edges. Try Nebraska Storm for those hard-to-get places. I remember how you used to go for that teeny-bopper in Boston with the safety pin in her cheek.'

'She just did that at parties.'

'Well, Nebraska Storm might be appropriate in your approach to middle age.'

'I wouldn't take that from anybody but you, Maya. But I'll take Nebraska's phone number, thank you. I hope you'll get some vicarious pleasure out of this.'

'Oh, maybe I'm just longing for my former fans to look *me* up and idolise me, in spare moments away from the chickens. Here's the number, and the address, if all else fails.'

I found myself wishing that all else would fail. Maya was right; I was ripe for adventure.

'And Emma . . . I sure am glad you moved to California.'

I was too. I hardly had to consider that moving was a geographic cure for a broken heart. The broken heart I'd arranged myself, with the help of a secretive, workaholic physician in Boston. I spent so much time figuring out that her secrets weren't so bad I hardly noticed that she wasn't around for the climax. The denouement was better spent in California.

'And now, I'm going to go and feed chickens,' Maya announced, giving me a quick hug and pausing when our hips touched. Maya always paused like that when she hugged you. It was her way of saying you were special to her. The problem was she did it with everyone. At least I had never interpreted it as an offer and hadn't had to suffer rejection at the touching hip bones of Maya Russgay. Others weren't so lucky.

She opened the door and stepped out, scattering a group of nervous Barred Plymouth Rock hens. Maya Russgay, the singer with the guitar, who had led thousands from long playing records into the streets when we all saw revolution around the corner, if not in our daily lives. She crossed the driveway, and a flock of fat Jersey Giants parted for her big boots and regrouped in her wake, scratching and pecking in the dry dirt.

I sat a moment looking at the valley. I thought about a gay man I knew who worked for what used to be the Ma Bell phone company. He might help me with the phone number of the Women's Freedom Foundation. I went out into the beautiful California weather and shut myself in the sheet-metal box where I spent most of my Californian life, a beige 1973 Plymouth Satellite Custom Sedan. I put the key in the ignition and the engine slowly turned over.

Maya appeared from a barn, hauling a sack of organic starter feed. 'Thanks for checking out this Women's Freedom Foundation thing, Emma,' she blew me a kiss.

'I'm not doing it for you,' I said.

'I know, you have a true revolutionary soul, Emma.'

I let that one go. We both knew about my revolutionary soul. It had been relativised away. What was left over was an inclination to work on projects that went in the right direction, and if a few thrills came with the territory, that was okay too. It was time to clean up a few loose ends. Fetus fanatics and the verbal agreements of rock stars. I didn't know then what a dirty job it would be.

Three

I could have gone through menopause waiting to get Nebraska Storm's manager on the phone. After twenty calls I'd gotten no further than her press agent's secretary who didn't know anything about the Women's Benefit Concert or a signed contract. I began to wonder if Nebraska Storm still existed.

The news of Nebraska's drug débâcle had made me sad. I had liked that green mohawk and the way her voice could shriek as if a large dragon were being pulled from her oesophagus and released in the auditorium. We had let that dragon enter us until

13

Nebraska brought us down with a whisper. We gave up our souls to the music that came from Nebraska's diaphragm, lungs and throat. But maybe we were all just vicariously celebrating the drugs which coursed through her system, turning her into a nightmare goddess. It had been a nightmare that her drummer, Edwin Anvil, had never awakened from.

When I got tired of calling Nebraska's answering service I did a little research in the rock and roll rags. I found out that Nebraska had washed up on the surface of newsprint one last time four months ago. It was a short story about drug rehabilitation and therapy in Taos, New Mexico. I hoped she was on the up; it was time to find out, in person.

So I pulled the address out of my pocket, straightened up newspapers and files littering the walnut table in my dining room, and left the little bungalow. On the way out soft Japanese maple leaves brushed my arms. I looked in the mailbox but it was empty.

I checked a map and gunned the Plymouth up the hills to a quiet deserted street. I found the number on a wrought-iron gate and parked. I listened to the doves. I looked around at the Californian horticulture and tried not to think about how sporty murderers were in the American West.

A little gravel fell down the incline and bounced to the edge of my toes. It was a hot, still day and the eucalyptus trees didn't move a limb or drop a button. That was why it was so easy to hear the purr of the Porsche engine and the wide Gatorback radial tyres crunching the gravel. That was also why she had all the windows up. Air conditioning. I positioned myself between two massive wrought-iron peonies on either side of the gate. A remote buzzer was pressed, a chain pulled the gates apart on a track and the Porsche came into sight.

I gave her just enough room to get the car past the gates and then I moved out in front of the sharknose hood. I hoped my imitation Ray Ban sunglasses and knife-pleated tuxedo shirt would make a good impression. The vehicle stopped. It was a pity that the two white women behind the smoked windshield couldn't appreciate my plaid tennis shoes from where they sat.

The driver wore wrap-around shades and the woman sitting next to her sure looked like Nebraska with a hat on. The woman in the

14

wrap-arounds didn't have a lot of time to be friendly. She beeped the horn which sounded as if it drew a lot of power from the batteries; it didn't sing any songs for me but could have caused some inner ear problems.

I leaned over on the hood, hoping the driver wasn't in the mood for inflicting massive internal injuries. She wasn't. An automatic window rolled down.

'Would you get out of the way, please?'

'Hi, I'm Emma Victor. I'm leaning on the front of your car because it really seems to be the only way to get in touch with you folks.' I smiled. The woman I hoped was Nebraska was holding a notebook in her hand. 'Honestly, I don't want to cause myself injury. I'm on the organising committee of the Women's Benefit Concert. You know, Menstrual Pad? Next week Nebraska is honouring us with a couple of sets.'

'Yes. So?'

'You neglected to return our contract.'

'What? Oh, wait a second.' Wrap-arounds reached down and pulled a thick, bound datebook out of a pocket in the door. She split it open where a yellow ribbon landed between two pages. I moved around the side of the car and leaned on the moulded metallic body.

'Contract. Right. You should have gotten it back last week. George must have forgotten to send it.' She put a gold ballpoint pen on the paper and scribbled something. Then she put the car in gear and lifted her foot off the brake pedal. I felt the warm sheet metal slide under my shirt. It was time to let go of the car, but I wasn't in the mood. The concert was too important and I was getting too nervous about it. The car slid by and my elbow landed in the corner of the window.

'Is there anything else I can do for you?' said the driver, pressing a gold-sandalled foot on the brake pedal again.

'I was just dying to see Nebraska in person.'

'So you thought you'd hang on to the car?'

'Yes.'

'Okay,' Wrap-arounds said, with a sigh reserved for the pesky public – nerds who need to be humoured. 'Let me introduce you to her.' She whispered something across the seat. Nebraska leaned forward and stuck a hand out over the high-held tits of the driver.

It was hard to believe it was Nebraska Storm sitting there. She had metamorphosised since her punked-out-edge city days. Gone was the pasty white skin, translucent and lightly green under a spiked mohawk. Gone were the spindly arms which had offered their veins to the needle. The mouth that had collected a few festering sores visible in her last public photo was smooth and cherry red. It spoke to me.

'Nice to meet you, Emma.' She gave me a limp fish and retreated. Her complexion was good and normal-size pupils had looked at me. She was wearing an enormous turban of creamy gauze and enough folk-art jewellery to endow a museum. An elaborate knotted necklace circled her neck and ended in a step-cut purple amethyst resting in the deep cavity of her collarbone. From the looks of her transportation it wasn't lack of money that had kept Nebraska underfed.

She went back to her reading material, which looked like musical notes punctuating a five-line staff.

'And I'm Portia Fronday. Glad to meet you,' said the driver. Portia was dressed in a chiced up sheepherder's robe that kept slipping off her shoulder. No straps. Either the woman, in her late forties, had the highest tits I'd ever seen or she was wearing a strapless bra in eighty-degree heat. Both bad signs.

'I'm sorry that you didn't get the contract,' she said. 'Nebraska's cutting her new album and we're really busy. Details have been escaping us.' A phone rang in the car and she picked up a receiver from a matched-grain walnut dashboard. 'Hmm. Yes. Okay.' She hung up and turned to me. 'We've really got to be going now. That was the producer and we're on studio time already. And don't worry about the concert. Nebraska will be there for the sound check. You gals are really lucky. This will be the premiere of her new album.'

'Really?'

'Yes, but don't put that on the poster, please.'

'You mean, let's not confuse Nebraska's Real Career with Good Works.'

'Put it any way you like.'

I found myself bending my knees to peer into the car at

Nebraska. She was chewing her thumbnail and looking out of the window, away from me. Big deal.

'Nebraska is really glad to be doing this concert.' Portia stuck a henna-rinsed head out. 'She stands firmly behind projects which help women and is glad to donate her time to you ladies. Nice to meet you . . . ' She paused.

'Emma.'

'Right, Emma. Goodbye.' She pulled her head back in and the smoked-glass window slid up from the felt-lined slot in the door. Goodbye Nebraska, I thought. See you next week on stage. I hope you haven't had a vocal chord operation or grown any nodes in the meantime. At least you look like you can still stand up.

I looked at the funny kicked-in backside of the Porsche. Somehow aerodynamics are not the same as aesthetics. Unless you're Nebraska Storm. I wondered if she still had the green mohawk under the turban. After they drove away a little shower of eucalyptus buttons fell on my head, but that was just the beginning. A lot more was going to fall on my head after that.

Four

I drove home over the freeway, through the beginnings of Friday traffic jams, off the ramp and past the public tennis courts, one of which was vacant. I saw a good future for myself in this fact, even though my mailbox was still empty.

Japanese maple leaves petted me soothingly on my way up the walk to my new home. The bungalow was beautiful, with small but well-proportioned rooms, cool and sunny spaces and a kitchen with built-in flour bins, a bread drawer and a pantry. I walked in and called the velvet-throated man who worked nights for a phone company.

Charles was going to pick up his cheque at noon and said that he'd call me back with the number of the Women's Freedom Foundation or Bu Mper Lee or both. When he called he had three numbers.

'It's not really unlisted, Emma. As usual, you just don't know where to look, girl. The Women's Freedom Foundation is listed under the Divine Vishnu Inspiration Commune. I've got their financial office, the number of Ananda House, where your Bu Mper officially resides, and the main switchboard for information and reservations. Take your pick.'

'Give me all of them. So do you know where this place is?'

'But do I ever know where the Women's Freedom Foundation is! It's paradise in Moraga City.'

'Moraga City? Industrial ghetto?'

'That's right. Across the tracks and jumped the tracks. There's a big crowd of women on the corner of Beach and Eighth every night at six waiting to get in. They all wear yellow clothes. It's a trip! You'd really go for it, Emma.'

'Give me a break.'

'Don't you know about the Divine Vishnus? Dinner at six, meditation at seven and the Kama Sutra at eight.'

'Just so long as they're good for five grand.'

'Maybe it would get your mind off Boston.'

'Leave it alone, Charles. Ever since I've moved here you've taken a suspicious interest in my non-existent sex life.'

'Sorry Emma. A non-existent sex life *is* suspicious. Besides, we boys need to take lessons from our gay sisters. Safe sex is making me an honorary lesbian – doing that crazy hand jive.'

'Well this lesbian is waking up alone and liking it. I'm staying honourable.'

'And boring.'

'Thanks, Charles. I need that these days, I really do.'

'Well, don't do anything I used to do,' he warned.

'I can't.'

As I broke the connection, pushing the button down, the phone rang immediately, as if it didn't want to be alone.

'Emma – glad I could reach you,' said Maya's voice. 'I've called all day and you weren't home. What's with the Storm contract?'

'They assured me it was an oversight and mouthed their further

18

good intentions. Nebraska's agent didn't have the most pleasant mouth, and Nebraska's mouth was hiding behind her fist when I saw them.'

'You saw her? How'd she look?'

'Healthy and converted to folk-art fashion.'

'Must be an improvement over that leopard-pelt corset with the prehistoric hairdo.'

'Not really. I liked her more hard edged.'

'How would you like to escort her to the concert?'

'What?'

'I talked to Roseanna about it. We want you to drive Storm to the concert. Good luck. She's got a sense of timing like Marilyn Monroe. Her idea of a good audience is thirteen thousand waiting for forty minutes. I don't want the crowd to boil over in the heat. It's happened before. You go to her house at seven and get her in the car and on stage on time. We're offering it as a favour.'

'Do I get to drive the Porsche?'

'I doubt it. You may get to twist an arm.'

'Or set all her clocks ahead.'

'Good luck,' Maya said again, and we hung up. Escorting Nebraska Storm was making me feel better about tracking down religious freaks. I couldn't really complain; California was turning out to be one big colourful carnival. Loud, full of fast-moving machines and honey-toned hawkers. It was just what the heart specialist ordered.

I called the first number Charles had given me. It was the Divine Vishnu's Financial Office all right. That's the way a character named Lailieka answered the phone; but when I asked for Bu Mper, pronouncing it 'Boo Mumper', like a children's disease with its own dialogue, I must have missed the secret password. She put me on hold long enough to put me in my place. 'Hello,' said a deep female voice finally.

'Hi, is this Bu Mper?'

'Yes.' Sigh. Was I pronouncing her name right?

'I'm Emma Victor from the Women's Concert Steering Committee.'

'Emmm-hmmm. Yes?' Her voice had all the comforting tones of an amplified wood rasp. I heard papers shuffle.

'Well, your cheque for five thousand dollars bounced yesterday.'

'*What?*' More paper shuffling.

'Your cheque for five thousand dollars – '

'That *can't* be!' A notebook ringbinder snapped shut. 'Wait a minute.' A keyboard and two beeps. 'No, it's okay,' she seemed to say as much to herself as to me.

'What do you mean, it's okay?'

'The money's in the bank. Just call them if you want.'

'Great. Actually, Ms Lee, I was wondering if we might be able to meet just for a few minutes.'

'Well, I'm really busy.' A typewriter clacked behind her words.

'I think it's important. We want to have some personal contact with our sponsors before we put their name on the programme and thank them formally.'

'Emm-hmmm. Sure.' A buzzer sounded. Then silence.

'Are you there?'

'Oh shit, the deposit boxes are closed for lunch. And it's Friday too. Well, I guess I have time in between. Meet me at the Palace. Twelve thirty?'

'I'll be there.'

I hung up and listened to the hum of the freeway through the open dining room window. Their cheque signer was smart to go eat on the cool waterfront. I hoped she didn't pass any bad cheques at lunch; the Palace was a real home of cool interior, cool food and the cold shoulder. They wouldn't think twice about calling a cop on a dine and dash.

It took me twenty minutes through late lunch traffic to get to the waterfront eatery sporting perforated sheet-metal doors and handles big as shoeboxes in satin stainless steel. It was speaking architectural language and it wasn't a dockworker kind of lunch-box any more. I struggled with one of the doors and won. The Palace had probably not looked much different on paper from the way it did in real life. The designers were crazy about right angles and had probably given a platoon of welders a few months' employment. All the surfaces were covered with materials as hard as tooth enamel. Stainless steel frames supported smoked glass slabs for tables, diners perched themselves on tubular chrome chairs, leaning over the slim pickings of nouvelle cuisine lit by halogen lamps. It looked like an intensive care unit for food.

A maître d' stood behind a Tennessee marble reception pulpit and raised his eyebrows at me. He smiled.

'I have an appointment with Bu Mper Lee,' I said, wondering if he knew how to pronounce it. He did.

'You mean Boo Ma-*Per*.' He emphasised the last syllable. 'Ms Lee is seated by the window there.' He pointed with a stainless steel fountain pen towards a plate glass window and a cloud of screaming red hair.

'Thanks,' I said, and trotted over the shiny floor towards the table where a big-boned woman sat under the flaming mane. She was drinking tea and reading some loose papers, and she didn't notice me until I was standing next to her. I was looking down at the fuzzy layers of bright curling hair trying to get a glimpse of scalp. A pleasant, slightly distracted face rolled up at me, two aquamarine eyes took me in carefully, and two large hands started shoving papers quickly into the leather pouch by her elbow.

'Oh, hello!' said a broad thin mouth with big, white, slightly protruding teeth. She held out one of the hands that had stopped fussing with the papers, and I sat down in the chrome chair across from her.

'I'm Bu Mper,' she said in the same raspy tones as on the phone. She leaned forward and her large breasts in crushed silk brushed the edge of the table.

'That's just how the waiter pronounced it too.'

'Oh, call me Bumper. Most people do. And you are Emma Victor. Glad to meet you.' She picked up a leather file, tilted it towards her and zipped it shut in one fast motion.

'Would you like some tea?' she asked. I nodded and she put the folder on her lap and poured me a thimbleful from an ebony and chrome teapot.

'Nice to meet you,' I said. I was surprised to feel that I meant it. I picked up the tiny teacup and sipped a flowery-tasting liquid that stayed on the light side of sweetness. It wasn't bad either. I poured myself another few hits. 'And nice tea.' Bumper slipped the leather portfolio on to the floor, where it stood on its spine between her feet.

'I always come here after my noon jog. Haven't you ever been here before?'

'No. I don't lunch out often.'

'Oh, the food is really wonderfully prepared. Just the right sauces, and just the right portions.' She winked and indicated her waistline in the crushed lemon silk body suit. Then she plucked a menu from the plexiglass holder. 'Look, they have a fresh pasta salad with salmon. And a lamb cutlet with quince jelly, if you're not veggie.' Being in a restaurant seemed to make her much friendlier than on the phone. And much more talkative. 'Look here, peperonata with basil and peeled tomatoes. You know,' she leaned forward even farther, her bushy hair remaining behind her shoulders, 'they take such *care* with the ingredients.'

'Yes, except sometimes I feel like eating food and not someone's accomplishment,' I said. But she was still reading the menu as if she could almost put that in her mouth. The waiter appeared and carefully wrote down our orders, resting his pad against a black plastic apron. I looked out of the plate glass window at Alcatraz Island while Bumper ordered, and Bumper looked at me while I ordered.

'So, Emma. What's on your mind?' her deep voice rumbled, and I wasn't even irritated with her too-familiar tone in using my first name.

'Well, the Women's Freedom Foundation is a little hard to get a handle on.'

'What do you mean?' She drew her lips over the big teeth.

'It seems you folks aren't listed under the Women's Freedom Foundation.'

Bumper smiled. 'Are you worried about the WFF? We have a storefront where we have nightly meditations for women, that's all. It's one way we can serve the interests of the women's community. We don't need a phone. Women know where to find us if they want to.'

'You must admit, the name sounds pretty Moral Majority.'

She laughed and crinkled two small aquamarine eyes at me.

'I didn't think it was so funny.'

'Oh you would if you knew. Some people would say our family makes the gay baths look like *Father Knows Best*.'

'From what I hear these days the gay baths do look like *Father Knows Best*,' I said, but Bumper was busy brushing the left hand side of her mane over her shoulder. Long strands of red hair slid off her silk shoulders.

'The name was a last minute late night meeting disinspiration,' she explained. 'We had to sign the incorporation papers that night. Someone came up with something about lotuses and somebody else said that sounded like footbinding. It was getting to be an all night discussion and we got tired so the words women and freedom got stuck together with foundation because we were trying to get a tax-deductable status.'

'And . . . ?'

'No go. Tax deductions are pretty hard to come by these days. The government is really coming down on alternative religions. Especially ones that run businesses.'

'So that's where the Women's Concert comes in?'

'Exactly. We're in need of tax shelters. I heard about the Women's Benefit Concert and thought it had merit. Why give money to museums when humanitarian services are going down the tube?' she explained. Just then our soup arrived. Large enamel bowls of miso broth were placed before us with perfect crescent cut leeks floating on the surface. Bumper wiped off her soup spoon with a napkin and we both started sipping.

'I see. So your donation is just a way of getting a tax write-off. But isn't this Women's Freedom thing associated with – '

'Yes, with the Divine Vishnu Inspiration Commune. Go ahead and laugh,' she said.

'I think I will.' I allowed myself a grin that got out of control. Bumper was not turning out to be what I expected.

'My parents nearly died when I joined,' she continued. 'My dad said I was regressing and adopting a Thai Santa Claus as my new father figure. He's a shrink. Beverly Hills.' She laughed, slowly raising the teacup to her wide mouth and sipping. 'And he was right,' she tilted her head back and opened her mouth, smiling at some delicious memory. Dionysian daughter revenges Freudian father.

'But now they're actually glad. Can you believe it? Santa Claus has gotten me to take on more responsibility than any biological fathering or Ivy League education ever did.'

'That's what people say about the army too.'

'But I'm not making missiles. I'm making love. And money.'

'Sounds too good to be true. Is it?'

'You'd better believe it. What do you think people can accomplish if they give up their individual goals and create something together? Anything. Almost anything is possible. And it can be true for anyone, if you are brave enough to surrender. The first beginnings of joy and trust.'

'Sounds like a bank.'

'It's a gold mine,' she laughed, putting the teacup down and dabbing at a little drip of tea on the saucer with her linen napkin. 'I know. I do the books.'

'Why the Women's Freedom Foundation? I mean, what does Vishnu's philosophy have to do with women?'

'Well, Emma, if you're a feminist you should know. Our whole culture is left hemisphere biased.'

'Run that by me again?'

'Left hemisphere – linear, scientific, absolutist. Masculine. Aggressive.'

'Don't go any further. I'm still looking forward to my lunch.'

'And the right hand side' – she raised a hand and tilted it from the wrist, towards Alcatraz – 'the other side of the coin has been ignored. I don't need to tell you that.'

'It seems like in certain areas you don't need to tell me anything.'

'Intuitive, receptive, feminine . . . ' her fingers extended one by one towards the window and the prison outside.

'But who does the dishes?'

'We all do, Emma. Don't go making up stories in your head. We're not talking either/or – this is real integrated energy. And we're not just talking about it either, we're doing it.' She smiled, her big teeth like white triangles, trying to escape her mouth.

'You're quite a saleswoman. I guess this is where I'm supposed to sign up. But how come I haven't heard more about you Vishnus? In one Californian month I've run into Moonies peddling flowers, Krishnas peddling records, Bhagwans peddling ecology and Jehovahs peddling the apocalypse. How could I have missed someone peddling paradise?'

'We aren't actively engaged in increasing our membership. We don't need to be. Just to stand in Vishnu's presence is enough. Once you experience that, you know you don't need to advertise. You've arrived at the ranks of the privileged.'

'So Vishnu's the key. What's he like anyway?'

'New members come to him, he doesn't go to them,' she confirmed in a schoolmarmish way that I was to become unfortunately familiar with. 'He doesn't need you, Emma. But you might need him.' Her lips curled over her big teeth and her mouth closed with effort and finality. I hoped the lecture was finished, but I wasn't that lucky. I didn't need any divine inspiration, but I did need more of the miso soup and I knew that there weren't going to be any refills.

'Look at the sixties and communal living,' she went on. 'Those were the days of adventure, and discovery of group possibilities. The eighties seems to be about single mothers on welfare who can't earn any money and men in bachelor pads with quadraphonic sound lusting over pornography.'

'And you've got a corner on squeaky clean sex that stays exciting?'

'People need meaningful relationships,' she continued. 'I'm not a cynic and I don't want to give up certain dreams. I've found joy in the discovery that I don't have to. I'm not trying to convert you, Emma. I just want to share how happy I am.' She laid her last card on the table and I ate a last leek out of the miso soup.

'And *I* just want to make sure that your involvement in the concert is on the level,' I said.

'Listen, I make the decisions about donations. The Women's Benefit Concert was recommended to me by our governing council. I didn't see any reason against it. Don't worry, we're not going to try and take over your benefit.'

'It would be pretty hard to, as you say, take over.'

'To tell you the truth, Emma, I'm always surprised at what strong reactions people have to our movement. I can hardly talk frankly to anyone outside our organisation. It's as if people endow us with greater powers than we have. We don't proselytise and nobody can force someone to have a unifying group experience. Fears tell a lot about a person, about a culture. I'm not the

25

daughter of a shrink for nothing.'

'I think I know what you mean.'

'What are people so afraid of anyway?' She shrugged and the red curly mane ascended and descended with her shoulders. 'Forbidden attraction?' she suggested.

'Like lesbianism,' I offered. I watched Bumper's face, but it didn't try to rearrange itself. She looked at me and carried on smiling.

'Denied attraction makes people hostile, even if they're melting in the best places,' she confirmed.

'What's your organisation's policy on homosexuality anyway?' I asked.

'We only have a policy about pleasure. The rest is finding your own compatible energy partners.'

'Unifying group experience?'

'If it feels good, do it.'

'Wearing yellow clothes seems a little fanatically unifying to me.'

Bumper smiled and put her elbows on the table. She lifted the enamel bowl of miso soup and drained it without spilling a drop. She raised her napkin and touched it to her lips. 'How is it any different to nuns going into a convent? They wear habits, have for centuries. Or what about the old feminist flannel shirt and blue jean uniform?'

'That's not the same.'

'Why not? It's all external identification with principle.'

'We never claimed that unshaven legs gave us special vibrations.'

'Are you sure about that?' Bumper's smile showed white sharp incisors parted by her big front teeth.

'Okay. I don't want to underestimate symbolism.'

'Neither do we. We just respect it more than you do.'

'Undoubtedly.' We looked at each other and I saw a pleasant face and eyes that could meet mine directly. I sort of liked Bumper Lee; if I had met her anywhere else, in any other colour, I wouldn't have taken her for a New Age Clubwoman.

Our salads came. Bumper had chosen the pasta, a small number of curled shells scattered over her plate with a few scraps of see-through salmon and a grilled pepper next to it. I looked down at a perfect specimen of radicchio lettuce, four circles of cucumber bisected by a carrot and a diced courgette. The brightly coloured shapes were sprinkled with blue cheese. I speared a few pieces of the carefully prepared vegetables and crunched them in my mouth. It was like eating jewellery. We ate in silence. Bumper's joy and the need to share it was fortunately outweighed by her appetite.

'So what's working on the Women's Benefit Concert like?'

'Hard work, nice people, high hopes. Maybe some good prospects for fund raising.'

'Sounds all right to me. What's your part in it?'

'I do the PR for Maya Russgay. When I'm unlucky I spend all day trying to get hold of Nebraska Storm and if I'm lucky I get to drive her Porsche to the concert on Sunday. If we're all really lucky she'll get there on time.'

'Sounds pretty exciting,' she said slowly, her eyebrows going up and down. Someone had plucked them recently.

'I probably won't get to drive her Porsche,' I said. Bumper was chewing slowly and she wasn't looking too sympathetic. Maybe her ambitions had included Porsche chauffeur before she turned the steering wheel over to the guru. It was nice to know that the woman could include some regrets in her otherwise flawless repertoire. Our plates were emptying fast when our black-plastic-coated waiter appeared with a telephone. He placed it carefully in front of Bumper on the glass table with something between a curtsy and a bow and walked away.

'Sorry,' Bumper said to me, took the receiver and said, 'Yes, yes, no, no' into it in a light growl. Then she hung up. 'I've got to get back to work,' she apologised, but she wasn't really sorry. We'd both finished our meagre meal. She looked at her watch. 'Oh shit, gotta run to the bank. It was nice to meet you Emma. I always enjoy meeting women who are also involved in good work. You may not realise it, but our hearts are a little bit in the same place,' she said with a kind of intonation that made me think that our hands had been in the same kinds of places too.

She grinned and looked into my eyes and paused for a moment to let the red hair, crinkly eyes, big white teeth and happiness sink in. They didn't sink that far, but retained a kind of superficial

27

excitement. California was all right with me.

She reached down to pick up the leather portfolio, parting her knees to get it. She'd been holding it between her feet the whole lunch; it had to be the most guarded purse since the first twelve year old transported her first Kotex to school on the bus. Bumper tucked it under her elbow and stood up. I couldn't help gasping. She must have been six foot two in high top gymshoes. And she wasn't just long; the silk suit pulled at her hips slightly and a belt cinched her ample waistline. She was enormous and she was a knockout.

Bumper crinkled her small blue eyes at me and pumped my hand for a minute. 'If you have any more questions, don't hesitate to call.'

'I won't.'

But it wasn't questions I wanted to ask Bumper Lee, although I was afraid the guru would always be along for the ride. Bumper put her smile and big teeth away and turned, a long yellow shape topped with red hair, like the head of a match, striding across a polished floor. People turned in their chrome chairs and looked. The maître d' nodded goodbye at her and Bumper parted the heavy entry doors with the flick of a wrist. I looked down at the remains of a carrot with a little bit of blue cheese clinging to it. A piece of paper had been slid under my plate and another non-adventure was at an end. I'd found out something about the kind of people that follow a guy named Vishnu, and chalked up a twenty dollar lunch bill on a nearly empty stomach. None of it made me feel any better.

Five

Even the summer heat couldn't penetrate the cool Bay breezes or the feeling that I was on a marvellous carnival ride, spinning over loop ramps and zooming on to overpasses. I was anxious to call Maya but I didn't want to do it in a urinal masquerading as a phone booth. It was easier to stay on the freeway and aim towards home.

Both tennis courts were empty and I'd gotten a letter, not postmarked Boston. It was from an aunt describing the annual Fourth of July family picnic including a detailed account of a sparkler accident.

I went into the kitchen and poured myself a beer in a tall fluted glass. I put some peanuts in a bowl. Then I walked into the cool dining room and reached for the phone. It rang. It was Maya.

'You've got another errand with the pillar of punkdom, Nebraska Storm. Roseanna Baynetta needs the lyrics for her new songs down at the office. Apparently the American Sign Language Institute has found us a feminist with fantastic fingers – she's their state of the art signer – but we're worried about getting her the material on time. So you've got to get to Nebraska Storm and get those lyrics today. Or tomorrow at the latest.'

'You mean Storm has made us wait this long for the lyrics?'

'You'd think they were the Dead Sea Scrolls.'

'I'll do my best.'

Maya hung up. I had forgotten to tell her the reassuring news that the Women's Freedom Foundation was good for five grand without strings.

I called Nebraska Storm's press agent and got an answering service. He'd left a message that the lyrics would be ready the day of the concert. It wasn't the message I wanted.

I called Roseanna, office anchorwoman of the Women's Benefit Concert and a personal hit with me at Maya's barbecue.

'I'm not a happy woman,' she said when I told her.

'I can imagine.'

'I'm probably going to have to come close to humiliation to beg that signer to learn this stuff the day of the concert.'

'If you want a good lesson in humiliation you should try the organisation around Nebraska Storm. By the way, I hear our signer has talented fingers.'

'She needs rehearsal time too. I gotta have those lyrics, Emma. I know you can get them for me. Women who come from Boston

29

can get tough with the organisation around rock stars when they have to.'

'No, I think I'll just humble myself with simple pleasantries instead.'

'Pity,' Roseanna said. 'How Californian.'

I called the press agent back and got an original voice, not one for hire. And I didn't have to eat any dirt or lick his heels. He gave me an opportunity I never would have expected.

'You may pick up the lyrics tomorrow at ten o'clock, no earlier. 479 Panoramic Way.' He hung up.

That meant that I would be visiting Nebraska Storm's private residence again. I called Roseanna and gave her the good news.

The rest of the day was spent rewriting a press biography for Maya, sanding three pine boards I was going to use for bookshelves and trying to stay cool. I put an undercoat of primer on the cheap grade timber and leaned them against a wall to dry. I wrote a letter to Boston that wasn't particularly entertaining and didn't mail it. I did a load of wash and hung it up to dry. Two T-shirts dried in a record three minutes, waving on the line in the California heat. I leafed through a museum catalogue of futuristic lighting fixtures. I fell asleep.

I dreamt about a woman in a white coat, her pockets filled with ballpoint pens which kept falling out and stabbing me as she leaned over my body. Meanwhile a red-haired nurse offered me medicine that I knew was deadly, and all this to a steady percussion beat like a disco drum solo that was the requiem for my own funeral. I awoke with a jolt. But it was only my heart pounding, and I lay still for a few moments, reminding myself where I was, and fighting the nasty dream edge that was still leaking in from my unconscious.

I didn't become any happier even when the phone rang and I heard the sound of Jonell Flax's voice. It wasn't that it was a bad voice, it's just that I heard it in stereo with her mother's. My best friend from Boston was doing a conference crisis call.

'Hi, Emma!'

'Is this Emma Victor?'

'Wait a second, Mom. Emma, is that you? Baby, how are you?'

'Hello, this is Jonell's mother. You're her friend who moved to

California, right?'

'That's right.'

'Emma, how're you doing? Surviving the sunshine? Emma, your last letter sounded so down. Isn't the concert going well? Or do the mellow vibes have hard edges?'

'It's more the pace and the space – ' I started.

'Hey, you're not going to go for any prepackaged instant therapy things?'

Jonell's mother piped up, 'That's *not* funny.'

'Oh, Mom,' Jonell whined.

'Stop whining!' Jonell's mother and I said at the same time. But only Jonell and I laughed.

'Emma, we're calling because well, maybe we need your help,' Jonell explained. 'It's about Lana.'

'Lana moved to California some time ago, didn't she?' I asked. Lana was Jonell's little sister.

'Right. She moved to Santa Monica last year,' Jonell began, taking a breath. 'She had a job in the physics department of a lab. She found out after six months that a lot of the work she was doing was being used for weapon manufacturing. But it wasn't just the principle of the thing. She felt used, betrayed, by the people there. We got some pretty hysterical letters. On the phone she acted so outraged, well, we could hardly make head or tail out of what had happened. We were thinking discrimination, possible sexual harassment; she had had some kind of relationship with a guy at work. Then the next thing we knew she . . . she made a suicide attempt. Aspirins. Damn near burned out her stomach.' Jonell took a deep breath.

'We tried to get her to come home,' Mrs Flax's voice chimed in. 'I don't understand why she didn't want to be with her family. She's just a child really.'

'She was making more money than a Wall Street Broker in a bull market,' Jonell reminded her mother.

'And she's of age,' I said.

'Anyway,' Jonell continued quickly, 'Lana agreed to go and spend some time with Mom's sister Ida in Taos, New Mexico. You know, the sun, the rest cure, and Aunt Ida like a mother hen with a newborn chick.'

'And Lana seemed to be doing okay there,' Mrs Flax said.

'Well, not entirely. Ida wrote that she was very quiet, withdrawn even. I didn't think it sounded so good. And she didn't express any interest in writing or calling us either. It was all Ida could do to get her to write a postcard.'

'What'd she say?'

Jonell sighed. 'She said she'd gotten involved with some *real* people. It seems you only have those in the West. The rest of us are androids. Anyway, she went on some retreat, a meditative healing in the desert, and pretty much left Aunt Ida with an apple pie cooling on the windowsill. She came back once to Ida's place to pick up her stuff and told Ida that she had seen the light or something like that, and had fallen in love to boot.

'So she moved into some farm in the desert, a place Ida had never heard of. She called a few weeks after that sounding totally ecstatic. It seems Lana made a quantum leap for somebody out in the desert and subatomic particles flew with the speed of light. All this happened in between workshops where Lana was getting rebalanced, rebirthed and – '

'Removed from her common sense,' Mrs Flax sighed.

'It's all relative, I guess.'

'That's pretty much what she said too,' Jonell confirmed. 'She said ''We all make our own reality.'' The last we heard was a postcard saying that she was moving to the Bay Area. She said she'd made some friends, and joined a religious youth group, and gotten a job.'

'A job!' Mrs Flax spluttered. 'She said she was going to take cleaning work. A laboratory physicist – cleaning toilets!'

'Anyway, that's all she wrote. We haven't heard from her in six months.'

'Not a single letter,' Mrs Flax said with a catch in her voice.

'We're worried about her, Emma. She left Ida's so suddenly, she was so wound up over that job, and after her suicide attempt so withdrawn and then hysterically high. Mom can't sleep at night for worrying, and we're thinking maybe we should come out there. I suggested we call you first – '

'A cleaning lady. Lana!' Mrs Flax broke in. 'I couldn't even get her to clean her *room*! I raised a physicist to become a cleaning lady and trip off into never-never land with a guru and a bunch of honkies – '

'Mom, Emma is white.'

Pause. 'Oh, I'm sorry. I'm just very upset.'

'I understand, Mrs Flax.'

'Emma, could you please try and find out what's happened to her?' Jonell asked quietly.

'Jonestown!' sniffled Mrs Flax.

'Mrs Flax, I understand your concern, but there are many groups in the Bay Area and there are big differences between them. Jonestown and the Moonies get all the press. There must be some alternative religious groups that serve positive functions,' I mused out loud. 'And maybe Lana's just very busy. After all, you said she was in love – '

'I'm afraid it could be serious,' Jonell interrupted. 'Lana said she'd found the answer to life. As if there was a question. Emma, will you do your best to try and get in contact with her?'

'Of course,' I said.

'And I want her to come home,' Mrs Flax said.

'Mom, we have to approach Lana diplomatically,' Jonell interjected. 'After all she's made a free choice. You have to respect that, even if you don't like it.'

I asked Mrs Flax for Lana's last address and phone number. I heard her shuffling through some papers and she mentioned several addresses in San Francisco. But I didn't need to write it all down; Lana's last forwarding address was a cosy sounding joint called Ananda House.

'It's some Eastern sounding organisation,' Jonell explained.

'The Vishnu Divine Inspiration Commune?'

'That's it.'

'I was just working my way up their alley. I might even have a contact there. I'll find out what's happened to Lana.'

'Thanks, Emma,' Jonell said. 'Take care of yourself in sunny California. We're all waiting for you back here if you ever change your mind.'

'Who's we all?'

'You mean you want to know if Frances is waiting for you?'

'I guess it's unlikely that she's eating her heart out in between the blood and guts of the surgical department.'

'There wasn't much left over, huh?'

'No, not much. But I think it's time to cook up a two-fisted backhand. The weather here is beautiful.'

'Jonell, this is long distance.'

'I said I'll pay you back, Mother.'

'Goodbye, Mrs Flax. Try not to worry. I'm sure Lana's okay.'

We all hung up.

I got off the sofa and splashed some cold water on my face and ran a cool stream from the tap over my wrists. I washed my feet and dried them off. I sat down and reached for the phone again.

'Vishnu Divine Inspiration Commune. Management and Financial Office' said a clipped voice. 'Lailieka speaking.'

'Hello, I'd like to speak to Bumper Lee please.'

'Bumper?' The voice paused. 'She's in a meeting.'

'Could she call me afterwards?'

'It's going to last all day.'

'Do they take a coffee break?'

'They don't drink coffee. To whom am I speaking?'

'Emma Victor. I'm from the Women's Benefit Concert.'

'But that was all straightened out, I heard.'

'This is about something else.'

'So you're *not* calling as a member of the Women's Concert committee, hmm?'

'It's personal.'

'Maybe I could help you?'

'Well, I was hoping Bumper could help me locate someone at Ananda House.'

'Who's stopping you from seeing her? Why don't you just call?'

'I wanted to talk to Bumper first.'

'You don't need to talk to Bumper about that, do you?'

'No I guess not. Could you give me the address of Ananda House?'

'You don't know where it is? Maybe you'd better call first. To make an appointment. Is this a friend you wanted to see?'

'No, not really. I'm a friend of the family.'

'Oh. Of the *family*.' Pause. I heard a line being drawn somewhere. It was an enemy line. 'I see,' said the voice, coolant having been added. 'The phone number is 777-1019.' The number matched the second one Charles had given me.

I pressed the button down, released it and dialled again. An irritated male voice answered.

'Ananda House.'

'Hi. I would like to get in touch with a friend of mine who's staying there.'

'Staying?'

'Well, living there.'

'Right. Which working unit is she in?'

'I don't know.'

'You don't know?' But the voice wasn't really asking. It was confirming and I felt myself shoved behind enemy lines again.

'Am I supposed to know?' I asked. 'Some say ignorance is bliss.'

'Have it your own way. What's your name and who are you looking for?'

'Emma Victor. I'm trying to reach Lana Flax.'

'Oh, Lana. I'm sorry. She can't come to the phone. I can give her a message.'

'Ask her to call me. Emma Victor. Tell her I'm a friend of Jonell's and to please call me this afternoon or evening.' I left my phone number.

Conversations with Vishnus on the phone were enough to make me voluntarily commit myself. Instead, I washed and dried the breakfast dishes, arranging the pink glass cups and matching plates on the open kitchen shelves. I went shopping. I made a salad that was heavy on the avocado side with a walnut cream dressing and ate it.

I waited for Lana Flax to call. She didn't. At three thirty I tried to reach her again.

'Ananda House? I'm trying to reach Lana Flax.'

'I gave her your message,' said the same irritated voice.

'I'm really surprised she hasn't called.'

'The phone system is going through an overhaul.'

'I'm a good friend of her sister Jonell's. I'm sure she would have called me back if I said it was important.'

'Like I said, the phones are being fixed. I'm sure when a line is

35

cleared up she'll call you. If she wants to.'

'How come I can get through, but she can't?'

'Look lady, I don't *make* the phones, I just answer them.'

'It's important. Couldn't you just ask her to come to the phone?'
I wondered suddenly why I was pleading.

'I'm sorry, but we can't do that.'

'But it's really rather urgent. Can't I get any kind of message
through to her?'

'Sure,' he said, gave me their post office box number, and hung
up.

I looked at the paper with the three numbers that Charles had
given me. I'd used 'Financial Office' and 'Ananda House'. It was
time to go in through the front door. I called 'Dinner and Meditation reservations'.

I was asked to choose between the women's and mixed meditations. I didn't figure guru girls were much different to guru boys.
But at the women's I still had a fifty per cent higher chance of seeing Lana Flax. I was told to bring a towel. It was one way to spend
an evening in California and one more way to spend money. After
gas, it would set me back fifteen bucks. I wondered if what
Charles had said was true, that women would be lining up around
the block. I looked in my closet for some yellowish clothes. My
financial situation hadn't allowed me to refurbish my wardrobe for
California heat and leisure lifestyle. Except for a ten-year-old tennis outfit, almost everything I owned was black.

Six

I settled for a short sleeved tennis blouse on the ivory
side of yellow and the most faded blue jeans I had. I didn't want
to be an imposter anyway; I didn't even want a vegetarian meal
or an intensive meditation. I wanted to see Lana Flax with my

own eyes and that was about all.

A small breeze had started to work its way through the flatlands and brushed past me as I opened the front door on the way to the car. The day's heat was starting to leak out of the pavement and the Plymouth still felt like an oven. I opened the windows, gunned the engine and headed on to the freeway. After the overpass the Plymouth merged with the Interstate, full of diesel fuel and coastal breezes, California perfume. A spectacular Bay view was gearing up for sunset to the throbbing of a disco radio station. Eventually a long stream of vehicles split off on to a double lane exit, leaving the rest of us to sail past the skyscraper condos hugging the Bay shore. They offered empty spaces at double digit interest rates.

When the condos let up, the houses got smaller and the California dream melted into an industrial reality. It wasn't the territory of high interest high hope lifestyles any more. I glanced at the map and traced my way another ten blocks to the Vishnu Divine Inspiration Commune. What a place to pick for paradise.

I passed a few cement block warehouses being built, an old frame garage being torn down and two empty lots for sale. It was a ghost town of big concrete cathedrals inhabited by fork lifts. And it was probably the last piece of wasted waterfront real estate existing in California.

I parked my car next to a cement block warehouse landscaped with cyprus trees. Looking across the street I connected the address of the Vishnu place with a rambling redwood complex at the top of the small incline. I could hear the distant lapping of water from behind it.

But that wasn't all I was hearing. The sound of laughter punctuated by bells drifted my way. Soon I saw a group of people, a host of giggling daffodils, swaying on the edge of the road. They were dressed in every tint, tone and shade of yellow. Mixed with brown to become ochre, mixed with blue to become chartreuse, or with synthetic agents to become day-glo, they were all wearing garments in the family of that sunny colour. Underneath the clothes all of them were white and none of them was Lana Flax.

A pre World War Two Duesenberg made its way slowly along the pavement, parting the citron sea of bodies. So this was the man himself. I mentally geared myself for the moment. I couldn't do otherwise. Bumper had done her PR work well. I had to admit I was curious to see him. The rapt attention of all the people gathered around the car made me focus on the vehicle as if it were the chariot of a god.

I could just glimpse an ageing man inside the auto. He didn't seem to have to crack any jokes to keep the crowd laughing. All the windows were rolled up anyway. Two people sat on either side of him, but, like everyone else, I found myself straining to see his face. He looked just like another satisfied senior citizen to me, celebrating his golden years in cash. It was easy to tell he was enjoying the whole thing.

I got out of the Plymouth and mingled with the crowd. It would have been simple to slip amongst them; all I had to do was force laughter out of my mouth to blend in. I couldn't imagine anything that funny any more, but no one was watching me anyway.

'He went to the airport to pick him up,' I heard someone say.

'For Vishnu it's probably just another ride. But for Sadhima it must feel like a great honour.'

'I've heard about him from Delphy. She knows him from the Eastern Commune. She said Sadhima is the most multi-talented individual she's ever met. He's got a pilot's licence and knows fifteen kinds of martial arts.'

'I heard he was in Vietnam.'

'No, Yale, I think. Anyway, we should expect things to really start happening now that he's arrived. The start of the International Membership is going to happen right here.'

The Duesenberg had come to a halt and the faithful folk did too. They swayed gently in their places, keeping a respectful distance. A young man stepped out of the car. He was a pretty boy, with long, shiny black hair and the right kind of shoulders. It must be Sadhima. If he lost his job for the guru he could easily find work in the rag trade modelling shirts. Now he got to ride around in Duesenbergs; Lana was right. Everyone makes their own reality.

Pretty Boy put a small Persian rug on the concrete in front of the car. He extended an arm into the interior of the car and slowly a brown hand came out, then a light brown foot in a worn, chewed sandal. It stepped softly on to the carpet. Another foot followed. The young man pulled slightly and the car gave birth to the complete presence of the man everyone had been waiting for.

Vishnu wore a long pale blue gown and although his figure was thin, perhaps even shivering, he stood with the ease of a dancer. A long curly beard, groomed and fluffy, rested on the gold-embroidered front of his garment and a large emerald earring hung from his right ear. The gown shimmered as he raised his arms above the people. He shared an unspoken joke with them and they burst out laughing, kindling a warm smile on his face.

He turned back and forth, including everyone in his gaze. His eyes rested for a while on Sadhima and then went back to the crowd. A silent introduction.

The people laughed harder. He smiled wider. Sadhima grinned. This went on for a while. It didn't seem like such good show biz to me, but because everyone else was enjoying themselves, I tried to too. Suddenly, Vishnu focused his attention on one young man. 'You,' Vishnu said slowly, walking towards him. He took the man's hand, who looked like he was so overexcited his vital signs would soon have to be checked.

'You didn't think,' Vishnu said carefully, with an accent as thick as his beard, 'you did not think,' he repeated, 'that I was looking for *you*.' Everyone waited for the punch line. His emerald earring shimmered. 'But I was,' Vishnu confirmed with a twinkle that sent everyone into spasms of laughter. It was a joke I didn't get.

'And *you*,' Vishnu continued, his voice rising, his attention turning to a middle-aged woman with silk flowers in her hair. She moved towards him and he held a hand over her decorated head. 'You didn't expect me to find you either,' he teased her. Her blush confirmed the fact.

'You see,' Vishnu turned his gaze to include all of us. 'Everyone thinks I am greeting someone else.' This sent the crowd into a collective paroxysm of glee. Released by the recognition of their own silly egos, they started holding and fondling one another while Vishnu looked on approvingly. But he wasn't entirely approving. He'd seen me. And I wasn't feeling anybody up, nor had I ditched my ego.

His brown eyes found me, and I noticed his pleasure increase. The people stopped and Vishnu edged along the tassels of the

39

carpet towards me. I found myself moving forward, as if I wanted to help his eyes get me into focus.

'Your doubts,' he grinned slowly, the edges of his moustache rising, 'they do not matter.' The people around him smiled. I smiled. 'Your doubts do not matter,' he repeated slowly, 'at all. And that' – he looked at all the people gathered around him: this was clearly the punch line of the day – 'that is wonderful!'

I felt a curious elation. This sort of nonsense was contagious.

'But you,' he continued, 'you are watching everything. Watching and very far away.' I kept my mouth shut. He wasn't a person to have dialogue with anyway. He wrote all the lines himself. But I still wanted to hear what he had to say. There was something riveting about his attention. I started to feel a little paralysed. Like I couldn't, like I didn't want, to move.

'No, you're not watching,' he smiled in sudden recognition. 'You're looking. Are you looking for someone?' he enquired liltingly. I felt the blood drain out of my face and I started wondering who really did write his dialogue. But then he turned away. He shimmered triumphantly at us all for a few more well-chosen moments. But then he turned away. He was a class act, a stand up cosmic comedian who didn't have to stand up for long. In fact, he was already preparing to enter the Commune.

But not without help. If it hadn't been for her deep brown skin I wouldn't have recognised her. Vishnu's first lady in waiting had emerged from the car behind him, and he leaned on her lovingly. It was Lana Flax, metamorphosed from science nerd to femmed out hippie princess.

I got a good look at her as she escorted him into the building. Small boned, she looked like a collector doll, perfectly dressed in updated guru chic. A starched kimono floated around her small figure. She almost cradled Vishnu in her arms, golden bangles falling to her elbows getting lost in the folds of her sleeve. And little bells on bracelets circling her ankles tinkled as she gently led the scintillating figure up the carefully swept walkway to the door.

The young man with the long, shiny black hair followed and when the door closed behind Lana and Vishnu he stood between the entrance and the crowd of followers. After a moment a few people cautiously approached him. He held them in conversation in front of the door. After about five minutes he stepped aside and let them enter. Apparently Lana and Vishnu wanted to make a getaway all by themselves.

Seven

The crowd filed after him in an orderly fashion, the giggling subsiding and turning into the more normal hum of everyday life. It was a happier sound, to my ears, than all the giddy laughter. I still had fifteen minutes before the services. A hiss echoed low upon the lawn and suddenly hidden sprinklers spewed out circled fans of water on the grass strip surrounding the building.

I opened the redwood door and walked into a reception room. Mellow meditational sounds oozed into my ears from hidden speakers. The cool, large lobby with flagstone tiles was lit by yard wide skylights. Redwood planters hung beneath them and poured out golden heart ivy, Boston ferns and asparagus plants. There wasn't a dead leaf or needle to be seen on any of them. A larger than lifesize portrait of Vishnu, laughing, hung on the right hand wall in a brushed brass frame, flanked by two coco palms. For a photograph he seemed to be getting a big kick out of watching all the activity in the room.

Yellow figures strode back and forth across the lobby looking as if they knew where they were going. Giggling groups conversed animatedly, gesturing to each other on their way to another part of the complex. A couple sat engaged in conversation without words on a sofa. The only person in the room who wasn't having a good time stood in the corner across from the door, his eyes flickering every few seconds to the tones of a tuneless melody leaking out of hidden speakers. He was observing every movement

41

of the devotees. It was Pretty Boy with the long shiny black hair.

Before me was a massive white desk which stood in front of a white fibreglass curtain, a waiting area with magazines and imitation Barcelona chairs to the right of it. No one was waiting, so I didn't see why I should either. Behind the desk sat a fresh young white woman dressed in full silk, a cream-coloured blouse under a raw silk jacket. She had done a good job with three-tone eye shadow and her blue eyes looked as big as saucers and just about as deep. A picture of the Vishnu, framed in desktop plexiglass, sat next to a name plate which read 'Delphy'.

Before I knew it, Sadhima, his full-length tumble curls falling to the collar of his designer sport shirt, loomed behind her. He bent down to say something and gave me a shot of his parted hair and clean scalp. A baby shampoo commercial grown up and gone testosterone.

'This looks pretty complicated.' His tone was soothing.

'Bu Mper ordered it. It was her idea. We can tape and receive messages, in addition to automatically routing all calls. Lailieka is teaching me.'

'That's just wonderful,' he said in a way that made it sound not wonderful at all. 'Since you've got such good tabs on things, could I ask you for a volunteer from the cleaning crew? I'll need a room made up downstairs for two sisters next Friday.' He grasped the back of her chair with his soft hands. Delphy tilted her head back and looked up at him.

'Of course.'

'And I might need you to make some reservations for me.'

'Airlanka, or Air India?'

'Cathay Pacific.' He lifted his eyebrows and brought his face down slightly towards hers.

Then a buzzer sounded and the woman leaned forward, her silk jacket rustling, and fiddled with some toggle switches on an intercom board. Sadhima looked up at me, with two clear and very light grey eyes, so light that the black pupil and dark iris rim seemed to make two bullseyes in his eyeballs, like an Alaskan Malamute dog. I was glad when he peered down to look at the receptionist's long white hands working the toggle switches.

There were a lot of little boxes wrapped in plastic, and several coils of thin coloured wire on the desktop. When Delphy was done she leaned back again. Sadhima said something that was a profession of happy ignorance about the telephone system which she so deftly worked with her long fingernails. It was a scene which could be happening in any office building in town.

'Hi,' I said, and after a moment they looked up.

'You wanted something?' Breck boy perused my clothes and I felt like a wash-basket refugee.

'Hi, I'm Emma Victor. I have a dinner reservation at five thirty –'

'Yes, I see.' She leaned back to whisper something at the man who was leaning over her. He whispered something back and she nodded her head. He took his hands off the back of her chair and bent down lower.

'I hear the chow is swell.' I smiled. Uninterested smiles passed over their faces.

'Don't forget to keep in touch with yourself,' I heard him say, with a pious smile worthy of a budding saint. His hand in her pocket was not worthy of a budding saint. Then he stood up and strode away.

'Dinner,' I repeated. Delphy licked her lips and bent a small head with a groomed auburn cap of hair over her papers on the desk. She peered up at me. Nothing was left from the look with the grey-eyed man.

'Did you bring a towel?' she asked crisply.

'No. I forgot.'

'Oh.' She frowned slightly and folded one glossy lip under the other before she said, 'Well, you can get one from the facilitator after the dinner.' She scribbled something down on a pad in front of her. A buzzer sounded by her elbow.

'Oh. Yes, Bu Mper.' I noticed Delphy didn't rate the use of the informal 'Bumper'. 'Yes, of course.' She hung up and looked at me. 'Go and wait with the others in the coffee shop. And that will be twenty dollars please.' A little adding machine clicked alongside her.

'Twenty dollars?'

'Dinner plus towel rental,' she explained, taking my Andrew

43

Jackson and giving me back no change.

'I knew I had a good reason for coming here,' I mumbled.

Her eyes brightened, but with a brightness that only seemed to shine inwards towards herself. 'We all do.' She tilted her head, her hair swung to the left and her pencil pointed to the right. 'Coffee shop's that way.'

I picked up the beige card she gave me with a number forty-two on it. There were only five minutes until dinner and I wondered why I had to wait in the coffee shop. I didn't find out the answer to that but I did find out why the beige card said forty-two. I parted the swinging glass doors into the coffee shop and found forty-one women in yellow.

But there was a lot more to see than yellow people and squeaky clean interior design. A plate glass window took up the entire space of one wall overlooking an ornamental garden. Raucous colours of azaleas and phlox were dimmed only by the fading sun-set. White-washed stepping stones wandered through a close green lawn of diacondra and moss. A rose garden could just be seen behind a splashing Florentine fountain of cast birds and cherubs. The upper part of the window sported rectangular ventilation windows which were open and the splashing of water mixed with the sound of laughter floated in with the dusky scent of honeysuckle vine.

I looked back at the buttercup crowd at the bar and saw that I was the cause of no attention. I didn't see why exactly. Out of forty-two people I was the only one wearing blue. I walked over to a metal-grid bulletin board that was bolted on to the tiled wall. Notices about apartments to share, music lessons to take, and kitchen tables to sell fluttered around a 'Workshop List and Schedule' in the middle. The therapies and courses listed were a cornucopia of Me Generation muddle. A lot of words, signifying nothing, except maybe the Drug Rehab programme offered bi-monthly.

'Let there be spaces in your togetherness and let the winds of the heavens dance between you.' A quote from Kahlil Gibran read across the top. But could the winds of heaven tell where the spaces were if everyone was wearing yellow? I didn't want to find out. I looked at what the courses promised and knew I was a candidate for all of them. Step right up, Emma Victor. In just a few hours, through dramatic ritual action I could create for myself the childhood of my heart's desire. If I could only find the willingness to take the risks, greet the challenge of surrender, I could join this carnival of creative functioning and spend the rest of my life drawing mandalas. And when I was finally finished with this life, others were waiting. There were mediums ready to introduce me to parties on the Other Side, workshops ready to propel me by means of astral projection into past lives. And all for fifty dollars (dinner included). Weekend workshops two hundred and twenty-five bucks (bring your own sheets).

I picked up *Celestial Call*, the house publication. There wasn't a lot in it. When they weren't talking about cute duckies being born in springtime and how to read your mood ring in conjunction with your daily chart they were writing a lot of poems about the guru. An editorial by First Secretary Bu Mper Lee asserted that the Vishnu movement also had an urban soul and that part of their mission was to sustain meditative values in the marketplace.

The bell rang and the women abandoned their soya appetisers and formed casual groups, arms circled around waists, hands reaching for hands. As they moved away from the bar another portrait of Vishnu, the laughing man, was revealed on a wall. I could see what he thought was so funny. If I could say to a group of people one morning, 'Now I want you all to wear purple' and know that they would do just exactly that, down to their socks and underpants, I'd smile too. The man had amazing confidence. After all, what if you threw a religion and nobody came?

As I followed the last crocus-coloured caftan billowing through the door, I wondered what dinner would be like.

'So how's the food here anyway?' I asked a woman at the rear of the moving flank. She was the only person not hugging or holding someone.

'You've never eaten here before?' she asked suspiciously. I didn't bother to give the obvious answer. Her straight blonde hair hung on either side of a horsy face with a recent history of sunburn. She glanced back at the yellow group continuing on without her. I was forcing her to slow down, separating one of the sheep from the flock. 'The food is good.' She looked at me carefully. I wasn't yellow and I wasn't eager enough.

'I guess I'm really lucky to be able to experience this whole thing for only fifteen dollars.' I tried. That was the ticket.

'Vishnu says you have to put effort and investment to get into anything,' she burbled.

'I guess I haven't tried hard enough.'

'But that's the secret,' she raised two pencil-thin eyebrows, 'You have to learn not to try.' She parted another pair of doors and we found ourselves in the buffet room. Horseface gravitated towards the pack, as if my bad blue vibrations might be catching. The women were lining up on either side of a buffet table. I had expected brown rice and lentils; but I found a horn of plenty, right in the middle of oil refinery land.

There were vegetable pies and nutburgers, spinach lasagne and stuffed mushrooms simmering over candlelit hot plates. Whole wheat, seven grain and rye breads with iced dishes of butter curls next to them, a green and white hill of broccoli and cauliflower blooms with a pool of walnut cream sauce waiting at the base. Caramel cakes, blueberry muffins, chocolate brownies, raspberries and red currant yoghurt were lined up for dessert. The finale was at the end of the table. A candelabrum with twelve tapers flickered and shone over an impossible mound of melons, pomegranates, mangos shining with dew, and sea-green guavas. At the bottom three pineapples lolled on their sides in a lake of seedless grapes. From time to time people appeared from the kitchen in white caps and aprons and rolled by with stainless steel trolleys to fill up the table as portions were used up. A tall woman on the sidelines oversaw the operation and mumbled to kitchen workers in between arranging napkins at the end of the table or replacing a fallen serving spoon. The scene alone was worth fifteen bucks even without the food. I wasn't sure about the towel.

I picked up a tray and perused the fruit trying to decide. Horseface had skipped the breads and was trying to initiate a conversation with a couple who were popping grapes into each other's mouths.

'Don't eat with your hands from the buffet please,' said a passing kitchen worker, replenishing some muffins from her food cart.

'Oh, yes, of course. Sorry,' said one and moved on.

I followed the last group of women into the dining room where small white tables were placed on four different levels opposite a similar plate glass view of the garden. Carpets softened the acoustics and a bubble gum tune was played note for note on Tibetan bells through four speakers in the corners. A sunken pit with five tables was already filled, and a raised area with a brass railing had been taken by a large group who knew each other and had pushed their tables together. Two quiet couples gazed into each other's eyes in a corner nook overlooking a magnolia tree, and three women ate while earnestly talking and pointing at some papers spread out at their table. That left the long-faced woman, who was looking around for a place for herself and resting her eyes nervously on the only available table left. I was sitting there.

'Have a seat,' I invited her. 'I only bite food.'

She sat down on the white plastic moulded chair provided.

'The food looks great,' I said. She nodded, breaking apart little flowers of raw broccoli. 'It's very nice that there is a women's meditation . . . ' I began.

'Yin energy,' she explained without looking up. 'Vishnu wants us to be able to get into it, completely, together, before we can go on to the next step – '

'The next step?' I asked. 'What exactly is this meditation?'

'You don't know?' she asked.

'Do I have to know?'

'No, it's just that, well, I mean most people who come here know what they're looking for.'

'Oh, I do.' I said, and I wasn't lying. I still didn't see Lana Flax anywhere in the dining room. 'I just hope I recognise it when I find it.'

'When you find it, recognition is never the problem.'

'Then I just hope I'm looking in the right direction.'

'There is no right direction.'

I sighed and ripped the skin off a banana. I thought these people liked to discuss problems. 'Am I just lucky or do you talk to all the girls in Disneyland this way?' I grumbled, but the woman didn't answer me. Someone was flagging her from the raised platform, waving a yellow-sleeved arm. My eating partner couldn't get her food, tray and citrine self up the carpeted stairs fast enough.

47

I sat ripping little succulent spheres out of a pomegranate and crunching the seeds between my teeth. Eventually a vibrating tone was sounded through the system and everyone gathered up their plates and trays and headed towards a pass-through, sorting out paper into one container, silverware into another and handing dirty plates to steaming rubber gloved hands which reached out of the wall opening to accept them. These women knew everything; they knew where to put their silverware and they knew where to go when the bells sounded. It was just like being the new kid in school. Yes, it was clearly worth fifteen dollars, maybe even twenty without the towel. We filed into a locker room of sorts. They all had their towels and blast off clothing stowed in gaily painted cubbies lining the walls. I stood and watched them and wished I had a cubby too.

I turned away and then I saw her. Lana. It was still hard to believe how much she'd changed. Somebody had done a makeover job that turned the skinny, insecure perpetually pubescent whizz kid into a perfectly groomed princess. The broad, square face was the same, the thin nose with wide fluted nostrils and the determined, swelling rosebud mouth. A braided thong necklace hung around her neck. A little laugh fell from her mouth and she had that same dizzy look as Delphy the receptionist. It all made me feel very cold. She glanced around and some of the yellow crowd turned to look back at her. I remembered what Jonell's mother had said, one black woman in a crowd of honkies.

'Lana!' I said loudly in the silence.

She turned, her eyes following the voice and finding my face at the end of it. She put my face together with another world. 'Emma?' she gasped.

'Yeah, hi. It's me.' I walked to her and took her in my arms and gave her a hug. When I drew back she looked like a person waking up from a cat nap where only big fat kitties slept.

'What are you doing here?' Her face was guarded and surprised at the same time, like a child with an unexpected gift from a stranger. She'd obviously not gotten my message and I decided not to tell her that her mother had called me. That was the first big mistake I made.

'I'm going to the meditation,' I said. And that was the second.

Eight

'You *are*?' Lana grinned with a kind of smile that had never been there when she was the science nerd. Contact lenses floated over the warm brown doe eyes which thick glasses used to hide. She'd smeared copper eyeshadow above them.

'How did you hear about Vishnu?' she bubbled, smiling expectantly, but not waiting for an answer. 'Sometimes I can be so surprised at the people I see here.' She looked at me closely with her big brown eyes, and seemed to find something. 'Sometimes I'm not surprised at all.' Suddenly I was one of the family.

'This is some place. And you live here too?'

'Here is where I *worship*,' she corrected me. 'Where I've taken swimming lessons in the transcendental oceans of bliss,' she tinkled. Her almond-shaped eyes squinted and she looked as happy as a kid in a candy store. She even had the lollipop in her mouth already. 'Of course, on the material plane the garden is beautiful,' she conceded for the sake of conversation. 'And we are making it more beautiful all the time. But the possibility of improvement in outer things is endless and leads nowhere. To me the world is perfect as it is. You can walk to the ocean but the most beautiful sunset is contained in his words. Oh Emma, I think it's so exciting that you've come here!'

I looked at Lana, or was I letting her presence fill me? The place was affecting me already. She was like an angel-food cake, sweet and slightly sticky – light and warm, full of airy whipped-up egg whites, leaving her a little frothy at the mouth. It wasn't at all unpleasant to stand next to her. I almost had to remind myself that I was disappointed that the promising young physicist had ended up a dedicated soldier in the battle for selfhood. Or was anything, even this, an improvement over high-tech weaponry?

'To surrender yourself Emma, is the only release from this reality . . . ' Lana glowed with the high wattage of super servitude.

'I'll bet – '

49

'You'll have to meet him in person,' she went on excitedly, out of breath. 'It's hard to get an audience these days, but – '

'Slow down, I've only just gotten through my first dinner.' But her face dimmed slightly and once again I realised I was lacking the spirit of cheerleading enthusiasm. I sounded as if I was afraid dinner would be poisoned, or that I was diving into a pool of yellow-bellied sharks, not seeing the blissful opportunity that was there in front of my eyes. But I didn't want to have to play out any charades with the laughing man himself.

'You know we all are afraid when we can see the barriers but cannot cross them.' She smiled, darting her eyes at me. 'The meditation is great. It really opens you up – I hope you're ready for it!'

A stream of yellow people was filing out of a door and I could feel Lana drawn magnetically towards them. I took her arm and a noseful of patchouli oil and tried to prepare myself for the meditation. It wasn't the right moment to tell Lana to call her mother. She circled my waist and pulled me closer and I didn't wonder why the development of breasts was referred to as blossoming. We climbed up the brightly lit stairway, Lana's bangles clanging, her braided necklace bouncing and her ankle bracelet jingling. She winked and pulled away, hurrying to catch the yellow file of women. I ran my hand along the railing just like they did, hopping up the stair to the next class.

The room we entered was dominated by another large plate glass window. The sea stretched out from a scruffy beach, and after that there was just a view of sky, and sun disappearing behind the horizon. I walked to the window and looked down. The Vishnu property line seemed to end with a fence, and beyond that a path led away through clumps of marsh grass, quillwort and retired truck tyres down a hill to the water. But the effect mostly was of sky and sunset, and mirrors on the opposite wall reflected the scene so that the room was drenched in pink light. I sat down in one of the seven cushioned chairs which faced the view.

'Those are for the midnight meditation,' Lana said, pulling me back to where the women were settling themselves on the floor. 'Sometimes Lailieka sings, and her beautiful voice fills even the garden.' Lailieka. Bumper's secretary, with the terse telephone manner, honcho of the guru elite who hadn't been sent to charm school.

I sat down with a thump on one of the high-density foam rubber mats. The women around me were assuming variations of the Indian squat that we were taught in first grade. Wrists were finding knees and resting on them, pulses pointed towards the heavens, and faces creased with laughter became smooth and solemn. One woman's head was drooping and then started to roll around slowly. I looked over at Lana.

'Lana doesn't have any social skills . . .' Jonell said once when Lana disappeared into her room for a few weeks. It was a family crisis they didn't share with friends. I looked over at her now. Loosened black curls bobbed as her head started to swing back and forth rhythmically. The prodigal physicist wasn't exactly a unified field. And I didn't think this place was doing a lot to help her.

Drooping heads snapped up at the sound of the door closing. The woman who walked in wasn't my idea of somebody you'd want to be mistress of your mind; she had black hair pulled back tightly, stretching the skin over the ridge of her eyebrows and falling in a long braid when it got free of her scalp. She had translucent white skin and the only nice thing about her face was a pale beige wash of freckles that splattered across her nose. Her whole being seemed sharp, pointed, and as she looked around I imagined a mosquito ready to suck blood. She stepped in, baggy harem trousers flapping at the ankles with her jerky walk. She had a folded towel across her arm which she put down in front of us. She went over to the window and strutted around, reaching up to the big linen shades covering the windows, her black braid twitching as she stood on her toes and back again. The room softened to a filtered pink. The towel in front of the group was still sitting there. It was calling out my name.

'I guess this is for me?' I asked, as she walked back towards the middle of the room.

'You're the person who rented the towel?' she said and I felt an uneasy memory stirring. Don't talk out of turn. Don't ask stupid questions.

'Yes, I rented the towel.'

'Then take it,' she shrugged. She turned her back to fuss with

51

some candles in a cellophane-wrapped box while I gathered up the deep-pile towel and went back to my place on the mat.

'I think you all know me,' she lied through evenly matched teeth. 'Oh, of course not,' she beamed my way. Did she have to emphasise it so much, or did I need recognition in my role of new girl? Somehow I became grateful for the attention. Until she said, 'I'm Lailieka.'

So this was Bumper's receptionist who seemed to have learned her trade at a security school. She probably had a memory for names like a phone book.

'I'm here to facilitate the activation meditation,' she continued. 'There are three parts. The first is current space where you will sit and empty your mind. Just try to empty your head of thought, breathe gently through the nose and out through the mouth,' she recited, like an airline stewardess with a litany about seat belt fasteners and air flotation cushions. And the meditators were paying as little attention as any flight passenger. They rustled in their places. They were restless. They knew all this already. They wanted to get high. 'Then comes the second part,' she continued, 'the rahami breath flow for ten minutes. When you hear the music we begin with movement mandala. And that's your cue, try to find *your* dance: swinging, jumping, howling, spinning, doing anything you want. Try to experience yourself as you are spontaneously.' Lailieka looked at us one by one. Somebody giggled. 'Not *that* spontaneously, that's another meditation,' she said, the corners of her mouth curling up anyway. It was meant to be a frown as much as a stage whisper was meant to be quiet. I felt like I was in a gym class where the teacher was a little wicked and the children were very very good.

'Then we go back to a rahami and a final emptiness.' I hoped I could remember everything she said. It sounded a little like a wash cycle to me. More laughter as Lailieka told us to be careful of flailing arms, and reminded us to take care of each other.

'Now we're going to begin,' she warned us. We rustled into stillness and I could feel the others fastening their mental seat belts. I was glad Lailieka couldn't see into my mind. I was sure that my cosmic tank read empty and whatever was there would probably make her scream and run away.

'Okay. Close your eyes. Now just relax, but try to sit up straight and follow the flow of energy through the chakras and down to the base of the spine.' Silence. I tried to find my energy. 'That's right, follow it down there,' she said. I was just starting to find the energy, I thought maybe it was hanging out . . . 'Now let that energy come back up.' Wait, I thought. I haven't followed it down yet . . . 'And let it flow faster and faster out the top of your head, leaving your mind completely and totally blank, filled with the absence, emptied and left with . . . nothingnesssssss.' She hissed slightly and her voice faded out. But I wasn't left with nothingness. It happened too fast. I wasn't going to find nothingness; I didn't come in time.

I tried breathing very slowly, in through the nose, out through the mouth. But I felt myself sampling the taste of unpleasant anxieties, dental problems, debts, an insecure future, and a tennis backhand that had never made the grade even when I was in practice. Not to mention an ex-girlfriend who loved me but never had the time. Be here now, I used to tell her, not laying a career foundation for four years from now. But who was I to talk? I wasn't discovering the present. Where was that energy anyway?

I listened to the steady breathing of my companions. I would soon reach one of two potential tennis partners by phone. One was a woman I knew by face in Boston. She had a murderous serve and, I'd heard, a good sense of humour. But wait. I was supposed to be in the present. Shit.

The next part was easy. I heard a bell and everybody stood up. I did too. The rahami breathing exercise was essentially high-paced hyperventilation. It gave me a light head and I saw little yellow lights in front of my eyes and almost fell over backwards after ten minutes. For a while there I had felt very much in the present. I could see the women around me throwing their heads back and forth like forty-one potential whiplash cases. One or two also stumbled backwards so I knew I was getting some of the right effects.

Suddenly a drum beat popped out of a speaker above my head. Another pop and the rhythm started to pick up, and so did the women around me, who started shaking their arms and legs. Soon the room was full of furious pummelling figures, dancing with a combination of demonic possession, St Elmo's Fire, and lack of deodorant. Lailieka opened a window. She turned around and caught me peeking. I closed my eyes and hopped higher. Eventually the drums died down and we stood in our places, but there was no breath left to catch. The rahami bell rang and we were throwing any available oxygen back into the room and out of our brains entirely. This time I got a spectrum of lights doing a feature film behind my eyelids and the beginnings of a cold sweat rush. Suddenly, we got to lie down.

I couldn't think about anything any more. It was enough to be in silence, and it was more than enough to lie down. A surge of energy started to play up the back of my spine and the part of my head touching the mat wasn't there any more. Would all my brains leak out on to the floor?

'Do not look to the fruit,' said a deep, slow voice with a heavy accent. It was Vishnu. What was he doing here? Was he counselling me on my financial problems? 'Do not even look at the tree.' I forgot my questions and concentrated on the voice speaking only to me. The fruit, it didn't matter, Vishnu was saying. Neither the tree. 'It is the seasons that plant and ripen. It is all the parts and no parts at all.' The voice was green with endless chlorophyll. At that moment I thought I knew just what he meant. Later I wasn't so sure. The words became flowers, opening up and blooming like a time-lapse movie, red roses bursting open with every word he said, red roses, contained in the voice but so different to the skin, cold and grey. A breeze must have rustled over my skin, damp with sweat, almost bringing me back. But I didn't want to return. Just to follow that voice, that was all I wanted. What was it saying now? The words upon the wind, the lack of words? It wasn't making any sense.

Little orange sunbursts started flashing behind my eyelids; they made a firework show in the blackness in front of me. I was falling and as long as I didn't look down it would be all right. But I did look down and it became a bad, bottomless pit. The voice was gone, I couldn't find it. It wasn't anywhere, and I thought I heard a phone ringing somewhere, and footsteps running. I heard the laughter that was supposed to be there change to weeping. I was frightened, my heart was beating and the voice tried to come back but it was getting fainter and fainter.

Click. The tape was turned off. I opened my eyes and the room flashed in front of me. But it was nothing compared to the nightmare flash I'd just had. The sun had set. Lailieka was lighting candles. I saw my fellow travellers unfold and rise as if it had been a complete vacation. So why had I resided in purgatory? Or was my attitude bumping me off the only charter flight to nirvana I'd ever been on? I looked around at the yellow crowd grabbing their towels. Lailieka came towards me.

'You can go to the showers if you like,' she announced.

Turning to the doorway I caught the corner of Lana's kimono disappearing through it, and felt another stab of disappointment. A woman who could add seventy figures in her head was making a practice of over-oxygenating her brain cells and I stood drenched in the cold sweat of a meditation bummer. Maybe a shower would wash it all away. Gathering my wits together I followed her escaping figure.

Nine

I put my blue jeans and T-shirt on a peg next to forty-one yellow articles of clothing in the dressing room. The shower room matched the rest of the building in its interior design. It was well built, in the best materials, spacious and complete with yellow-clad attendant. She was slowly going over the floor with a squeegee mop. I went to one of the many stalls. I adjusted the shower nozzle to a softer flow and watched the space under the door. Two dark brown feet flashed white soles at me as they headed towards the dressing room. I grabbed my five dollar towel and followed them.

'Lana, I want to talk to you.'

'Sure, Emma. I have a few minutes.' She stopped expectantly.

'What I have to say won't go over real well in the shower room. It's important.'

'Yeah, well, okay.' She looked a little puzzled. 'I'll meet you in the coffee shop.'

I dressed and went downstairs to the busy coffee shop. Lana joined a clot of comrades at a table where Delphy the receptionist commanded everyone's attention with her anxious vibes.

'But, I thought it was supposed to be *mine*!' Delphy spluttered, looking around at Sadhima and the four others sitting there.

'Mine!' echoed somebody and the dirty word sent a wave of suppressed giggles through the group.

'Yours?' Sadhima smiled. Delphy was playing right into his hands.

'Yes – you said that – how could you do this to me?'

'Why, I'm not doing anything to you, Delphy,' protested Sadhima gently. 'I'm just telling you about a job reassignment. Vishnu has given certain instructions.'

'And I think it's a good idea,' somebody piped up. 'You're obviously too attached to the job of receptionist.'

'I think you're on an aggression trip,' somebody else offered.

'Yeah, bad vibes, clearly broadcasting bad vibes,' said another yellow party.

Delphy held her breath and looked around her uncertainly. It was Sadhima's moment.

'You see, Delphy,' he said in honey tones, 'Nothing is yours. You don't own the job as receptionist.'

'It's not, it's not just about that – ' Delphy began.

'And you don't own me either,' Sadhima said with a patient smile, settling back in the deep cushions behind him. I noticed two female followers purring on either side of him. He smiled complacently. 'Isn't that what this is really about?'

Delphy kept her mouth shut. It was a good idea; she only provided them with more ammunition.

'It's clear you need a lesson in humility, Delphy,' someone repeated.

'It's clear your old pals from India here *don't*,' Delphy said, losing control again. The group smiled, happy to find their suspicions confirmed.

'I shouldn't even justify myself to you, Delphy,' Sadhima began.

'Your personal work should be on acceptance. But, yes, Cathra and Juna both worked with me in India. And I want them to work with me on the International Membership. The receptionist must play an important role in this process –'

'But Lailieka has been teaching me about all the equipment. The recording, sending functions. It would be a waste of time to have to start all over . . . '

'Nothing is a waste of time. Unless your time is worthless.' Sadhima sighed. The child wasn't learning her lesson. 'You're too attached. And I think it would help Juna to be receptionist for a while. She needs to work on imaging herself vocally. And the laundry can be wonderful.' This last statement sparked a smile on all faces except Delphy's. It even sparked a smile on mine.

'I love you, Delphy,' Sadhima moved forwards, and peered closely into her face. 'Why don't you stay on as receptionist until, let's say, next week. That's when we'll be receiving more overseas guests. That will give you time to accept your new task. You must learn this lesson, Delphy. You must learn it, not for us, but for yourself.' Sadhima's sermon was over.

The lines around Delphy's mouth softened. Tears welled up in her eyes.

'That's it,' Sadhima encouraged her. 'Give up. Surrender. You know the laundry could be the greatest thing that ever happened to you!'

At this the tears rolled down Delphy's cheeks and she smiled ever so slightly. Juna and Cathra waited expectantly on either side of Sadhima, but the others started to laugh. Eventually Delphy began a cautious grin. A yellow comrade took the opportunity to tickle her in the ribs. She giggled and that set the whole group off into the laughter of hyperbolised happiness.

Lana turned to me, 'You see, Emma, it's joy.' But I wasn't convinced. A grouchy bad humour had never looked more attractive in my life.

'Let's take a walk, Lana,' I suggested, breaking into their psychotherapeutic moment. I got three turned backs and Lana stood up. I took her arm. 'Can we go outside?'

'Sure, we can go into the garden.'

'Well, I was thinking more like outside outside, like the Dairy Queen, but I guess the garden will have to do.'

'It *is* a beautiful garden,' she said, begrudging the material plane. We walked through french doors into the greenery, hushed and humming in the dusk. She sat down on a curved-back wooden bench under a mimosa tree. I sat down next to her and looked around at the delicate little mimosa blossoms at our feet. The garden was bordered by lit up hallways, and yellow people striding purposefully back and forth down the corridors.

'What's that over there?' I pointed to one wing of the building with an imposing entryway, an extra pond with lilies and a miniature rotunda with a cupola over the doorway.

'That's Ananda House. It's where I live.'

'Kind of a dorm situation?'

'No. Ananda House is different. Only some of us live there.' She shrugged and I wondered what 'only some of us' meant in the cosmic scheme of things. Did the less enlightened get to bunk down in the barracks?

'How did you get involved with Vishnu anyway?'

'Oh, it was easy. It was so easy. I was staying with my Aunt Ida in New Mexico. I used to go to the sauna in town. Just to get out of the house. I had – well, I'd been feeling pretty depressed. I noticed that it felt good to go into town. There was a sort of alternative bookstore. They had a sauna.

'I liked to just sit there, in the heat and the dark. I was trying to forget a lot of things you see. Boston, my mother's ambitions for me. That whole crazy scene in the physics lab. I just wanted to be left alone. But I didn't want to be alone. You know what I mean?'

I nodded. I knew what she meant.

'So I met this guy there. We talked. I thought maybe he was on a sexual trip. But he was cool. He invited me over to his house. He was a silversmith. And he had this beautiful place. I would just go there and visit and he'd go in the back and work and leave me sitting in his living room.'

'A great host.'

'It was wonderful. I felt like everywhere I've been people have wanted something from me, you know what I mean. It was just

58

what I needed. Just to sit there, during the day. And then he played me some Vishnu tapes. I heard his words. I knew right away. I knew that I wanted to be there. He told me there was a commune in the mountains.'

'And then?'

'I packed my things. As any pilgrim I needed very little. I wasn't alone. The hills and the wind sustained me. I walked into the desert along the highway. But I was not alone. He was in every stone, he spoke to me on every breeze, he loved me and accompanied me and his infinite caring permeated every lizard and cactus and stretch of asphalt on the way to him.'

'Yow.'

'And when I got there they had work for me right away.'

'And when did you meet Vishnu in person?'

'When I had my first darshan – audience – with him. It was like I looked at him, and his eyes reached into mine. He was looking into my soul, Emma. For the first time in my life I wasn't alone. I transcended myself. I had found sanctuary.'

She looked at me and brightened up, 'It's hard to believe how unhappy I was!' I tried to smile at her joke. 'And now, I live in this community of love. And healing.'

'Like Delphy just got healed.'

'Yes. Exactly.'

'And then?'

'Then I had the most wonderful opportunity. Vishnu wanted to improve his English. And you know how Mother is. If ever a black girl learned how to speak blue blood WASP English it was me.' Lana was right. I'd never thought about it, but she and Jonell both sounded like Katharine Hepburn.

'So every day I gave him lessons. We went over pronunciation for hours. He even had a portable language lab flown in. It was great fun. We laughed and laughed. It was marvellous.'

'So you spent a lot of time alone with him.'

'I have been very, very privileged. And it did raise the spectre of some jealousy. We are all seeking, but some of us are still working on the perfection of loving.'

'Are you still giving him English lessons?'

'No, Vishnu is brilliant, that lasted only a few months. He

picked up the whole thing right away. He's finished now.'

I remembered Vishnu's voice as it spoke to me from under his beard. He didn't sound like Katharine Hepburn.

'So what are you doing now?' I asked.

'Oh, you mean busyness, things to do. I know the dead space well.' She looked at me indulgently.

'Have you totally traded physics in for – '

'Being in the magic presence of a realised being? Yes. Yes I have.' I wondered how much Lana was in his presence. I wondered how perfect her love was.

'And I have the loving meaning of daily tasks, Emma.'

'Cleaning?'

'Cleaning is another form of meditation, if it's all in his service. But I'm not cleaning toilets, Emma, not that it would make much difference. I've been endowed with the greatest task of all.' She paused to let the suggestion of her ultimate task form in my mind.

'What's that?'

'Cleansing *him*,' she said almost defiantly.

'Come again?'

'I'm his assistant in kryia. The cleansing process.'

'What is that exactly?' I asked, thinking it would be one more thing I wouldn't be able to understand. But I was wrong.

'It takes different forms. Sometimes Vishnu ingests quantities of salt water and after very specific movements he expels the water from his body.'

'And you're ready with the pan?'

'Or sometimes a receptacle in which to receive the yards of gauze material he swallows in order to clean his intestinal tract.'

'Oh. Yards?'

'It's a longer process, of course.'

'Of course.'

'I'm very privileged in my personal contact with him. He's helped me so much. Remember how shy I was?' She flashed her copper eyeshadow at me.

'You were always busy computing the probability of black holes with the given data. It wasn't exactly grist for the conversational mill.'

'That was probably closer to a liberation than I realised at the time,' she said. 'But you see, all the different aspects are one phenomenon. Vishnu taught me that.' She glanced at the sky conveniently above us as her example. I couldn't help looking up and seeing stars beginning to prick the darkness above us.

'But what about your career?'

'Oh, Emma,' she laughed tolerantly. 'I have learned the ability to arrive at concepts *without* logical processes.'

'Oh, swell,' I said, but Lana was immune to everything from sarcasm to honest goodwill.

'How'd you like the meditation?'

'I'm afraid it gave me a headache and not much else. Actually, Lana, to be honest, I didn't really come here for the meditation.'

'What do you mean?'

'I'm here because Jonell and your Mom called today and they're worried about you – '

'What?' The word fell softly from her mouth and I felt the sky above us begin to slip. She said nothing for a moment. I heard gravel crunch somewhere on the far side of the garden. '*What*?' Then the transcendental smile fell from her face and something crashed in her eyes.

'Hey, it's not a trick, it's just that – '

'It's just that you lied to me.' The words came through tightened lips.

'Hold on a second,' I soothed her. 'I couldn't get through to you any other way. I've been trying to reach you through the switchboard at Ananda House – '

'I don't believe this!' Her face drew into an angry knot. She looked up at the sky that was no longer her friend or example.

'They seemed reluctant to connect me with you,' I continued. 'And I asked them to give you a message to call me back, and you didn't.'

'The phones are being repaired. And I was busy,' she said angrily.

'And the switchboard operator got a little rude – '

'What did you say? That you were a friend of the family?' She shook her head slowly back and forth.

'Something like that.'

'What did you expect? We've had kidnappings here, Emma. I'm

61

not a prisoner. Jesus Christ, what paranoia. And I suppose my mother works right into this.'

'She's worried about you.'

'She's worried about her child prodigy finding happiness instead of reflecting glory on to her.'

'She said you called her "flesh mother".'

'Yeah, well, I guess she took that the wrong way.'

'Tell me the right way to take it.'

'She didn't have to take it so personally. I needed to separate myself from her. I was just an extension of her ego trip, I wasn't supposed to have any happiness of my own.'

'Give her a chance. Nobody's done the job of parenting right yet. And maybe she's blowing it. But she deserves to know where you are, and that you're okay.'

The coffee shop was filling up and getting noisy, and laughter spilled out into the garden.

'Call her,' I said quietly, trying to get into one vulnerable spot the guru had maybe left behind. 'Don't question all her motives for wanting to be in touch with you. If you've got the wisdom you say you have, then you see that she has things to work out too. Try and forgive her.'

Lana looked at me, the copper eyelids were puffy and her voice fell to a carefully controlled low tone. 'It hurts. It hurts too much.' We sat there together, under the inky sky, in the beautiful garden with the sweet breath of night-time flowers and trees, transcending nothing.

'Without getting into a complicated discussion about different kinds of freedom,' I began, 'I'll call your mom and tell her you looked beautiful, and for the most part as happy as a clam.' The brown eyes warmed a degree. But I wished to hell Lana wasn't happy as a clam. I would have liked to see her troubled neurotic soul work things out in the real world.

'You're damn straight I'm happy,' she said under her breath. 'And I am starting to understand these things, not with a rational egoistic mind . . .' she went on. But I was hearing a pretty egoistic feeling of revenge in her voice.

'Emma Victor?' The words split the warm night air. Bumper Lee's big figure appeared in a dress with cucaracha ruffles on one shoulder. Her springy red hair was entangled in lace.

'You know her?' Lana turned to me. 'Hey, what's going on here?'

'Beats me,' Bumper shrugged with a little smile, looking from Lana's face to mine.

'Hi, Bumper,' I said.

'I hear you tried to reach me at the office today.'

'I ended up taking a meditation instead.'

'How do you two know each other anyway?' Lana had gone back into her defensive posture.

'I was doing some fund raising and met Bumper. It's just coincidence that the WFF is funding a project I'm helping with.'

'Oh.' That seemed to be a solvent for the crinkled eyebrows. Lana looked at her watch. 'Shit, it's nine o'clock. Gotta go.' She got up in a near panic. Vishnu sure knew how to make people jump. He had even made me jump out there on the sidewalk. I wondered, when he saw Lana's face now, as she walked in, would he also in some way see mine? Lana turned back and looked at me a moment.

'I'll make that call,' I said, not knowing if I was making a threat or keeping a promise. Well, Lana and her mother would have to figure that out for themselves. Lana nodded vaguely and hurried through the coffee shop and down a corridor. I wondered if it was cosmic diaper duty that was calling her.

'What phone call is that?' Bumper asked me and I looked into the careful, hidden face, so different to Lana's. Yes, Bumper was cut from a different bolt of cloth and I knew what made her so attractive. It had nothing to do with humble servitude.

'Don't meditations bring about mind reading?'

'I'd rather not tax my intuition if a direct question and answer can fit the bill.'

'I'm a friend of Lana's family. They wanted me to find out if she was okay.'

'And? Is she okay? What did you decide about Lana's personality?' Bumper raised her reddish eyebrows.

'I didn't see much sign of it.'

'Lana's upper percentile brow chakra but she's a flunker on the fourth,' Bumper shrugged her shoulders and then continued at my quizzical glance, 'Fourth chakra, the heart. The ability to merge, with another person, with yourself.' She smiled and showed me her big teeth. 'Or with a group.'

'Looks like she's doing a great job of that.'

'You're only seeing the most superficial level, Emma. Lana has problems. A mother who's stifled every essence of her being for nineteen years.'

'She had two parents, Bumper. Your Freudian bias is showing.'

'I'll tell my father you said so,' she laughed.

'So which chakra are you big on anyway?'

'Me? The spleen chakra. Located three fingers below the navel.'

'And what does that do for you?'

'I feel the emotions of other people. Clairsentience. And it can go so far as to,' Bumper stepped in front of me, blocking out the bright light of the coffee shop, 'lead to the duplication of the emotions in others.' I looked up into her face but her expression was lost in shadow, 'But only in very extreme cases. What did *you* find for yourself here, Emma?'

'That I can't get the hang of your meditation and all I do is worry about my debts and my tennis serve. But I see you have that all worked out.'

'Yes,' Bumper smiled. It was cold in her shadow so I got up and stood next to her; she towered over me by big inches. I looked at the mimosa fans littering the ground. I bent down and picked one up, playing for time, finding a delicate smell in the pink and white hairs. Bumper nodded her head towards the doors and I walked alongside her, her cloud of thick hair rustling on her shoulders. We went through the french doors into the garish, bustling room. Yellow groups were laughing, confronting, carousing and making a lot of physical contact. But I wasn't to be a part of the golden gladness; Bumper was hurrying me through the crowd and into the hallway.

'I'm sorry you didn't get anything out of the meditation,' she was saying. But she wasn't sorry. She'd pegged me for a parental spy in the house of happiness. We were coming into the low-lit lobby. Closed for business; my fellow meditators had either left or decided to stay for the night.

'I didn't really come here to meditate so I couldn't,' I confessed.

'Maybe you should give it a try, for real. Or are you so satisfied with life, with yourself? I don't think so, Emma Victor.'

'The way I've usually heard about it, from the people who should know, meditation isn't something that brings you nirvana like a fast-food hamburger. I understand it takes discipline, and a lot more time than a crash course in hyperventilation can give.'

'You disappoint me, Emma. Your cynicism is so transparent. I had higher hopes for you; you know the experience of putting a principle before your individual concerns. The inspiration of being in a committed group! The thrill of finding a way to live that is new. The hope – our hopes – of a women's movement were high. But things have changed. I can look back on that time and those feelings but I can't feel the feelings any more, can you? Where did they go? You're mostly thinking about making a buck, while we've got excellent living conditions, good food, purpose and the promise of a happiness developed from within, a promise only you can make, or break, for yourself. And the women's movement, what has it given you, Emma?'

'It's left me with a mind,' I said, but my reply was killed by three quick beeps from the reception telephone. Bumper strode to the desk and picked up the receiver. Something unpleasant registered on her face and she turned her back to me and hung up. Suddenly she wasn't so interested in politely getting me out of the building. Pushing and shoving would do just as well and she took me by the elbow and propelled me past the picture of the laughing man and out of the door. I dropped the flower fan and reached into my pocket.

'Let us know when you're serious about meditation, Emma. I'm sure with a little attitude improvement you'll be able to make some progress with that bulky ego of yours. Goodbye now,' she ended on a false sing-song note and sailed back through the lobby as fast as she could without running. The door hissed slowly, closing on pneumatic hinges.

I had the feeling something wasn't good at the Vishnu Divine Inspiration Commune. I wanted another look at how things were going there and I knew just how to do it. My bulky ego had slipped a matchbook in the doorlock as it closed. I opened it up and went back into the lobby. I crossed the dark interior to the white

65

reception desk. I moved the curtain behind it to get a view of the garden. I didn't see a lot. I just saw the long expanse of hallway behind the coffee shop lit up like an airport terminal. And Bumper Lee running through it like a bat out of hell.

I heard laughter renew itself from the coffee shop. Such attractive, happy people. Healthy, sensitive, seemingly intelligent. I wondered what made them want to give up secular life for their cloistered joy. I wasn't sure I wanted to find out. I'd hardly had time, anyway, to find out what the laughing man was saying. Mostly I had just felt nervous about belonging. Bumper was right about the fact that they didn't recruit. They were as welcoming as the cashmere sweater and circle pin set in high school. I wondered what that had to do with his supposed wisdom. What did making the yellow leap guarantee anyway?

I turned away from the window when Bumper's figure disappeared into a doorway. It was none of my business any more. I could call Mrs Flax and tell her Lana was okay and would probably get in touch with her soon. My part in it was finished. I did think Bumper Lee was sort of attractive though, even if she was as two faced as a rupee. And what had made her run off like that? But it was time to get home and go to sleep. Tomorrow was another day, where I could at least enlist my minor talents in service of the Women's Benefit concert. There were lyrics to be picked up and dropped off, a concert to get on its feet and money to be made to supply the coffers of more urgent causes.

I turned my back on the garden and walked over the cold hard flagstones of the high-tone lobby. It was one way to save your personal world, all right. Especially if you were upper middle class. Find big Daddy, hole up with some finely furnished digs and overload your brain with oxygen.

I closed the door of the Vishnu Divine Inspiration Commune without regret, and walked out into the night. I saw the double-decked chrome grille of the Plymouth grinning at me from across the street. One trip to the Vishnu Divine Inspiration Commune was enough. I thought it would be just swell to get into my own bed and sleep the sleep of the sleeping.

Ten

I liked waking up alone in my sunny California bedroom. I lay peacefully with friendly fantasies and only the sound of birds, my own breathing and the far-away hum of the freeway breaking the silence. I had painted the room a milky white, but left a William Morris wallpaper border running under the picture rail near the top. I traced a dark green vine as it grew olive leaves and small crimson berries, a printed paper trail under the ceiling without a trace of yellow in the pattern.

The morning paper banged against the door. Full of sport, diplomatic blundering, gossip and snappy columns, it was just my cup of mental tea. The jogging murderer I could have done without, he was scoring more hits in out of the way places, but the day still looked friendly.

Nor did I mind filling the Plymouth up to the brim and handing over a big piece of money. Today I wasn't going to God, I was going to visit the next best thing, a punk rock queen who'd hit bottom and was coming up on top. For a Women's Concert, no less.

I drove way back into the hills to Panorama Way, escorted by grass, sage and verbena burnt brown by the sun. It made this area the biggest firetrap of the rich next to LA. If you could afford the house and the taxes, the fire insurance could squash your status like an old tennis ball. I came to the iron gates and stopped the car. I walked to the speaker box set into one of the cast iron peonies and spoke my name. The gates rolled back to let me in. The Plymouth rattled its valves up the steep incline and I couldn't have been more surprised to see what was there than if I'd found the lost city of Atlantis.

Some pretty racy architect had gotten hold of Nebraska when she had more money than sense, and had erected something like the Taj Mahal on an acre of Piedmont Hills real estate. A tiled pathway led between two pentagonal reflecting pools towards a building which would have made the art directors of *Sinbad the*

Sailor blush.

A square building in the middle was topped with a monumental dome, which ended in a petaled cupola shaped like a lotus blossom. Two three-storey towers clustered on each side and tall pendentive windows marched around the curved surfaces like slotted eyes. Glazed tiles ran along the corbelled arches and under each windowsill. Copper planters belched raucous pinwheel petunias from every parapet and ring moulding around. It was the Ayatollah goes to Hollywood. I walked towards the entrance in the middle building between the reflecting pools. A half-moon bell was set in the pink stucco for me to ring. The door was answered and Portia Fronday stood there with an open mouth which exhibited a high level of dental artistry.

'Yes?'

'I've come for the lyrics – ' I said to her questioning glance.

'Oh, of course. I'll get them. I'm on the phone. Just wait here.' She let me in and strode off, leaving me in the tiled entryway with a pair of oversize brass oil jars big enough to hold a couple of monkeys.

I looked around. The domed ceiling had a trompe-l'oeil design of flowers twirling in and out of woodwork bowers. The latticework stood out in high relief along the convex surface. It had nothing aesthetically in common with the geometric design of the tiles on the floor. California wealth. I let out a sigh and looked at my watch. I glanced at the empty space where Portia Fronday had stood and wondered if I should venture out into the thick carpet of the corridor down which she'd disappeared. I hummed a little tune and shuffled my feet on the tiled floor. They shuffled pretty good on the glazed surface. I hummed a little louder. I'd been waiting ten minutes. How long does a beggar at the gates of rock and roll wealth and bad taste have to wait? Suddenly I got the answer I didn't expect. A loud shriek split the silence and echoed along the hard walls. It came from the left and I walked from the hall to a corridor and another domed chamber, this one with an elevator. I looked back and didn't see Portia. I didn't hear her either, but a wail rose from somewhere above me. So I went inside the little panelled elevator and pushed the only button there was. The door closed; with a jerk and a tremble it started upwards.

As the elevator ascended a low moaning increased with every yard, like an impending orgasm. When the elevator stopped so did the voice. The black polished doors jiggled and parted, opening into a small hallway with more tiles and Ali Baba props, and a hammered brass door in front of me. A pair of slippers stood on the floor to the right. Like an actor who doesn't need stage directions I took off my plaid tennis shoes and put them neatly beside the other pair. I pushed open the brass door.

Behind it was a semi-circular room which featured a picture postcard view of the Bay eighteen feet wide and six feet high. It was the closest thing possible to being in a glider while standing on solid ground. Sky surrounded the room, clouds lazily floating by, and the edge of the world was visible beneath the Golden Gate bridge in the distance. The view continued through slotted windows which led around the curved walls of the room, to converge again at the hammered brass doorway where I was now standing.

Huge cream-coloured pillows embroidered with mirrors were flung across the room like balls of glistening cotton. I took a step and the white carpet absorbed my feet. I hoped my socks didn't smell. It was all very Moslem and I thought about women living in towers wearing veils. There was one person in the room who could have used a lot more than a veil. That was Nebraska Storm, who was leaning out of the window in her birthday suit and a purple cellophaned pageboy cut, howling like the minute she was born. She threw her voice across the water as if she could reach the sailboats in the distance, a nightmare Scylla from the land of rock and roll. So Nebraska was doing a voice lesson. As she paused for breath I cleared my throat and she jumped.

'What are you doing here?' The long woman drew herself up from a window seat and reached for a nearby robe.

'I'm sorry,' I said, averting my eyes, 'I heard a scream. I didn't mean to intrude.'

Nebraska appeared to think that over, slipping one arm and then the other into a Scheherazade robe. I was glad she took her time; I was still in shock from seeing her in the altogether, in front of a picture postcard view of the San Francisco Bay.

'I came to pick up the lyrics for the Women's Benefit Concert.'

Her shoulders relaxed and she slowly cinched the belt around her waist. She swung the long pageboy hair, a cross between black and magenta which fell in front of one eye like Veronica Lake. 'So now that you know I'm not screaming, what can I do for you? Sing?'

'That's a question you don't need to ask.'

She looked at me once and her eyes lingered on my socks. They were clean. She turned to the window and took in a lungful of air and leaned out. The melody floated clear above the mountains and seemed to hang there. The words were Italian. She threw the last note over the water, paused a very correct moment and turned to me. 'It's from *Aida*,' she said. 'I guess there's nothing quite like being entombed alive, underneath the God you've offended,' she muttered.

'Or any God at all,' I said.

'Or any God at all.' Her words drifted out of the tower window.

'Of course together in tomb or tower has something over dying alone,' I said, noticing Nebraska's posture and forgetting for a moment how to make coherent conversation.

'But not over dying,' Nebraska said. I wondered if she really did hold the needle for Edwin Anvil. I decided to look out of the window with her. The view was the same, stupendous, but neither of us was noticing it.

'This is quite a place you have here,' I said, finally.

'Yes, it is quite a place. I'm glad you like it.'

'I didn't say I liked it; I said it was quite a place. Who was the architect anyway?'

'A former acquaintance. He used to be my real estate adviser. Now he's into design. He was big on the Middle East. The cradle of civilisation and all that.' She was being very friendly, but friendly with the egotism of stars; it was the kind of familiarity that presumed you already knew each other. And according to Nebraska we did. I'd seen her on stage and heard her voice a thousand times, and that was all that mattered. Or maybe not. 'So you're one of the ladies from the concert production; I remember you, in front of the car. I've never seen any fan put Portia in such a snit.'

'I was concerned about the concert.'

70

'You mean you're not a fan.'

'I don't go running after public figures I admire. I didn't mention to your agent downstairs, but I guess I'm elected to be your trail guide through the traffic to the concert tomorrow night.'

'Oh.' Her eyes wandered around the room. What I did with my time probably didn't interest her very much.

'Don't worry about your concert,' she said in a bored tone. 'I'm much more on time these days. I've learned the secret of managing time so I'm not late any more. I'm becoming a little more like . . . like everybody else I guess.' She looked at me with her cool eyes. 'I suppose you're one of those highly dedicated self-sacrificing political people. I can admire that. If you don't get into some kind of ego trip about it, I should think it would feel very . . . liberating in a way.' She looked at me but it felt like she was making me into something she wanted to see. 'Why don't you have a seat?' She sat herself down on a pouffe cushion. I chose one facing her and the Bay.

'I'm hardly self-sacrificing and there are a lot of women that work harder than I do.' I watched Nebraska look me up and down. Her eyes were doing funny things to me. I had said I wasn't a fan but I was wrong. 'Being a musician must be hard work. And sacrificing.' I watched the little sailboat triangles from the view glide back and forth behind her head, in one ear and out the other.

'Established fame,' she leaned her head back and smiled, swinging the black magenta pageboy. 'A contradiction in terms. Who pumps the fame machine? For a long time it feels like you do. You create the image, and you project it. And then one day, further down the road, you don't want to hear the voice of the image any more. But by then it's too late. It's telling *you*.' She turned her head to look out of the window. 'But I don't know why I'm saying all this.'

'It sounds like you need to talk about it.'

'The rest was a bad chemical vacation that nearly killed me. I'm just starting to get myself back together. I feel good, my body is healed and I've learned some of the tools to attain equanimity. I feel ripe to go out there tomorrow night. It's just the right moment to make the first step. I'm glad I don't have to make it alone.'

71

Baby let me drive your car, I thought. 'We're having the concert taped.'

'Have you sold it to the networks?' Her eyebrows flew up.

'No.'

Her eyebrows fell fast. 'Hey.' She seemed to be looking at me closer. 'Want something to drink?' she asked.

'It's eleven in the morning!'

'Tea. I'm off the sauce.' She opened up her arms to the view of the Bay. 'I was shooting heroin when I could have been drinking soma-roas.' She turned and looked at me. 'A celestial beverage drunk on the moon.'

She glided over to a carved table which supported a tray with a tea warmer and a pot of tea. She poured two streams into fluted porcelain cups and walked back. She gave me a cup and I looked down and saw two dragons winking from the bottom of the greenish brew. I sipped the sweet liquid and looked up. Nebraska was gazing out the window.

'You know,' she began, 'when I'm singing I sometimes feel as if my voice is only a vehicle for the pulsations of heavenly sounds.' She turned towards me and crossed one leg over the other. Her robe fell open and I could smell the sweet breath from her mouth. An involuntary heavenly sound was about to leave my mouth but the elevator doors made a noise and Portia Fronday entered the room instead.

'They're going to be here in twenty minutes – ' she started out to Nebraska and stopped when she saw me taking tea with her client. Portia wouldn't care how hard-working or self-sacrificing I might be. 'May I ask what you are doing here, Miss, Miss – ' she spluttered. I looked at Nebraska, who had arisen from the pouffe and was walking towards the window.

'Take it easy,' I said. 'I just heard someone screaming from this direction and thought maybe I could help.' I smiled at her. That was a mistake.

'I'm not in the mood to play games. Nebraska needs rest, time to practise and cannot be distracted. This is a breach of privacy.'

'You don't have to tell me that,' I said, thinking about Nebraska's robe.

'I've been in this business a long time and I've never witnessed such disrespect. You should be happy that we have troubled to give you these lyrics for the use of your – your – ' She shoved a brown cardboard-backed envelope at me.

'Signer.' I finished for her. The message was clearly that we'd better be grateful. I felt the steering wheel of the Porsche slipping out of my hands. I thought I heard Nebraska saying goodbye but she was only thumbing through some sheet music.

'May I escort you out?' Portia asked, through gritted dental work.

'Please forgive this unpardonable intrusion. I really meant no disrespect. I hope Ms Storm will have a pleasant productive morning.' Nebraska was watching the sailboats again. 'Ms Fronday, you needn't trouble about seeing me out, I can find my own way.' I bowed to each of them and high tailed my ass out of the hammered brass doorway. I just missed stepping into the elevator as the doors slid together in front of my face. I heard a sigh from within the room, the two women had waited until I was gone. I pushed the elevator button again. Then I heard Nebraska Storm whining in a way which recalled her old role as the punk princess of pissoffedness.

'What the hell am I gonna do?'

'You're working both sides of the street, honey. That's the way you started walking, so don't complain if you're getting bow legs,' Portia said.

'Well, what the hell was I supposed to do? I had to save my life, didn't I?'

'You have to save your ass.'

'Well, I didn't do it for *this*. Jesus fucking Christ, I'm gonna get *wired*!' Nebraska cried out. The worry wheels started grinding in my head. We didn't need Nebraska on drugs and out of her chemical balance on stage.

'If I could just reach him – '

'I've been trying. It's not easy to get through – ' Portia began.

'He promised me.'

'You can't order him around like a side man, honey.' Portia's voice calmed and counselled, but underneath I could hear she was worried too. Nebraska and her manager had their sights set on climbing the charts, only Nebraska was climbing the walls. 'I just hope a hundred thousand dollars is enough,' she sighed.

'If I could just get through – '

The elevator arrived. A hundred grand. Well, she could afford it. But it was definitely a high price for a drug man, sound man or side man. I hoped that she didn't make the score before the concert tomorrow.

The elevator let me out into the tiled entryway and I walked back over to the Plymouth. I put the lyrics on the seat of the car and said a little prayer that Nebraska would perform well tomorrow night and not give anybody any shit. I started the engine which rattled its valves at the turn of the key. What I wouldn't do for a new car or a hundred thousand dollars.

I shifted out of park when another, better car came up the driveway. It was a real normal kind of car, a light blue late model Chevy sedan. Two regular sort of guys were in it. They got out, closing the car doors quietly. They wore running shoes, dress Levi's and light windbreakers. Dark glasses sat on their noses. Two regular, normal Joes pushing the half-moon shaped doorbell on the quirky castle of Nebraska Storm, and probably pushing something else too. I hoped whatever Nebraska Storm was getting wired on would leave her system by the concert tomorrow. Suddenly, I didn't care about driving the Porsche at all. Driving the old Plymouth to a disco beat was just fine for me.

Eleven

'to da DISCO beat!'

BAM! The speakers turned off and along with it the light. I had been so busy visiting the past, drinking tea with Nebraska I'd almost forgotten the reality of the cell. White walls and foam mats. The thought of the beautiful interrogator who'd left me alone. I tried humming a tune. Two tunes. I tried to remember all the chart-busting hits of my pubescent years. Many had come back as nostalgia numbers. I tried cross indexing tunes to my grades in school.

After a while it didn't work. Either the room was getting cooler or I was suffering a psychological exposure that has become physical chill. My dried-out tongue was sticking to the roof of my mouth. Cold. I started to think seriously about peeing in the corner.

I was not going to be afraid.

'Da DISCO beat!' The speakers blared and then shut off just as abruptly.

'More tricks!' I yelled at my unseen captor. 'I always love a change!' Silence. 'I'm not ready to opt for a real bed. I love foam rubber mats! It reminds me of my gym teacher Miss Virangie in high school!' Silence.

I lay down and tried not to think about water. About murder. I had to keep my mind busy, organised around itself. I couldn't let the overwhelming changes in noise, light, and temperature take over.

Yes. The thing was to escape where no escape was possible. Maybe foam rubber mats and Miss Virangie was the way to do it. I tried hard to think about the high school modern dance class and how Josephine Hensler and I caught on to boys' wrestling. It started with going to meets. Miss Virangie was putting the moves on Mr Davenport the wrestling coach. She'd been putting the moves on Mr Davenport for seven years. Josephine and I didn't have that trouble. We loved the mats and the sweat and the grunts. Some chemistry was turning us on and we started trying the take downs and the double arm locks after school. Something in our teenage souls had left us free of the ambivalency that kept Miss Virangie and Mr Davenport in the bleachers, something naïve and wonderful, something that would have never packed my bags and brought me to California, landing me in a dark cell without a toilet, musing about murder.

But I was better off remembering the April day when Miss Virangie had gone out with the cheerleaders for practice. With a bang the heavy fire door of the gym had closed out the bright green practice field. Jo and I were left in the quiet cathedral of the gym.

We didn't hang with the cheerleaders and we weren't excited by the strange emotional choreography of modern dance. I went for tennis, and Josephine went for track, which gave her the long leg muscles that rode under the soft surface of her skin. I challenged her to an Indian leg wrestle on the foam rubber mat. Just like the mat I was lying on now, only now it was dark and I was cold. And old. How did I get this old anyway? Nebraska Storm and Bumper Lee had certainly helped me on my way. But I'd asked for it. I forced my mind away from them, away from my bursting bladder, and back to that teenage April day.

Josephine and I lay on the mat, and we raised our legs, once, twice and hooked on the third. Even the leverage of her long legs couldn't save her and I pulled her over to my side after a small struggle. We lay there panting in our royal blue official high school gymsuits, with our first names chain stitched in white above our left breast pockets. We looked at each other a moment, smiling. We held the glance for a while, until it was almost uncomfortable, staring into each other's eyes and then the uneasiness was gone and the nervous smiles left our mouths and we just kept on looking. She had two brown spots at five o'clock on her pale blue irises.

Suddenly Jo jumped me. I remembered the cheap square clasp of the belt flashing as she went for a take down. I cheated and grabbed her foot and sound exploded out of her mouth as she hit the mat. Her lips were forced into a tight rose as the air escaped. I spun and got my leg between hers and controlled her for a cross body ride. I could see the edge of her Peter Pan training bra with the expandable cups under the ironed flap of her uniform. She let her arm go, all the fight gone, so I pulled her over easily. Too easily. The next thing our fingers were finding their way under the elastic-banded bloomers of the regulation gymsuits made in Akron, Ohio, for thousands of high school girls in the Midwestern states of America. That's when cheerleading practice was over and Miss Virangie walked in.

It hadn't been so much fun then, but I was getting off on it now, the foam rubber mats, the smell of my own sweat and a tiny hard button after I unzipped and got my spit-wettened finger under the fleshy hood. I had read that most sensory deprivation subjects

76

masturbated after thirty-six hours, even in front of their captors. And I probably hadn't been locked up for more than twenty. I always knew I was oversexed.

They could have turned the light back on for all I cared. I had the most beautiful cunt in the world, but my underpants were falling apart at the seams. When mom mouthed the cliché, exhorting me to always wear good undies – 'You never know where you'll end up, dear' – she didn't have masturbatory exhibitionism in padded cells in mind. But dammit, I had to pee. Coming was out of the question. It was hard to imagine how I'd gotten in such a fix. But then, no one could have imagined the high price of driving Nebraska Storm's Porsche. And everything had gone so smoothly, just before the concert. I remembered fondly my house, my empty mailbox and the way Roseanna Baynetta had with obscene phone callers.

Twelve

Returning from Nebraska's I'd wanted to make sure my mailbox was still empty, so I stopped at my house on the way to the office. I thought I'd give Roseanna a call to let her know I was on my way. I picked up the phone.

'Yeah,' she growled, chewing on something.

'It's Emma. Are you chewing on your pen or your fingernails?'

'Better get over here with those lyrics or I'll chew on you.'

'Maybe I won't mind.'

'Cut the wise and get in the car. Oh, and – ' she broke off. I heard a button being pressed, 'Hang on.' I heard her pick something up and her voice became sweet and cloying. 'Still there, sweetie? Haven't you come yet? Well, why not? Something about the sound of my voice? What's it gonna take?' Her tones got softer until she cried, 'Hey! He hung up! Bastard!

Just a sec, Emma.' I heard her press a switch hook. 'Yeah, I know, not enough time. Well, I'm doing my best. Yes, yes, aren't we all. Okay.' She sighed.

'What's that all about?'

'I have a breather on the phone. He calls here once a day. I've got to keep him on the line, for at least two minutes for the trace, they say. I keep him going for seven and they still don't trace him! Either he gets frustrated or suffers premature ejaculation. Either way he keeps calling. I can't do the same thing twice or he'll wise to the trace.'

'Don't let it get you down.'

'Down? Hell.' I heard her push her chair back. 'It's the modern woman's daily sport. I'm just a creative person who enjoys a challenge, Emma – ' The phone rang again. Roseanna said, 'Yes, yes' into it a few times. 'Listen, Emma, get those lyrics over here now. That was the signer and she's tapping her fingerprints off. But you'll never find a parking place, it's getting into the rush. So just double park and stick 'em in the package lift in the lobby.'

'I'm on my way.'

I crawled to the Women's Benefit Concert Office with the lunch hour traffic. It was located in a building on the edge of the Oakland downtown renewal. I double parked outside which caused a panic in my lane of traffic, but I put on the hazard lights and didn't look back. I parted the glass doors and went into the lobby where a fairly good attempt had been made at restoring the marble vestibule. It still carried the memories of telegram, bus and bell boys whizzing out of Art Deco rooms in perky uniforms. The package lift was still intact from the twenties. I grasped the shiny chrome handle and pulled open the circular doors; I put the cardboard-backed envelope containing Nebraska Storm's lyrics in the dumb waiter. I pressed the button that indicated our office and sent the thing up. 'Thanks, Emma,' I heard Roseanna crackle through the speaker, and I walked back out to honking horns and unhappy drivers stuck behind my car.

I didn't feel like going back to my empty house. I was still eager to taste the atmosphere of the different Bay cities so I chose Berkeley where the parking was slightly better, and decided to drop in on the public library. The air was cooler there, and without the burden of rock stars, pissy agents and meditation hangovers I felt cooler too.

I walked past a storefront and a small black sign hanging by two chains from the ceiling. Three-dimensional wooden letters spelled out 'Life Move' and beneath it, 'Institute for New Therapy'. Seven techniques and sensation sessions were listed and three had little circled 'r's, the registered trademark symbol floating above them. It seemed like everybody had an angle here in California. Every time you thought of a happiness technique, you'd better trademark it fast. If you didn't, someone else would and your golden ideas would clink in somebody else's pocket.

I walked into a cookie collective which was on the verge of closing and bought a bear's claw that was still warm. I had sugar on the corners of my mouth when I decided to go check out the giggling man in the library to see if he had any special characteristics, or if he meditated with a trademark symbol floating above his head.

The library was still open, despite budget cuts. I sat in a high-ceilinged room with pitted wooden tables and low brass lamps. I made some notes and got some microfilm. I passed in some stack slips and got some books back. There wasn't a lot about Vishnu.

As usual, the greatest outpouring of material was his own press and propaganda office which he called an Educational Foundation. The hard news only mentioned him arriving on these shores. A food review of the Palace restaurant was also cross indexed. It seemed the Vishnus were into high-tech dining and one delicatessen. They had a lot of free labour but so far it didn't seem like they had enough venture capital to erect an empire like the Moonies. Vishnu didn't flash on the tube or give interviews. The only other story that cross indexed was one about a guy who had given up deprogramming. When I found it on the microfilm it was listed under 'constitutionality'. It seems that one Donald J. Morot had been a deprogrammer for three and a half years and was now into real estate. He had heavy questions about the ethics of deprogramming, but he had no regrets about 'returning' the twenty-seven Moonies 'to their families'.

His experience with Vishnu followers was different. He could discover no coercion on the part of the group to retain members.

The Vishnus were attractive; they had something tangible to offer lost souls. Members offered themselves voluntarily, like leaves waiting to be raked into a pile. He said the Vishnu followers were a good example of the difficulty in drawing the line between religions and cults. He himself had just come back from a trip to Japan where he had spent some time with Zen monks. So Donald J. Morot quit the deprogramming game and signed up for silence.

I found an authorised biography, issued by the organisation, a hard cover with deckle-edged paper. They weren't sparing the bucks on printing costs. I opened it and found a touched-up frontispiece printed in brown and black ink with a piece of tissue paper protecting Vishnu's image from scratches and greasy fingers. Even in photos he looked disarming. Or maybe I was just remembering the unsettled feeling of being in his presence. I was glad to be able to study his face from the photographs, where it wasn't going to look back, or talk to me. It was almost impossible to tell how old he was from his official portrait, and the clue wasn't to be found in print either. He was clearly pushing middle age to its limits, and his thin frame didn't make him look too healthy. The only thing that was for certain was his white hair. He had a lot of it, very clean and very combed, flowing from all sides of his head, even his face. He had bushy but tended eyebrows, and a ski jump nose that was the dream of every Valley girl. His eyes looked very flat and black, the irises like tiddlywinks against the white of his eyeballs. His smiling mouth was just visible beneath the ample moustache which joined his beard and the emerald earring hung as always from his right ear. Rumour had it that the gem was a gift from the Shah.

His press bio read like Siddhartha goes West. Javad Chaudhuri, or Aksobya Vishnu as he later became, was born in Bangkok. The young Javad left Thailand and was enrolled in a Tibetan monastery at a tender age. The monastic life demanded fourteen hours of study a day and three hours of examination by doctors of theology. His education continued for five years in this way, and then he became Master of Mystical Practices. It was hard to imagine that he used cribsheets or wrote the answers on his hands in ballpoint pen. Up until then he sounded like the real item.

When Tibet was annexed to China in 1950, Javad, now Vishnu,

returned home. Apparently mystical practices didn't go over so well and three months later he started a six-year tour through the Far East. Returning through Pakistan he gathered a crowd of faithful followers. It was a small group evangelism in which instead of singing hallelujah, everybody stands still – a not too uncommon occurrence in that part of the world. Travelling through to India, Vishnu founded an ashram at Adyar, not far from the spot where Madame Blavatsky and the Theosophical Society founded Huddlestone's Gardens by the Adyar River. It was at Blavatsky's that Vishnu first rubbed elbows with the West. He met two elderly students of Gurdjieff, founder of the Institute of Harmonious Development of Man. Gurdjieff was one of the first people to introduce Eastern Wisdom to the West, and his philosophies became a bridge linking Western people with Eastern thought.

Vishnu travelled that bridge in the other direction. He left the ashram and made a journey to Greece, Rome, London, and Los Angeles. His route not only followed the decline of Western civilisation, it also shocked him. Vishnu declared the West in a lockstep march to spiritual and physical extinction. As the West sat *in articulo mortis* Vishnu was waiting patiently in the wings with the answer in his soul, or a hardbound volume of nineteen dollars and ninety five cents (tapes available by mail for seven dollars). It was a tough job, but somebody had to do it.

The library had one publication describing his theories and principles. I went back to the stacks and ordered it, tapping my feet for five minutes of waiting. A young white man returned with the volume and put it in my hands with a cynical twist of his mouth. I was becoming one of them already. Excited at finding the real item I settled down into the wooden seat of the chair and leafed through the pages printed in purple ink. I read about chakras and saw a lot of diagrams with pentangles, lines converging into cones with big words around them like 'Present Day Reality', 'Ego-Tense', 'Possibility' and 'Time'. The Vishnus had a lot of complicated ideas about how the whole thing was put together. Not analysis, they stressed, but synthesis. They would call it a cosmic dance. On paper it looked like a knitting pattern.

I read all the words and understood all the sentences but my toxified, Western personality couldn't get into it. The emphatic phrases sputtered for a second like Roman candles in my brain and went out. My egocentric soul didn't kill them, they just died without attention. And I didn't care. I didn't want joy and ecstasy Vishnu-style. And even if I did want joy and ecstasy I certainly wouldn't want them all the time.

But Vishnu, they counselled, accepts the pace of everyone. Just be yourself, he said. It was what I was planning on doing all along. And that's just what I would have done, if Mrs Flax hadn't called me again.

Thirteen

I drove home and decided to clean the kitchen woodwork. Tomorrow was the concert and I would change the bed linen tonight and wash the pillowcases with lavender crystals. I would make a few phone calls and maybe acquire a tennis partner or two. The phone rang. It was Maya, reminding me to go to Nebraska's house at seven and get her to the concert by eight-thirty. She was so nervous she couldn't even tease me. Suddenly I wished I had signed up for food concessions or gate duty. I wanted to be working with the other women from the concert; escorting a rickety rock queen was looking less attractive and was no food for my feminist soul.

I was thinking all these cheery thoughts and arranging the cleaning supply area around the L-pipe under the sink when the doorbell rang. I dropped a cardboard canister of cleanser and went downstairs to open the door. On the right was the rosebush, home of several billion aphids, and on the left, a small apple tree. Neither of them had rung the bell.

I leaned out of the doorway and saw the back of a blue and white striped T-shirt on an individual under five feet tall scurrying away from the house and down the path. It turned around.

'She couldn't get to the bell,' the pubescent person explained, and jerked a thumb in the direction of the driveway, where a shiny old wood-panelled station wagon was parked.

I went down the steps and around the little path, past the Japanese maples. The ancient car was in the middle of a questionable restoration process. It looked like some mechanic had the shakes when the bondo was applied. The hardened goo was hanging off part of the back wheel guard. The wagon was much higher than it should have been, even for the days when cars looked like bowler derbies. The whole thing was resting on an expanded chassis and its windows were smoked so dark I couldn't see inside.

I stepped over the kerb and the rear door opened with a hum that gave away a technology inconsistent with the exterior. I walked around to the back, and looked inside the boxlike woodie. It was Roseanna Baynetta who smiled and said hello from within and rolled towards me on to a perforated metal shelf that was slowly extending out the back.

She came into the sunlight which flashed off her shiny brown hair and the gold embroidery on her bolero jacket. She leaned forward from the waist with a straight back; she held a small bunch of purple freesias delicately in her hand. Her torso turned and light shot off the gold embroidery again. She was wearing a white T-shirt underneath, blue jeans, and heavy duty tyres on her Everest and Jennings wheelchair. Her arm extended and I could smell the flowers in her perfect tapered fingers.

'I realised you wouldn't be heading down to the office any more,' she reached down and put on a wheel brake, 'so I thought a delivered token of our appreciation was in order.'

'Thanks. It's been a long time since I've had any floral fan mail.' I buried my nose in the blooms to hide a warmth in my cheeks. 'What kind of buggy is this anyway?'

'It's a 1949 Chrysler Royal. Ashwood panelling on the sides, all original exterior. Except for the fibreglass and the smoked windows.'

'And the chassis.'

'Well, I thought a Jeep chassis was a good idea.'

'You did?'

'Sure.' Roseanna pressed a button and the platform on the back

83

of the car descended. I looked over at the little kerb that separated the driveway from the garden. After the driveway came a two-foot drop to a pebbled path, then three steps of flagstone and a concrete stairway leading to the front door.

'My abode is sometimes not so conducive to entertainment.'

'The view from your driveway will do. The freesias reflected her violet eyes.

'Would you like tea, lemonade, or a Boston Overhand Twist?'

'What do you think? I've never been to Boston.' She smiled and I went back into the house. I took two tall tumblers and frosted the rims. I put ice, pineapple juice and sangria into them. I cut up a lemon and floated a slice on the surface of the liquid. I poured some almonds and peanuts into two nesting bowls and put it all on a tray.

I went back downstairs. Roseanna was looking out over the driveway into the street where my low juniper bushes were being taken over by Bermuda grass.

'It sure is green and pretty here,' she said, lifting the sweating tumbler from the tray. She held it in her lap where it made a moisture stain on her T-shirt. She tinkled the ice back and forth in the glass and looked down with the eyes that matched the flowers. I guessed that the ice was looking better than I was.

'Well, the yard should be greener. I water the hell out of the lawn and I don't do much of anything else. The weeds love it and they're healthy at least.'

She took a sip. 'Hey, this is great.'

'It's our Boston survival recipe. Eat peanuts, get your salt in-take, sit in the shade and drink an Overhand Twist; and if you close your eyes you can almost remember what it's like to be out of the city. How *do* you get out of the city in the summer?'

'Mostly I never am in the city. The greater part of the year I raise bean sprouts with my ex out in the sticks.'

'Bean sprouts?'

'They don't talk a lot and I like the delivery work.'

'How long have you been doing that?'

'Oh, four years now.' Her forehead had a little shine, from a thin layer of sweat. The Twist didn't seem to be doing its trick. The ice cubes in my mouth were making my fillings cold.

'What did you do before bean sprouts?'

'Hang on to your hat, Emma Victor. I was a classical ballet dancer. I had an agent and a closet full of tutus.'

I wasn't sure I could handle it. I could see Roseanna springing out of her chair, standing on her points and doing a jeté, extending her leg and executing an arabesque in my imagination.

'You're seeing me leap out of my wheelchair, an adolescent Makarova,' she said. 'You're thinking, now she's sitting down all the time.' Roseanna clanked the ice cubes in her glass. 'But how do you think I got here in the first place? Ballet triggered more than my toes. On the way home from my début I was in a four car collision. But that was a long time ago.'

'Well you still have the same hand action,' I said, remembering the way Roseanna had of extending her fingers and moving her head to watch them. But I was still imagining Roseanna doing arabesques in the driveway when I heard the phone. 'I'll just be a minute, I hope.'

'I'll just stay here and enjoy the view.'

I turned and went up the path. I took the phone in the living room and sat down on the sinking sofa-bed couch.

'Hello? Hello?' the receiver squawked. I put it to my ear.

'Hi, this is Emma. I was outside – '

'This is Mrs Flax, Emma. I heard you went to see Lana. And I want to know what the hell is going on out there!'

'I beg your pardon?'

'What's going on?'

'There's not much to tell. Lana looked swell, and talked a great ecstasy line. Everything seemed in a holding pattern to me, and not very exciting. I've got a classical ballet dancer sitting in a wheelchair in my driveway. I probably have more to worry about than you do.'

'What? Listen, I just heard from Lana and she sounds desperate. What did you say to her anyway? I'm thinking I'd better come out there and see for myself.'

'I'm sure everything will be all right, Mrs Flax. I'm not sure you'd get anything more from Lana and the Vishnus than I did.'

'Which was?'

'A waste of several hours of my valuable time, twenty dollars and a meditation which gave me a headache. Lana's firmly enrolled, I'm afraid.'

'Well, when I talked to her on the phone she sounded borderline ... bordering ... well, she's attempted suicide before – '

'That's funny. When I saw her she was catching mimosa blossoms in her hair and talking about finding true happiness. She's determined to stay there. And she looked beautiful and healthy.'

A pause. Then a snurking sound on the phone that might have been someone crying or a plumbing problem in somebody else's L pipe. 'I – I'm sorry,' she said. 'I'm just at my wits' end. I want her home. She disappears for six months and then calls me and says maybe she would want to return to Boston. Then she changes her mind. That's all.'

'You mean Lana really wanted to come home?'

'That's what she started out saying. She sounded so utterly lost and desperate.'

'And it doesn't sound like the same Lana I talked to.'

'Could she have been hypnotised when you saw her?'

'No,' I said, remembering her response to my hidden motivation for going to the meditation. 'No, her responses seemed quick and genuine. And she didn't look too tired of summer camp last night.'

'Do you think she's been brainwashed, Emma? Tell me about this, this cult thing. It sounds so weird. Are they making her crazy?'

'They would probably have a good laugh at your words. They'd say the point was to go crazy. That if you can see through this layer of reality – '

'Sounds horrible, just awful!'

'Really? I don't know. Although I am rather fond of this reality at moments. It's just that I think this guru guy is looming large in the picture.'

'Oh God, is it dangerous?'

'Less people get hurt from it than Agent Orange. I would hardly call it an emergency-creating situation. But I don't think it's a swell place for her either.'

'What did it look like to you?'

86

'A lot of people wearing yellow clothes enjoying themselves in a pleasantly decorated highly sanitary situation. The members are busy doing therapies and meditations and in between they clean all the time and make great food and eat it. What time did Lana call? Did you have the feeling she was alone? That she was free to talk?'

'Eleven p.m., just after the rates went down. Oh, I'm getting more worried – do you think they're really doing some kind of personality destruction?'

'About the phone call, Mrs Flax – what was happening in the background?'

'What do you mean?'

'Were there background noises of any kind? People, music?'

'No, it was very quiet.'

'As if she were alone in the room.'

'Wait, there was music of some sort. Very simple sort of melody, the effect was tranquil. Some kind of organ?'

'A casio organ doing Eric Satie?'

'Something slow. And then it stopped towards the end of our conversation. I guess someone was in the room with her playing music.'

'No, ma'am, the place is piped in with hippie music. They play it in a lot of the rooms. I don't think people actually hang out making that kind of music; it has too much the factory touch. No, I don't think someone was playing music in the room. I think someone turned the music off.'

'Oh, God, they're monitoring her. Maybe she won't be *able* to call me again. It is kidnapping!'

'Let's not jump to conclusions.'

'Why not?'

'Because it's going to cost you a plane ticket and Lana is legally of age to decide what to do with her life. Will you let me try and contact Lana again?'

Mrs Flax agreed reluctantly and we hung up. But I didn't like my conversation with her. I couldn't imagine what would make Lana fall off her transcendental cloud of bliss into despondency. I didn't like it that the angry runaway was suddenly considering going home. It was too much, too suddenly. The image of Lana, giving skinny Santa Claus English lessons, and performing even more intimate duties would hardly put Mrs Flax at peace. And withholding that information gave me a heightened sense of responsibility and involved me more, not less, in the situation. I looked out of the window at the neighbours' side of the street where a land cruiser and a low rider were parked. I remembered Roseanna sitting in the driveway and hurried downstairs.

'Sorry,' I said, panting. 'Some old friends from Boston with a California problem.'

'Are you the problem?'

'They'd like to think I can help with the solution.' I looked down the driveway with her. It looked the same as it did ten minutes ago. 'My best friend's sister seems to be ensnared in a cult group.' I told Roseanna about the Bumper lunch, the Flax phone calls and my meeting with Lana the night before. I told her that I didn't like the set-up or the selected intelligent attractive women with their hippie hair, beaded headbands and vulnerable unshaven armpits who so often form the inner circle around spiritual leader types.

'Well I think if you go back there, there's one thing you should keep in mind.'

'What's that?'

'It's unlikely you'll be able to shape events. The whole situation seems pretty strongly off course to me.' Roseanna looked at me a little too long for comfort. 'You going to take Nebraska to the concert, right? Want to go to the party afterwards?' she asked.

'I think I'd better leave it open,' I said.

'Not too much happening after the concert,' Roseanna pressed. 'The party will be where it's at.'

'But I'm not sure where I'll be. It's part of the problem I'm supposed to solve.'

'Yeah, sure, okay.' Roseanna undid the brake and wheeled her chair on to the lift platform. 'I've got to be getting along. Work is backed up at the typesetter and I had just enough time to drop by.'

'Thanks for the flowers,' I bent down and kissed her cheek and she helped me by turning her head. The kiss landed somewhere around her ear, far from her violet eyes. I stood up and she reached over and pushed the button to elevate the ramp. We'd both been lying. Roseanna didn't have just enough time to drop off the flowers. She had all the time in the world. And I didn't think any minor solution I might supply to the Flaxes would get in the way of going to the party after the concert with her. But Roseanna made me nervous. And it wasn't her problem. I could see the woman dancing on the driveway in a bolero jacket shot with gold embroidery. And I could feel attraction, but the object of my attraction was sitting in a wheelchair. I felt confused and generally shitty walking towards the front of the car to say goodbye.

I leaned in the passenger side window and got a good view of the Baynetta style of transportation. In front of two swivel bucket seats was a dashboard cluttered with a CB radio, a quadraphonic tape player and a laser decimal disc turntable, dashboard telephone and something that looked like a radar screen.

'Aren't you worried about all this stuff getting stolen?'

'I've got tamper switches and an ultrasonic motion detector working for me,' she wheeled herself over the carpeted interior of the wagon. 'It's all fitted into the bakelite dashboard.'

'Where'd you get all this stuff?'

'My dad. He works for the big fashion houses. You know, investigative security is big business with the skirts. Rip offs before the runway. "Dahling, I can't believe our models are wearing the same dress!" So that's what he tries to prevent. He *says*. I think he's been a counterspy.'

'And he just lays this stuff on you?'

'He gets a lot of it as samples and I get to score it that way. Or it's slightly out of date. Sometimes I just borrow the gadgets. He doesn't seem to mind.'

'That's great.'

'Not entirely. He's never said it, but I think he imagines me in one of those haute couture dresses he protects. He could probably get me a few of those, but he figures I couldn't pull it off in a chair. Maybe it's only subconscious on his part, but I think he sees it as a kind of technological compensation. And I see it,' she did a quick transfer out of her chair and into the bucket seat, 'as just one more way to get something I want.' She leaned back in her chair, and suddenly everything tightened in her face, and just as suddenly, relaxed. Roseanna Baynetta had pain. She started the engine and ran her hand over the other bucket seat. 'Original highlander plaid upholstery,' she smiled, and began to back slowly down the driveway. I wondered if she used radar to do it.

As I walked back to the house my thoughts went back to Lana. I had to talk to her again. Face to face. But my cover was blown at the Commune. I couldn't really be the enthusiastic meditation goer or truth seeker of the evening before and I didn't think I'd be welcome as a drop-in visitor. But I was saved from worrying about that. I heard the phone and an allegro pace brought me up the stairs to answer it. Of course it was the solution to my cosmic predicament. I was hearing the voice of the guru Giselle, Bumper Lee asking me for a date, saffron style. I should have stayed with freesias; one more date with Vishnu was going to be one too many.

Fourteen

'And first there's a rebalancing workshop that you must experience.' Bumper was adding an unwelcome addendum to her invitation in her happy, hoarse voice.

'I'm not a tyre. Just dinner with you would do. Besides, I've got a lot of things on my mind.'

'But the concert isn't until tomorrow night. And you have to play chauffeur to a chronically late performer. Maybe a quiet evening here would be just the refreshment you need to release tension, Emma.'

'I doubt that rebalancing is the way to do it, but I'll agree that I'm tense. And you're not making it any better.'

'You can get in touch with your inner resources here, Emma.'

'And get pushed out the door again like last night?'

'I'm sorry; I also had some things on my mind. And to be frank, we've become a little paranoid. But maybe we have reason

90

to be, when someone comes to a meditation as an excuse to make contact with one of our family.'

'Only because she's somehow unavailable to make contact with the rest of the world.'

'Our phones have been down. And it was her choice not to call you back. But let's not quibble about that.'

'No, let's quibble about something else. You're inviting me to an evening at the Commune, to save my soul, or to make up for your inhospitable behaviour?'

'No. I'm past the karma of complications, Emma. I just like you. And I used to *be* a lot like you. I was a lesbian feminist too.'

'You just got unlucky and happy one day.'

'Come to the workshop and have dinner with me tonight. I don't want to convert you, Emma.'

'No rahami breathing I hope. There's better ways to practise panting.'

'Don't forget your towel this time.'

We hung up. Another evening filled in California. I would see Lana Flax once more, and maybe not for her own good, whatever that was now. I hoped to destroy any suspicions her mother had and some of my own as well. And maybe I hoped, more than a little bit, for the opportunity to hang with Bumper Lee, the biggest woman I'd ever met and, next to Roseanna, the only turn on I'd felt in months.

I walked into the lobby of the Vishnu Commune at six o'clock with my towel and a better attitude. The lobby looked just about the same as the day before, the same guard was flicking his eyes about, and the same clots of yellow people were drifting happily back and forth through the spacious room. The same people lounged on the long burgundy couch with foam partitions, talking into telephones. Hippie muzak oozed and bonged out of speakers at an almost imperceptible volume. Only the desk had changed. I could see the tall figure of Lailieka bending over Delphy, her white face pinched. Her sharp nose pointed at something under a raised counter that had been attached to the desk. One long bony finger extended itself slowly; she looked like a mosquito taking aim. I went over to them, leaned over the countertop and glanced under the ledge to see liquid crystal numbers floating in an elaborate PBX switchboard system cluttered with headphone jacks and polished brass knobs.

Delphy was pushing buttons on the new equipment and gave us a great view of her three-tone eyeshadow. She and Lailieka turned their faces towards me, like two secretaries in the principal's office. I was the student without the note from Teacher.

'I'll deal with this,' Lailieka said quietly to the smaller woman, who nodded and got up without looking at me. Lailieka touched Delphy's sleeve, caught her eye and pushed a button on the switchboard. 'You can take the other line now,' she said to her.

'And I'll take this one,' I said, just under my breath, but my breath didn't cover it.

'What kind of line did you expect?' Lailieka asked as Delphy waltzed away between two plate glass doors. Lailieka straightened up into a more direct firing position. She pushed back a strand of black hair that had escaped from the french braid trailing down her back.

'I've come for another meditation.'

'I'll bet. And what did you expect to get out of it? A more convincing way to lie? All you want to do is spy on one of our members.'

'Bumper invited me,' I said, and watched Lailieka's face fall off an emotional cliff and climb back up again. 'I guess she wants to have dinner with me,' I said apologetically.

'I see,' Lailieka looked as if she was eating rat turds. They weren't going down well but she was swallowing anyway. It was a long time since I'd seen anyone so obviously jealous. She must love Bumper a lot, in a bad, old-fashioned possessive way.

'You don't mind, do you?' I said. 'I brought my own towel.' Rat turds with green gut dressing.

'How nice. How very nice. For both of you.' Lailieka started scratching on a small memo pad with a pencil. I leaned over the counter and looked down. She was writing 'wwwwwwwwwww' all joined together like a sharp little chain.

'She suggested I try the rebalancing workshop.' I did my best to sound enthusiastic. 'Before we have dinner, that is.'

'Fine.' Something like a smile curved the lips and a light gleamed in her pretty green eyes. 'I'm leading the workshop. It's very intense, so be prepared. You'll be contacting a lot of tension – '

'Gee, I thought I was already doing that.'

' – in a structured risk-taking situation.'

But I was already doing that too.

'You know where the coffee shop is?' And Lailieka pointed her pencil just like Delphy had the day before. I went towards the room filled with the busy yellow laughter so I could have the wonderful feeling of being something short of a leper. I walked up to the bar where yellow bodies parted and made a big space, colour quarantine keeping me safe from any feelings of claustrophobia. I ordered a peach kefir and sat down. Lana wasn't to be seen. I noticed a woman who wasn't wearing yellow. Another blue sheep. She was staring at her gymshoes and fiddling with the edge of her aqua T-shirt. I was grateful to find someone who had not merged with the whole.

'Are you going to the rebalancing workshop?' I said to her quick glance as I walked towards her. I sat down next to her and we look-ed out at the multicoloured garden waving at us from the big window.

'The rebalancing workshop. It's going to be a trip,' she said.

'It's very heavy, I hear. How did you get interested in rebalan-cing, anyway?'

'My boyfriend did it. He's taken prayamis. Last week.'

'Run that by me again.'

'Prayamis,' she said with finality, as if explaining to an idiot, and it dawned on both of us that I was more of an outsider than she was, blue clothing notwithstanding. 'Prayamis, that's when you officially join the family.'

'So you haven't joined?'

'Not yet. I started wearing yellow clothes a few weeks ago. It felt a little silly at first, but look.' She pulled up her faded jeans and showed crocus-coloured socks. 'I really am, like, starting to feel the power.' She glowed with a happier expression which must have come straight from the yellow ankle energy. She looked in her early twenties.

'How did you feel when your boyfriend became involved?'

Her eyes shifted back to the shoes. 'Oh, I was scared at first. You know.'

'No. I don't know. Is it so scary?'

She reached down and retied her laces. 'It's like, really, really hard. I just didn't understand. He had new friends and they just talked about Vishnu all the time. That was before I, like, started listening to the message instead of the words.'

'Right. And then you started to get the message.'

'Sure. I mean, I have things to work on. He's right. I've got all kinds of ego trips going. I lay it on our kids all the time. I keep them from having their own, like, self concept. I guess. I mean that's what Johnny – I mean Prhrrnina – keeps saying.'

'He has a new name?'

'It's, like, part of surrendering.'

'And rebalancing helps with surrendering?' I was getting worried.

'You've got to work through all this stuff first. But the exercises really help. It's, like, brutal.'

'Swell. Where's your boyfriend now?'

'He lives on the other side of the Bay. He moved out when he started living the life. He's really in touch with himself.'

'And you have the kids?' She nodded. 'So you're really in touch with the laundry and the cooking. Sounds like a good reason to be aggressive. I'd be stockpiling tactical ballistics.'

'Well, he might move back in. I guess I have to see if I can, like, find myself.' She looked up and had a small battle with words. She frowned and lost the war. 'We all need to, like, get in touch with the autonomous expression of who we really are, I guess.'

'I guess.'

Just then Lailieka marched into the coffee shop and the young woman and I stood up and followed her into the stairwell. The giggles and cheery commentary of the yellow people who walked behind us became hushed. I was on my way to experience the process whereby they came to terms with themselves and became so happy. I felt as if I was going to an execution.

'One of the ways to enlightenment is confrontation with self,' Lailieka was explaining. The room was dim, with musty orange curtains hiding the garden behind a big window. Two bare light bulbs gave off thirty watts apiece, hanging from brown wires, swinging slightly. 'You have to learn to empty yourself of thought

94

to make contact with the world.'

But do we have to do it in such an ugly room? I thought. The Vishnus clearly splurged with their decorating budgets on the more public areas, like lobbies and coffee shops, just like two-star hotels and nursing homes. I wondered what the barracks looked like.

'And to begin, you have to learn to contact your emotions, head on.'

My heart was sinking. I didn't have any insurance for emotional head-on collisions. My policy was up, it had lapsed in Boston. But maybe a collision was just what the doctor ordered.

'Through a series of exercises and rituals we will begin to trust each other . . . ' Lailieka was saying.

I looked around the room and saw twelve other people, two white gawky boys, four earnest looking young women. Two men on either side of Janine, the abandoned mother, were decked out in official guru jewellery. A large white woman with big unmade-up eyes and lots of little teeth overshadowed a hippie prince boy with flowing locks, long eyelashes and a mouth as luscious as a Belgian bonbon. And there was a Farrah Fawcett Major blonde.

' . . . so we can get in touch with the essences of each other.' That seemed like a really good idea; there I was summing up the group members by complexion, age, and dentistry.

'But first, a rahami breathing exercise to loosen us up.'

Oh Christ, I thought, Bumper had promised me that I wouldn't have to do this. She didn't tell me I'd be doing it with boys either. But I martyred myself and started bellowing huge breaths out with the rest of them. The pleasant spots of light, the twinkling wallpaper appeared and lined the chamber of my consciousness, or nearly unconsciousness after a while. During a rush of dizziness I took it easy and took a peek. My compatriots were still puffing away, heads whipping back and forth, portraits of their leader bouncing on their chests, breaths coming out in blasts from lungs. A few stumbles, Lailieka was looking at me, I closed my eyes and shifted into some hearty sounding pants. A bong sounded, everyone stopped but me, one phoney sounding aspiration ending just after theirs. I was the last one clapping in a silent auditorium.

A few giggles and I turned to the man next to me. 'Glad that's over, I've really blown my bagpipes,' I confided. His gaze fell a few degrees in temperature.

'Now I want you all to just look around and make eye contact with each other,' Lailieka was saying. 'Just look at everybody. That's it.' We gazed around. Everybody looked just the same, except for an occasional pinpoint of light that flitted across my viewing screen.

After that we had to choose a partner. The large white woman and I gravitated towards each other. She had a twinkle in her eye, which helped me get through a variety of activities with her. Then we had to hug for fifteen; her body enfolded me pleasantly for five, after ten I was sweating, and I started getting anxious just as the exercise ended. Then we had to gawk at each other again for a while. Moving our arms up and down, we squawked like chickens on command. After we finished making fools of ourselves, we stood up for a long time with slightly bent knees doing a variation on the hyperventilation, this time making a hissing sound. The hissing began quietly and got louder and louder. Then I realised that the sprinkler system had been turned on in the garden.

A sudden sob and I peeked and saw Janine stumble and then retch. 'I'm going to throw up.' She loped towards Lailieka who gave her a paper bag with a neutral nod. She grabbed it and tossed her cookies in.

'Whoooaaa,' somebody wailed and I jumped. Then a sniffle. God, they were all going into the main wash and I was still on fill. It just wasn't happening.

Janine was still retching into the bag and one of the men with jewellery was driving his voice into a crescendo that threatened to take the lead over all the other sounds. Suddenly my partner pulled out in front with a cry like a banshee thrown out of hell with blood-sucking leeches attached. Her large chest heaved in and out. Great sobs stuck in her throat and were released with gulpings, as if she was drowning. She bent over and wheezed and wailed, snot coming out of her nose. Finally, she was sobbing. I put my arms around her big round shoulder.

'What's it about?' I said. 'What are you thinking?' She just broke into snivels. 'Say a word.' I implored. Her giant torso

96

clenched and relaxed and her head came up with an expression that was a lot farther away than her face.

'Be with yourself,' she said quietly, her nostrils widening. And then she bent over and started sobbing again. Well, the heavens could certainly find the spaces between us, I thought and got back to work.

Listening to the crying, sobbing, retching and howling was getting on my nerves. It was no use. I couldn't feel this kind of stuff. I supposed I could think about my ex-girlfriend back in Boston and wonder why I let her practise heart surgery on me when I knew she didn't have time to love anybody. The board of surgeons would issue her a licence, just as surely as I had done. But trying to bring up emotions with any particular train of thought was not the idea here. These people weren't trying; they were all acting as if they could spontaneously go bananas irrespective of subject matter. I couldn't just force myself to feel something just because I was supposed to. Could I?

I heard the abandoned mother of two starting to scream, 'Help! Help!' her voice rising in a room filled to the brim with cacophony. Nobody did anything, I guess we were all assuming that her cries of help were symbolic, a cry from a self-exiled Robinson Crusoe.

'Somebody . . . ' her sobs rose. 'Somebody hellllp meeeeeee!' she squalled and Lailieka strode over to the rescue at last. Redirecting Janine back to her partner, Lailieka arranged them in a pietà position: Janine continued to cry and her partner held her, but looking upwards in a detached way as Lailieka instructed, and stroking her back occasionally.

I shuddered and wished desperately that Bumper had gotten me into one of the parapsychology workshops. Maybe I could have met an attractive soul from the other side, or re-emerged as a pipe playing goat herder in Atlantis. Too late now. The workshop went on. We became apes and had to pretend that we were being hunted in the jungle. Lailieka sounded a gong that signalled the end of the first half of the session. 'I'll explain later about the sleeping areas, show you your mattresses et cetera,' she said. 'And the house doctor will be around to tell you about the contraceptives.' Then we broke for coffee.

My comrades emerged like those wooden toy figures made up of separate parts and held together by an elastic string on a pedestal. The button had been pressed in the workshop and they had disintegrated into loose limbs. But someone let go of the button, it was time for coffee and they stood up, their parts snapped back together and everything was instantly in order.

'Have you tried the kiwi kefir shake?'

'Have you seen Steven Spielberg's latest? The man is really into the reality of kids, I mean . . . '

'It's not enough to just get it on with somebody . . . ' my partner was saying to the long tall boy with pimples. I guess the barriers were breaking down. But I wanted out.

I walked into the coffee shop and found Lailieka talking to a woman in a cool yellow-green cotton suit. I walked towards them and saw the narrow eyes, the drawn up mouth, the sudden flush. A romance soured into resentment, I could smell it anywhere. It meant Lailieka liked girls, but she didn't like me interrupting her break.

'I don't think I want to stay in the group – ' I tried saying to her.

'We'll talk about it afterwards.'

'Could I just discuss it with you for a minute, I mean – '

Lailieka's back turned around one more time and her voice brushed me like a fly off her sleeve. 'We'll talk about it in the group, I said.'

In the group, in the group, in the group. Didn't two personalities ever get a chance here? Or just a bunch of bodies with one big personality for everyone? Did the spaces diminish so much better in the group that I could say why I wanted to leave? Would I be able to figure that out or express it in the chumminess of the group territory? I doubted it. It seemed to me the spaces between me and them would just get a lot bigger.

I went to the bar and got a thick yoghurt shake and tried to suck it up through a straw. I was pissed. The strawberry shake was great. Hippie Prince and Farah Fawcett Major were hitting it off at the bar, and one of the gawky boys was talking to my partner. This is really the essence, I thought, regression to a high school social predictability. The homecoming queen still got the football captain, even after enlightenment.

Lailieka signalled us back to the workshop. We sat in a circle.

The curtains were still drawn and the room was sour from sweat and forty cubic metres of bad breath. The two dim bulbs weren't any brighter.

I told them that I wanted to leave. It just wasn't my cup of tea, I explained. I couldn't get into the headspace, it wasn't really my bag and I could hear that I was losing the battle with words too.

'What does everyone think about Emma leaving the group? How have you *experienced* Emma in the group?' Lailieka squinted in my direction, then opened her eyes and carefully met each pair of eyes with something that looked more like a message than a question.

Twelve people looked at me from across their delineated emotional territories where they had just howled and barfed in front of this unmoved tower of emotional constipation, me.

'I didn't see Emma really getting into it,' one person said.

'Yeah,' one of the freshly scrubbed boys began, 'I think she has aggression to work out.'

'Well, I could see that she was playing games,' said a third.

'And I,' said Lailieka, 'saw you looking much too much at other people. What are you doing, writing a book?'

I got up, executing a perfect Indian Squat to Stand. Miss Virangie would have been really proud of me if this were high school, but it wasn't, and all the other tribal members were looking at me with suspicion or irritation or just plain confusion. 'Uh, I actually just wanted to come to dinner,' I began. 'I just want to say that I have enjoyed talking to some of you. No, that's not true, one of you.' I smiled at Janine.

Then I turned and tried to get out of the orange-lined interrogation atmosphere as fast as possible. I'd just gotten to the door when I heard Lailieka. 'Goodbye, Emma.' The words dropped like a body off the gallows. I went through the doors and tasted the space on the other side. Free. I hadn't felt so good since playing hookey and cutting the Ancient History finals.

I looked out at the garden from the long hallway. The sun shone on big sunflower blooms and a gentle breeze blew a spray of water beyond the edge of a fountain bowl. A bone-rattling scream issued from behind the curtains, but it was the rapid approach of yellow-sneakered footsteps that made me jump and turn around. Just my luck, a hall monitor.

And it was Sadhima, the pretty boy with the pearl-grey eyes. He looked calmly at me, with a smile of recognition. 'Are you a visitor?' he asked, and the whites flashed in his brown face.

'I'm a workshop stray,' I said. 'My flock is still in there.' I pointed at the orange curtains drawn against the glass behind me, where a wild elephant chorus was beginning. He looked me up and down carefully and I remembered how lovingly he had dismantled Delphy during the coffee confrontational therapy. His authoritarian glance wasn't above being flirty.

'You needn't bother checking my passport. I'm also here to have dinner with Bumper Lee,' I said.

'I didn't think Bumper had time to busy herself with new blood.'

'She didn't strike me as the bleeding heart type either,' I said, 'But aren't you doing some transfusions yourself, with the International Membership?'

'Are you interested in travel?' Sadhima enquired, in a way that made me sure that he had space exploration in mind for me.

'Not the kind that put Delphy out of her job without a thank you.'

'Why don't I just walk you to the coffee shop,' he said, his face never changing expression.

'Is that an offer or an order?'

'Perhaps you'd like a Divinity Yoghurt Shake? This way,' he said, and took me past pictures of god eye mandalas back to the coffee shop. He deposited me in one of the plastic booths and strode over to the wall, where he picked up one of the yellow courtesy phones that were hanging all over the place. He mumbled something and waited and mumbled something again.

I was getting a sour feeling in my stomach; I was getting tired of being led around and pushed around. Or maybe it was all that yoghurt. I sat down at a bench at the end of the bar and steadfastly studied the tiles on the wall.

Sadhima had seated himself at the entrance to the coffee shop. Two cuddling couples of heterosexual persuasion sat down next to him; a male asked him about possible excursions to India. 'We'll see,' smiled Sadhima and he leaned back and said something else that made his audience nod, smile and finally laugh.

He looked casually between the shoulders of his companions sizing up the coffee shop flock. My Divinity shake arrived. I glowered at it. Bumper didn't have much of a way with hors d'oeuvres, I thought, and even contemplated leaving. But that was before I found out what she was planning on for dessert.

Fifteen

The water had just started to separate out of the yoghurt and collect at the rim of the glass when the phone rang and Sadhima picked it up.

'You can go to Bumper's quarters now,' he said, leading me out into the garden and towards the kitsch rotunda and fountain. 'Here we are, Ananda House,' Sadhima extended his hand towards the building. It was the same kind of Far East Frangipani architecture I'd seen somewhere else lately. Someone trying too hard to make too much atmosphere with too much money. He opened the door with a flourish and extended his arm in the direction of a white-carpeted staircase. 'Up the stairs and to your left. It's the only door.'

'You mean I'm allowed to go alone?' I asked him, and he leaned over.

'You don't have to be alone if you don't want it,' he said, his eyebrows making soft porn suggestions.

'Loneliness suits me fine; I was just hoping I was too dangerous to let loose in this place.' I started into the building when I felt his hand on my shoulder.

'Oh, I don't think you're so dangerous.' He was grasping my shoulder firmly, making it impossible to shrug his hand off. I could feel his breath on my neck, and a cloud of Kama Sutra aftershave came with it, a cosmic sleaze breeze that wouldn't let up.

'According to your authorities I am chock full of aggression, envy, hatred and a bitterness that would shrivel your balls, buddy.'

'Oh, I get it,' he said. 'You only swing on one side of the street.'

'What makes it your business?'

'I just want to warn you about Bu Mper's dinners.'

'Just because you're feeling left out?' I knocked his hand off my shoulder, my fingernail tearing slightly at his skin, and he took his hand back with a laugh. He was probably a lights-on lecher; he just enjoyed playing in a vertical position.

I walked into the hallway with a mahogany table and a black vase with handles on its hips. Forty bucks worth of out of season lilies sat arranged under a portrait of the laughing man, pointing their golden pollen stamens out. The little reception foyer gave way to a high room with a vaulted ceiling. A showy white circular staircase curled up one end, just like in the movies. The perfect place to make an entrance in your new dhoti. A big chandelier of beaten copper with coloured glass inserts hung down in the middle like an oversize Hindu Christmas tree ornament. To the left of me a carpeted corridor stretched out and Lana Flax was rustling down towards the end of it.

'Lana!' I hissed, wondering why I was whispering. She didn't seem to hear me. She opened a door in the corridor, and disappeared. I heard her go down a few stairs. The tail end of her kimono rested a moment on the carpet, and then it too disappeared. I scuttled down the hallway and looked at the two wide marble stairs and the stairwell that curved to the right. 'Lana!' I hissed again, but the sound mingled with a whoosh of pneumatic hinges.

I looked back at the big quiet hall behind me and went down. I turned a corner, found two more stairs and then a heavily insulated fire door. I opened it and caught sight of the circular embroidered pattern on Lana's back bustling down a pink marble corridor. She stopped before another doorway and looked at it, as if hoping that it would open under the power of her gaze.

'Lana!' My stage whisper echoed in the air. This time she turned around.

'Oh, Emma, hello'. Her voice came from a deep freeze I didn't know she carried around with her. Her dark brown skin was pale and grey, and she'd left all her jewellery somewhere else.

102

'Why the hearty welcome? I mean – '

'Listen, I'm busy. Do you want something from me?' She looked tired, maybe English lessons were keeping her up nights. 'If you want to be sacrilegious, do it somewhere else.'

'Honestly, I was concerned about your welfare.' Just then we heard a tapping of heels and the heavy fire door opened. 'Dinner's almost ready, Emma,' Bumper called, her tall figure topped with red at the end of a long expanse of pink marble. She hurried towards me, a bunch of keys jingling at her waist.

Lana turned to me, 'So is this another coincidence? Or is this the second chapter of the story about being here out of concern for my welfare?' Lana shook her head. Bumper was approaching from the end of the hall. 'All these games you all play. It's beyond me.' Lana's voice started to rise. 'It's beyond belief.' She turned away and whirled back in the direction we'd come from.

Bumper arrived at my side, attempting to conceal her breathlessness. 'What was that all about?' she asked in the wake of Lana's kimono.

'It's about me confusing the hell out of my best friend's sister. Just a sec.' I started running down the hall after Lana. I opened the fire door to the stairwell. I didn't know what I was going to say to Lana when I found her, but she had sounded different to her mother on the phone. And even in the few moments I had talked to her in the marble hallway, she seemed different to me too. I heard her footsteps echo in the stairwell. And then they stopped. One flight above me I could hear voices echoing off the concrete walls.

'So Lana, you're interested in working on the International Membership,' I heard Sadhima say.

'Bumper suggested it to me.'

'Oh, she did?'

'Yes, my duties for Vishnu have been reassigned,' she said with a catch in her voice, 'Bumper is – Bumper is taking care of them herself.' Was that why Lana considered going home to Boston, I wondered.

'Perhaps you were getting too attached,' suggested Sadhima. He suggested that frequently, I noticed.

'It doesn't really matter now,' I heard Lana say. Attachment, non-attachment, these Vishnus could change with surprising frequency. Yesterday Lana couldn't wait to diaper the deity. 'I want to do anything that furthers our purpose,' she said to Sadhima.

'Perhaps we should consider something else for you. The International Membership requires a great deal of contact with people – '

'That's just what – just what I want. Right now,' Lana said stubbornly.

'But what you want doesn't matter, remember?' I heard Sadhima croon. A bracelet jingled, and I wondered if Sadhima was recruiting Lana for other duties.

'I – I have to go – ' Lana spluttered, and her footsteps started to descend again. I heard a door above me close. I had the feeling that Lana was ultimately heading for the laundry where Delphy would be folding sheets next week. So Lana wasn't going to fall on her back for the patchouli playboy. I heard her come slowly back down the stairs, where she was not happy to find me.

'So what angle are you working? The friendship angle? You wore that out already – ' she said angrily.

'Lana,' I started, 'I'm not betraying your trust. Not to anyone. Not to your mother. Or to Bumper. I only accepted her dinner invitation as a chance to see you.'

Lana looked at me with a twisted smile. She'd been little sister to Jonell for too long.

'Okay, and I think Bumper's attractive.'

Lana appeared to think this over, but it still wasn't the main topic on her mind.

'Your mom says you thought about coming home. And that you suddenly changed your mind,' I said.

'Yes. I thought about going home. But leaving wouldn't solve anything. It would only be running away – '

'From what? The emotional horror show of all these therapies?'

'I don't expect you to understand,' she snapped.

'What if your scene here deflates, or dissolves in the high tide of apathy?'

'That's pretty funny, Emma. That's funnier than you think.'

'Do you need money to get home on?'

'You fool, Emma. I would give it,' her mouth untwisted as the words fell out, 'to his greater glory.'

'Nobody is keeping you here? You won't let this guy Sadhima hassle you?'

'Perhaps his is an imperfect kind of love.'

'I'll bet that's generous. And Bumper?'

'She doesn't seem so spiritual on the outside, but I expect she has a great goodness within her. I admire her energy.'

'I think you admire her keychain,' I said, opening the door to the marble hallway where I'd left Bumper.

Lana's nostrils quivered and her brown skin flushed, but not with anger. 'The knowledge of human devotion is the gateway to heaven,' she intoned suddenly, and with an intensity that was nearly frightening. 'Heaven, heaven,' echoed back and forth down the hallway joined by regular, sharp taps, like a military drum and the jingling of keys. It was Bumper in her french court heels, striding towards us down the hall. Lana took an invisible cue to make herself scarce, and ran back up the stairway.

'I want to show you something,' Bumper said, beckoning me to follow her back down the pink marble.

'Why is Lana so unhappy?' I asked her.

'As Vishnu says, she has not learned to identify her being with the extraneous world. But let me show you something else besides one of our more troubled members.'

We walked back down the hallway, where Bumper unhooked the large keychain from her waist and opened up the door in front of us, the door that Lana had been so intently looking at. We passed into a tiny antechamber with a hissing ventilator fan. Bumper took a thick camelhair brush and began brushing off her caftan. Then she brushed my shoulders and jeans. It didn't feel too bad. We took off our shoes. She pressed a combination of numbers on a doorlock and a shell pink door slid open.

Gone were the marble and funereal atmosphere of the rest of the building. The architect couldn't get in here, apparently. A long window let in a rectangle of cool light on to a bleached stone floor. It was as quiet as a church, with muted colours; only the musk incense was loud, shouting in my nostrils. Lining the wall I counted seventeen ladderback chairs, with unfrayed rush seats and a pile of dark purple cushions stacked up at one end. A lapis-blue tapestry hung on one wall, with a dancing god in gold and silk appliqué resting in the branches of a bo tree. I walked over to the tapestry; the coldness of stone leaked through my socks. I looked up. The god's eyes were topped with a heavy black line and he peered out at me from under low pearl-seeded lids.

'The Divine Planamuni,' Bumper said quietly from behind me. 'Here we practise the Man-tray-aaana, the repetition of sound vibrations in definite sequence . . . ' She whispered in my ear, slowly, drawing all the syllables out. 'We are living in an ever-changing reality'. Her voice went on changing. She let that sink in. The dancing god was beautiful with his lightfooted dance and quiet pearly eyelids, a piece of art that was almost alive. 'The first step is knowing that.' My vision connected with a giant emerald, down around his lungi. 'And,' she continued, 'just imagine exercising control of that knowledge.' I felt Bumper's warm breath in my ear. Was she afraid the divinity was going to hear us?

The quiet and the musk hung heavy in the air; I shuddered. 'Is it possible – ' I started in normal volume voice.

'Shhh!' Bumper cautioned. After a moment she guided me by the elbow towards the middle of the room.

A light shone there, glowing from the floor. As we walked towards it I could see that a large section of the flagstones had been replaced with a twenty-five-foot square piece of thick plexiglass. And a flickering white and red light emerged from below. I leaned over, and peered down. The plexiglass was a see-through lid, a ceiling of an elaborate scene that played in front of my toes.

What was down there looked two hundred leagues under the red sea and I felt a similar pressure in my brain. Red flickering lights moved frantically over large stone figures, a third bigger than lifesize. They were leaning back and looking right at us; spiralling downwards they danced and fluttered, a stone staircase of beings beckoning us with willow-leaf eyes, curling fingertips, round bellies, conical breasts and secretive bud mouths.

'After having been born eight million four hundred thousand times the jiva is said to attain birth as a person,' said Bumper. 'And this one . . . ' she dared to nod at a large nude figure, twisting down into the glowing darkness. I saw a woman with open eyes and snake bracelets who was reaching up to offer me a polished coral pomegranate; fresh flowers were garlanded on her hips, her stone shoulders and neck. ' . . . Every night a sadhaka bedecks her with flowers at the time of sringara.'

I looked at the statue. Her mouth was open and a turreted crown grew out of her head and cascaded to her shoulders like a sand drip castle. She wore a necklace of tiny human faces which trailed down almost between her knees. 'She is the essence of five kinds of knowledge and is the embodiment of the Sahaja pleasure.'

'You don't have to tell me what that might be,' I breathed.

'Not so fast. She tramples upon the gods Bhairava and Kalaatri and wears a garland of heads still wet with blood, which she drinks.'

'A real scrapper, I guess.' I quickly moved my gaze to the painting which began where her pomegranate left off. It was a trip to yet another universe, where fourteen arms and fourteen purple heads multiplied on the body of one man, set against a brilliant Chinese red background. A miniature woman floated in front of his crotch, of which he only had one, and a pixie-like creature sat on a big olive green hat that covered all the heads. A hunter stood near by and prayed. I would have too.

Bumper looked at me as my eyes drifted past the little purple guy, along a drifting cloth of white, to a platform with a gathered circular canopy roof. Underneath was the thin Santa himself, Vishnu. His eyes were closed and he was wearing baggy pants topped by a thin linen T-shirt. The shirt was sheer enough to see his ribs. His earring glimmered. He looked as if he was sharing a very long, very private joke with himself. From the looks of him, it wasn't about food. I wondered if he knew we were standing there.

A sudden draught made the candles flicker still more and a few blew out. I stood transfixed in front of the quiet still scene inside the window, full of figures and spluttering flames. Somehow I felt something was wrong with the whole tableau. But maybe it was only Bumper, leading me away by the elbow.

'Was that Vishnu?' I pulled my arm away from her. She cocked her head towards the door.

'Shh. Yes. Samadhi, a state of trance. He's taken a vow of silence.' She was leading me across the room.

'He looks so thin.'

'It signifies an inner ripening, just as the seed gathers strength inside the withering fruit.'

'Oh. Who minds the store?' I was whispering as she opened the door in the wall.

'At the moment? I do,' she said. 'Come on, dinner's ready. You must be getting hungry.' We walked out of the cool room into the airlock chamber. We put on our shoes.

'What, what was that down there?'

'Hindu temples are never supposed to be engineered structures – they aspire to a condition of metaphysical monolith.' She opened the door to the brightly lit pink marble corridor. Her voice resumed the normal reciting tone, slightly bored, which I had come to associate with all the Vishnus. 'Many were just caves in the beginning,' she was explaining, tap, tap-tap-tap, tap-tap; we were walking down the hallway to the fire door. 'From the earth, of the earth,' she intoned.

'Seriously, those stone sculptures were really something else.' I shook my head, I could still feel the atmosphere of the cave room, even though I had only seen it through a double insulated glass peephole. The figures melting and merging into the darkness. I was sorry we were going away.

'Yes. Aren't they? Actually, Vishnu has rescued them from the hands of private collectors.'

'Isn't there a law about national art treasures, things like that?' my loud voice echoed.

'Believe me, the art is serving its true purpose, and not being traded around by a band of exotic art entrepreneurs in blue serge suits. Besides, we haven't crossed any borders with them.'

I squinted in the bright artificial light of the corridor. Tap, tap, tap-tap. I was still floating down into that room, like Alice in the rabbit hole, with the curvaceous statues dancing in the glowing light. My body seemed to flow out of the temple room, all the way up the stairs, into the funeral lobby. Bumper took me by the hand to hurry me into her quarters. She opened a door and broke the spell.

A massive oak table was waiting, with a small assortment of purple and white pansies in a small fluted vase. White curtains were drawn across the window, our polished silverware was ready and so was a menu.

'Menu?' I said, and sat down on one of the two rush-seated ladderback chairs. A simple calligraphy announced mushrooms stuffed with walnut ragout, miso soup, heavenly goddess greens and brown rice pilaf with vegetables. The rest of it looked safe, the wine was Californian and the dessert was Chocolate Sin.

'I'm starved,' said the big woman who was fond of food. 'I ran six miles today.'

'So what's it like, minding the store?' I asked her as she lifted the stuffed mushrooms from a dumb waiter. She proceeded to tell me about cosmic expansion, their building expansion and work-shop expansion, laughing a little too much and even crinkling her eyes at me when I wasn't saying anything funny.

'Can I talk to you, Emma?' Bumper was licking her lips as we started the second course.

'You're always talking to me, Bumper. I don't see any reason why you'd stop now.'

Bumper smiled at me indulgently. 'The Western world has opened up its soul to Vishnu. But it is a Western soul. And if you do not drop out, stay out completely, then you must come to terms with the organisational realities. There aren't many mountains or caves left.'

'I just don't like this New Age therapy stuff,' I said, after four glasses of wine had sufficiently loosened my tongue. 'It's too generalised, too instant. Too easy. There's got to be something wrong with it – ' I started, but the Chocolate Sin had just been plac-ed in front of me.

'I heard from Lailieka.'

'Did she tell you how I peeked when we all played ape?'

'Workshops aren't for everyone, Emma. It's only a matter of wanting to find the path.'

'Well I guess I don't want to.'

Bumper was cleaning off the last smudge on her plate. She looked at me and leaned back. 'There was a tale of a courtesan in India. She commissioned a hall to be painted with powerful frescoes. When her clients arrived she showed them into the hall.' The Chocolate Sin was great, infinite in the way only chocolate could be. 'I was watching you downstairs, when you were looking into the faces of the gods and goddesses.'

'And what about the courtesan and her gallery?' Red wine was snapping the thread of our conversation.

'She showed her clients into the hall, letting their eyes rove over the frescoes. And she watched them,' Bumper continued. 'She saw their expressions and she read the possibilities in their faces. This gave her the basis for selecting her clients.'

'She got to choose her johns?'

'It was a different era.'

'And a different kind of business,' I said. I was trying not to think about how Bumper looked like a Phoenician courtesan, billows of curly red hair and a build like a linebacker. I pretended to try and get the last streak of Chocolate Sin to curl into my spoon. Bumper took her napkin and wiped her mouth with it, hard, even the corners. It left her lips dark red.

'Do you have any more examples of the kind of statuary you keep in the basement?' It was just the right question, I could tell.

Bumper got up and went to the speaker in the wall, 'It's Bumper. Cancelling my herbal nightcap.' The speaker squawked something in return. She smiled and motioned me to walk with her to the door. Inside was her library, her bedroom and her playpen, overflowing with books and little statues of Shivas, paintings, candles in front of geometric clay forms, framed scenes of people with pale indigo skin playing musical instruments. A desk under a window looked out on the darkened inner garden, and a queen-size bed was the emptiest thing in the room. Hippie muzak oozed between all the objects and clutter.

'What's your pleasure?' Bumper leaned down and revealed a partition in the built-in bookshelf. A lot of liquor was sitting there.

'What kind of religion is this anyway? Hindu, tantric, gestalt, hyperventilation?'

'We take from everyone.'

'I'll bet. A kind of pot-luck of prophets.'

'What you are seeing is the adaptation of Eastern religion to Western life,' she said. What I was staring at was a fair amount of booze in her cupboard. She pushed the front bottles aside and found the one she wanted in the back.

'Sake?'

I nodded. She filled two jade thimble cups, gave one to me and leaned against her cluttered desk under the window. 'Cheers,' she said. She sipped, put the glass down and started to roll up some architectural drawings that looked like the building we were in, but with the surrounding space around marked off in squares. I saw two books, different publications of tide tables with markers in them. So maybe Bumper wasn't just fishing for recruits, although, as Bumper had it, she wasn't fishing at all. But I had a suspicion she was fishing for me.

She looked me up and down, she liked what she saw but her vision was aided by a half-bottle of wine meeting with some socko sake in the bloodstream. I didn't like the obviousness of her interior dialogue, but I did like her big teeth and abundant red hair, the way she always looked flushed and the way she walked into rooms. She took another sip and closed the rice-paper blind over the window and the view of the tree. Four glasses of wine were making me forget I was nervous, but I picked up a delicate little statue by its waist anyway. It had two figures: a golden crowned person accepting a full breasted woman into her arms, necklaces strung across her buttocks.

'It's Hevyara and his Sakti,' Bumper was saying, from close up. The figures were so lifelike they were almost squirming in my hand.

'His?' I said. They sure looked like girls doing it to me.

'Indian aesthetic theory is entwined with religious thought,' she was saying, her hand running lightly over my back. 'There were originally no portraits made in India, until the influence of the Aryans. It was all very pure.' She moved away and sipped her drink. That was very pure too, about eighty proof.

'What you felt downstairs, Emma, your face did not keep secret. You are not exactly open to influence, but you are certainly susceptible.'

'The sake is sure proving that to me.' I looked down at the little figures; they weren't sprouting any extra arms or heads as yet.

Bumper followed my glance. 'The characteristic of Indian sculpture that makes it so utterly unique is its sense of dimension, a sensuality that invites the hand.' She moved back and stood in front of me, her hand brushing up my arm, her thumb resting for a moment in the crook of my elbow, our breasts nearly touching. I looked down at the happy couple copulating in my hand with all their jewellery on. 'Hindu aesthetic theory recognises that of all the possibilities of aesthetic response, the erotic is the most effective,' she was saying, and of course, she bent over slightly and put her mouth on mine. Her hors d'oeuvre had been terrible but she sure knew how to end a sentence.

She didn't pull back and I didn't push her, I was too busy tasting her mouth and liking it, and feeling her red hair start to fall across our faces like a flaming lace curtain. I reached behind me and let the little statue drop upon the bed. Bumper was enormous, big shoulders, soft upper arms and an ample waist; she was holding my face, and her words rode on sweet vegetarian breath. 'You must learn to wade into the ocean of transcendental bliss,' she was saying, as my hands were wading into her hair, 'then you will get a complete image of the nectar' – I kissed her neck – 'for which we are almost always anxious.'

I unbuttoned her blouse and she helped me by pulling the tails out of her pants. Her large breasts ended in pale pink circles. My fingers found the tiny magenta centres and I felt her body tremble. She watched my fingers play for a moment, and whispered something about a demon, ravana, who could assume any form or shape to please women. I wondered if demons were homo-erotic but I was silenced by a hand rising swiftly between my legs. And then Bumper was gently bumping me and I reached my hand behind her and slowly began to explore her ample muscular backside.

Whoever would have thought I'd get it for a guru girl? Bumper let a moan leak out of her mouth. What would a surgeon in Boston think? Would she think anything at all? I didn't want to think about the answer to that question; mostly I didn't want to think that I was still asking myself that question. It was much nicer to feel the sexual riptide pull me under. I hadn't been excited in many moons, and now I was getting hot, wild. Bumper was amazing, all over me; she sure didn't learn all this stuff in rebalancing. Our bodies were rocking down to our toes, down to the cosmic orb upon which we were standing. The earth was a pinball hitting the bumper guards on posts that flashed and counted up infinite points. But behind the pinball machine was the cosmic pinball wizard Kali waving her various arms. And I was so excited, a multitude of

112

sexual reactions taking place all over my body. Too many reactions. And then all the reactions came to a stop.

The cosmic orb cracked and something went tilt. When I pulled away from Bumper I backed right into the owner of the extra pair of hands that had also been working their way across my body. And it sure wasn't Kali.

Sixteen

'I'm not really ready for close encounters of a third kind,' I said to the party behind me.

'I don't think you're ready for much of anything,' said Lailieka, her mouth curving up on one side, trying to snuggle into a crowd of freckles on her cheek. I looked at Bumper who was leaning back on to the desk, her wide flat hips shifting aside the papers and candles that cluttered the desktop. Her eyelids began to close like curtains in a play that had just ended. Her mouth mumbled, 'I suppose it was only an idea, a way to end the evening.'

Lailieka had turned her back to light a beedie cigarette and filled the room with acrid smoke in two puffs. It wasn't the kind of thing you did when you wanted to make love with somebody. I looked back at Bumper, still running on the low octane energy of alcoholic bliss. Lailieka walked over to her and perched her sinewy frame on the corner of the desk. She put her arms around the sliding Bumper and caught her head in her lap. That made Bumper smile in her sleep, which wasn't sleep for long. Her head moved across Lailieka's chest and nuzzled a nub that must have been Lailieka's breast through the thin material of her blouse. Lailieka smiled, and kept on smiling at me as she reached over to tap the tight ash off her beedie in a brass bowl.

I had the feeling Lailieka had played this one before, joining

113

Bumper's seduction scenes at the right moment with an extra set of hands. I had the feeling the scenes often ended like this, complete with Bumper passing out in a billow of red curls and Lailieka sucking on a beedie. It didn't exactly make you want to leap into bed with them. It was time to go home.

'Hey girls, you've got a cute scene but I'm not curious yellow. Not that curious, anyway,' I said. Bumper had joined her bootlegger in another dimension.

'Thank Bumper for dinner, and don't send me any junk mail advertising rebalancing workshops, okay?'

Lailieka just took another puff. I made for the door, turning one last time to see Bumper recover enough to say something to Lailieka that made Lailieka ditch her beedie and slide off the desk. I walked out into the hallway and it wasn't long before she caught up with me.

'What is this, another escort? I'm starting to look forward to being in the free world,' I said. We started down the circular stairway, Lailieka's hand brushed lightly upon the polished brass railing as we went down the stairs.

'There is no free world,' Lailieka was saying.

'Spare me that crap right now.' I stopped and looked at her. 'And get that stupid smirk off your face.'

'It's just that you have no idea what's going on,' she explained patiently, walking on. I heard myself sigh and followed her.

'I think your girlfriend invited me to dinner and I think you just have an interesting way of spoiling her party.'

'Well stop thinking. You don't know anything about Bumper. And if I were you,' Lailieka opened the door to the garden, 'I wouldn't try and guess.'

'I'm shaking down to my yoni. What's the matter, think I'll find out she goes for gentiles?'

'It's a little more complicated than that.'

'You can keep your revelations and your secrets, I don't want them bouncing around in my head.'

We walked into the deserted coffee shop. The empty pedestal tables on the checkered floor made the place look like a chess board. Lailieka stopped, rested a hand on a table top and looked at me. 'You think this is all some kind of game, don't you,' she said angrily. 'You don't understand that I'm trying to tell you something for your own good.'

'Everyone around here seems to be telling me things for my own good. I'm not in the market for your good advice,' I shrugged my shoulders; it was impossible. The followers of Vishnu had just one thing on the brain.

'Maybe you could use some good advice. Try educating yourself, and waking up to some hard facts.' She snatched a Vishnu newspaper from a wire rack and slapped it into my outstretched hand. 'Try believing me when I say it's for your own good,' she said pointedly.

It was no use talking. These people never gave up. And Lana Flax was a copy of the same basic programme that ran them all. I opened the glass door from the hall into the big dark lobby. I heard my footsteps cross the flagstone floor; they sounded very far away. It was time to head for the car. I turned back when I reached the main door. Lailieka was standing in the middle of the lobby, lit from behind, the shadow of her thin figure stretching out across the floor. The shadow pointed at me.

I heard her voice and what I thought were the tones of canned Vishnu sincerity. 'It's for your own good. Stay away from her, I said.'

'Tell it to your pillow.' I walked out of the door into the little vestibule. I took one last look at the laughing man in a frame on the wall. Someone had set fresh flowers on the polished hall table, under his brown and happy face. I had to hand it to the folks, they did have a way with housekeeping. I strolled out and got into the Plymouth.

As I reached for the ignition I heard a sound that made me drop the keys on the rubber mat. A tone as clear as a bell rang out into the night, followed by another and then another. Latin. I looked at my watch. Midnight, and Lailieka was singing the *cantus firmus* of a Gregorian chant. This was the other meditation Lana had mentioned. Lailieka sitting in the meditation room at midnight. Her voice was rolling over the beach, strong enough to reach out over the sea. I listened for a moment, transfixed. I'd clearly gone to the wrong service.

I started the Plymouth, turned on the quad headlights and drove off into the free world and back to my nest. When I sat down on the bed and finally took off my clothes I reminded myself never to wear black underpants while going out with a guru girl. There in the crotch was the sweet white kiss that was the evidence of how exciting Bumper's promise had been. I tore them off and aimed them at the closet where they rebounded off the unpainted plasterboard inside and landed on the edge of a yellow laundry basket. The Vishnus weren't doing a lot for my temperament or aim.

I tossed in the covers all night, making a sort of macramé out of the sheets while I slept. Eventually I strangled an artery in my leg. I untied myself and tried to massage the leg back to life, to still the sleepy panic that I had lost a limb. I turned on the light, destroyed the demons and did a lonely quickstep around the bedroom. I made myself a cup of warm milk and honey. I drank it and tried to still my thoughts.

Something was bothering me about Lailieka. I picked up the Vishnu paper, the *Celestial Call* and tried to let myself be seduced by the Vishnus for the second time that night. At least they were more honest about it in print and sometimes I could even get up a laugh. A slick biography of Sadhima introduced him as the new Director of International Membership. Although he'd been Harvard educated and spoke Spanish, Hindi and Portuguese, he'd never learned to see the world in relative terms. But that wasn't what was bothering me about Lailieka.

I found a fuzzy photo of Bumper Lee, who waxed poetical about the Commune. 'Here we have the maximum pleasure. Every comfort can be had, at your command. Yes, you can spend a few years in a world of beautiful men and women. People who re-create the splendour of their dreams, and are rewarded with the most refreshing drinks, the most healthful and pleasing foods, in surroundings designed for their comfort. You too can work, travel, make love, transform your life into something which is not just unique. It is perfect.' Too bad the price was so high. Lana had paid it. And Bumper said they didn't recruit. But Bumper did have a way with cult copy. After all, good marketing doesn't fill needs, it creates them. I could see what Lailieka saw in Bumper. But Lailieka wasn't a green-eyed jealous monster either. Her actions were more protective.

I turned the pages and after a while the effects of bad journalism and warm milk were making me sleepy. I was almost asleep when my eyes rested on a duotone print that took up the back page, reproduced in warm sepia tones. It illustrated what Lailieka meant by 'the hard facts'. A meditational pin-up pictured a woman in a gown sitting cross-legged in a pastoral setting. She graced a plateau, misty mountains floated in the distance. Flowers braided in her hair mingled with a knotted necklace. The necklace featured a large step-cut stone resting in her collarbone. The neck was thin and lovely, and it supported the head of Nebraska Storm.

Seventeen

'She's a no show,' came the voice over the telephone.

'What?' I asked.

'Nebraska Storm,' Roseanna said. 'She's a no show for the sound check. I called her manager about it.'

'Portia Fronday.'

'Right. She got all inflated and suggested we call her lawyer Willie Rossini. I told her that's just what we would be doing if Nebraska didn't show up tonight. I said Nebraska could open her coffers to a breach of contract suit and she wouldn't have to play at all.'

'Bet that went over big.'

'Aw, I'm tired of being pushed around,' Roseanna grumbled. 'So she's a big rock star, so she's a big name . . . '

'So she's sold half of our advance ticket sales.'

'We have a dozen other great acts . . . '

'Audience response isn't democratic, in case you haven't noticed.'

'And Nebraska Storm is a despot.'

'Let's hope she's not a drugged-out despot.' I told Roseanna

117

about Nebraska's last minute effort to score, and the kind of guys that were pushing her doorbell these days.

'Or a crackpot,' Roseanna grumbled.

'Settle in your seat, Roseanna. I'm going to tell you a story, and it's going to have the ending you predicted.' So I told Roseanna briefly about my search for Lana. If she ever met a Bumper or a Lailieka, I told her, wheel away fast in the other direction.

'So, you've met some rough trade in the soft sector, Emma Victor. I should have thought you could handle it.'

'Try handling this one. Nebraska Storm is one of them.'

'What?'

'That's right, she's pictured in their weekly good news bulletin.'

'That explains it, I guess.'

'What?'

'The donation from the Women's Freedom Foundation. They probably think it's fertile ground here to spread the message.'

'They said they weren't going to use the stage to proselytise.'

'They don't have to. All anybody needs to know is that Nebraska Storm is a convert. That's how she probably kicked anyway. They have a couple of drug rehab programmes running there. Works pretty good except you come out yellow.'

'Yeah. I guess it's not so bad. The Beatles had their guru too. Maybe it's just a phase,' I said.

'You should see the lyrics we've gotten from her. Maya and I have been laughing all morning. "Follow the stream to its source to find that it's an endless journey." '

'Hey, Roseanna, it's almost time for my major errand. I think I'd better go looking for my driving gloves.' My hands were getting clammy.

'Better pack some brass knuckles.'

'No, this is clearly soft touch work, Roseanna. Good thing I've got this job.'

We hung up. The phone rang again. It was Maya.

'Emma, I just called Storm's lawyer. It probably wasn't the right thing to do. I got pearly promises that she'll show; I just didn't like Fronday putting on her queen act.'

'You've got a much better one.'

'No kidding.'

118

'Maya, you've got to think about your performance tonight. That's what's important. Maybe it's time for you to soar into the void that Nebraska Storm is leaving behind. Give yourself a punky tilt; Storm sounds like she's turned into Rod McKuen.'

'Yeah. Okay. I'll try,' Maya sighed. 'But the thing that really got me was that I thought Fronday was putting on an act. Like she was scared. Scared that Nebraska wouldn't make it.'

'Go feed chickens, take a drive by the ocean. Clear your head before the concert, Maya.'

'What am I going to wear?'

'I don't know. But it's time for me to hit the road. Take it easy. Bye,' I said. It was not the moment to tell Maya that the colour of Nebraska's outfit was a foregone conclusion.

I called a cab and tried to avoid friendly small talk with the driver. Californian pollution and an olfactory memory of incense was giving me a headache. The gate was open and I started up the incline towards the house. I needn't have worried about Nebraska Storm. Through the oleander bushes that masked my approach I could see her waiting by the octagonal reflecting pool dressed in a gold glitter jumpsuit. She was pacing back and forth, glancing nervously down the hill and the access road. She looked like a woman who was being stood up. And I didn't think I was the one she was waiting for. I hoped it wasn't a junkie connection that was the no show. The air was still and I could hear Portia Fronday talking to her. I could see her making the kind of gestures I was familiar with. I had made them myself with Maya.

Except Maya had fortunately never worn a gold glitter jumpsuit to a gig. And she had never said anything like, 'He's with that black slut!' Which was what Nebraska was saying. The last three words seemed to hang in the air; dirty laundry that couldn't be aired enough. And Nebraska knew just what she was saying. Green jealousy transmuted into racism. And the princess of punk didn't care.

Portia had her work cut out for her and her hands flew up and down, cajoling, reasoning, trying to mould the woman into something reasonable enough to get onstage. 'When I get through they say he's unavailable,' I heard her explain.

'He promised me he'd be here.' Nebraska had plopped herself

on a marble bench and folded her arms tightly across her chest. 'You don't think anybody's – '

'At the moment it doesn't matter. Pull yourself together. You have to take responsibility for your own life. You can't break another contract. You know what Willie said.'

'But he said he'd be there. He promised.'

'This is your comeback Nebraska. You blow this, sweetie, and you can give up the mike and go back to your monkey for all I care. I'm out the door as your agent.' Portia turned and did her best to imitate a pillar of salt.

'I need him!' Nebraska cried, shaking her purple pageboy and banging her two fists down hard on the bench.

Portia walked over and slammed Nebraska hard across the face. 'You get yourself together, you hear me?' She put her face up close to the rock queen's. It wasn't the right response for a cold turkey withdrawal. That's when I realised what Portia had been dealing with all along.

The violent scene stopped me in my tracks. I watched a stillness descend on the two figures after the cracking slap had split the air. The sound faded and it was the moment to make my entrance obvious. Suddenly candlelit visions and late dates gave me the high card I needed to play. 'Hello, there!' I called cheerfully as if I had just arrived.

'Hi,' I got from the rock queen, and a begrudging nod from Fronday.

'I saw your picture in the Vishnu paper, the *Celestial Call*,' I said. A faint shadow of a smile grew on Nebraska's face.

'You're – you've taken prayamis?' she asked.

'I've seen Vishnu,' I said, ignoring her question and receiving a green jealousy flash. 'I mean, it was really just by accident. He's cut off from everyone. Absolutely. He's just taken a vow of silence.'

'He said he'd be here for my comeback.'

'Perhaps I have a special message intended for you.'

I saw Nebraska's face soften and I came into focus for the first time in our brief relationship. I wasn't a feminist or a fan, I was one of the family, and besides I'd seen Daddy in person. I felt all the cards in my hand, even Portia was ready to enlist with me. A royal flush, Emma Victor.

'Trust his love. Prove the strength he has given you.'

I watched the words work on her face and speak to the new
monkey that had moved into her soul. 'Portia, get my wrap and my
bag,' she barked. Portia took her orders and I took Nebraska's arm
and prayed the whole way to the stadium that the spell would last.
I got to drive the Porsche after all.

Eighteen

'Don't tell me audience response isn't democratic,'
Roseanna Baynetta wheeled by me. Her vehicle of the day was a
beefed-up Rolls All-Terrain wheelchair with speed kit. 'Thirteen
out of seventeen acts broke the needle on the clap-o-meter,' she
said. 'The Chicana Women's Choir got a gig on Public Broadcasting, and Juel Bloem and her band were just offered a recording
contract.' Roseanna stuck her tongue out at Portia Fronday's
back. 'And you'd better get what's her name ready; she's due on
stage in fifteen minutes.'

I bustled Nebraska along into her dressing room where Portia
started doing what looked like a fairly good job holding her hand.
But Nebraska was staring off into too much distance in the gold se-
quined jumpsuit. I didn't like what I saw. She looked like a woman
who needed a fix.

I started talking to her, slow and easy. I talked pretty words to
her like love and surrender. I got my hooks into her and I made
myself sick getting her up on stage. 'He'd appreciate a trooper, I
know it,' I guided her through the wings towards the stage where
her band had been set up and her remote pick up mike was being
adjusted. A woman in white was seated on a cushion fiddling
with the movable frets of a gourd-necked sitar. I could see the state
of the art signer waiting on the opposite side of the podium.

Nebraska stopped in the shadow of a curtain. 'You're right,' she said. 'I must do it for him. And I must do it alone.'

'And I think that means really alone,' I said, laying a hand on a gold-sequined shoulder pad. 'Don't mention his name on stage, okay?' Nebraska walked away, into the burning lights and thousands of dark far-away faces.

Her voice stayed in moderate range, her stage antics were minimal and the entire effect was somatic. Maybe there was some musical value, if you could stay awake long enough to concentrate. But the audience had a hard time making the adjustment. Nebraska Storm was supposed to challenge, prickle, even insult. There was vocal innuendo featuring Hallmark card sentiments. And some great sitar licks. Except for the sitar it wasn't my cup of tea. But then nobody was asking me to drink it. So the *soma rosa* of applause was muted for Nebraska Storm that night. And her face showed a guarded, almost bitter look as she left the stage. The glory of being good was reaping her little applause. But Nebraska Storm, disappointed twice in one day, was ready to reap another sort of harvest.

Nineteen

'Tell me that's not Nebraska Storm sulking in the corner in layman's clothes.' Roseanna and I were in the big tent at the after concert party.

'No lie, that's her.' I nodded to where Nebraska stood in blue jeans and a tiger halter. The tent was filled and Nebraska was finally getting some attention. After bombing out on stage, she was settling for the party and left-over glory of former times. She was even asked for her signature on a few old albums.

'Autograph hounds,' Roseanna mumbled. 'The hype around

women's music is taking on some of the overtones of pubescent obsession.'

'I remember Frankie Avalon,' I sighed.

'Doris Day,' Roseanna said.

But a lot more was going on than that. The big striped tent was filled with an organic buffet and good feeling. The concert had been a great success. Filled to capacity, the dollars had come rolling in and a few donations had exceeded four digits. The signer was laughing with the light technician over two Perriers. There were a lot of born-again types getting born again into all kinds of things. I was already mixing my water with wine. And probably so was everybody else. The noise and laughter picked up. Someone had hired a string quartet to play at the party and the music wove its way in between the laughter and the looks.

There was a lot to see. Roseanna, sitting next to me, was already working her way up the leg of the concessions organiser. When I caught her eye she let me know I'd missed my chance. I saw a woman in stretch blue jeans confer behind cupped hands with two other women. They trooped off, first blue jeans, waving aside the flap of the tent, and then her two companions, looking quickly around at the party before they slipped out into the night.

In about ten minutes they were back, wearing different expressions. They didn't need to look around at anybody any more. They were their own three-ring circus now, and they clearly had that carnival look in their eyes. The only people that noticed them were Nebraska Storm and me. I wasn't going to do anything about it. But Nebraska seized a moment when the circle around her were busy with each other and slipped away. The woman in the stretch jeans narrowed her eyea as Nebraska approached her. When her face relaxed you could feel the camaraderie in their common purpose. And you could sense that they were ready to go on a trip together. When they left the tent I went too.

I followed the two women outside into the night air. The stage lights were off, but there was a full moon. The red and white striped canvas shone eerily. And Nebraska and her new-found friend were disappearing behind a wing of the tent. The party sounds faded and I kept close to the cloth, stepping over heavy anchor ropes. I looked up around the multitude of seats which, hours

123

before, had been filled with the disappointed fans of Nebraska Storm. They couldn't see her now, like I did.

From around the wing of the tent I saw a spark kindle. A flame flattened out, playing underneath the bowl of a spoon. The woman fumbled in her pockets and handed Nebraska something. Nebraska leaned closer, and the two silent figures locked in a modern-day low-life embrace. The woman in stretch blue jeans was holding the two ends of a necktie in her hands. The necktie was knotted around one of Nebraska Storm's upper arms. She pulled it tightly. Nebraska's hand curled into a fist, and then relaxed a number of times. When she took the needle it was with an anticipation that could be read on her moonlit face. The necktie loosened. Nebraska continued with the needle, booting blood back into the cylinder. She drew the moment out, but I couldn't stand to watch any more.

I walked back into the tent, with its complications and good times. But I was tired. Roseanna was busy, but not too busy to notice the way I walked in.

'What's the haps, Victor? Still messin' with rough trade?'

'I don't know, it just seems to be messing with me.'

'Well, Roseanna's got just the thing for you, honey.' She wheeled over to the tent door which opened into the on-site business office, and I followed.

When the tent flap had closed off the party noises I saw her reach under the arms of her wheelchair and press a button. A moulded Samsonite briefcase popped out of the side of the wheelchair from under the seat.

'Open it,' she said. I flipped a catch and saw a lot of money, neatly banded and stacked inside. 'Over two hundred thousand dollars there, Emma. I want you to deliver it to the bank tomorrow. I can't do it. I plan to be busy.'

'Okay. I may as well give rough trade a good reason.'

'Here,' Roseanna reached over and pulled the case out, and I saw that it had a chain attached to the handle. The chain was looped several times and Roseanna lifted my arm and wrapped it around my wrist, snapping something closed. She produced a small key. 'You don't have to sleep with this on, but it might make you feel more comfortable on the street.' She undid the lock again, the briefcase chain fell off my wrist. She pressed the key into my hand. 'Another little toy from Pops. Hey, something else you should know.' She pointed underneath the handle of the briefcase and I saw a button. Then she pointed to the brass corner guard of the far edge of the briefcase where a small black hole had been bored. 'Mace,' she said. 'Point it at anybody who decides to get chummy with our money, and press.'

'Gee, Roseanna, I don't know what to say. I've never worn two hundred thousand dollars in a high security briefcase.'

'Just don't flaunt it.'

It was a nice end to the party and I got to ride home in another taxi, chained to a briefcase. Life was full of unexpected surprises and I had one more job to do, to be at the bank at ten. I didn't sleep with the briefcase but I had hard cash dreams on lavender-scented pillowcases. I was glad when the dawn rolled up and I could get rid of the dough.

Driving the Plymouth handcuffed to a briefcase wasn't easy until I discovered that the chain had an extendable-retractable feature. The chain slid in and out of the handle as I guided my gas-guzzling car downtown to deposit the winnings of our concert. I was finally forgetting about communes, mothers and rock stars. It was a lovely day and I arrived three minutes early.

The briefcase and I sat in the car, behind rolled up windows and locked doors, but I needn't have been so cautious. I hadn't really attracted any rough trade. The only other person who had arrived before the bank had opened was Bumper Lee.

Twenty

When a guard opened the door for Bumper I got out of the car with the briefcase. I went in, walked up to a teller and after a quick peek in the briefcase she invited me back behind

125

the security glass to start counting the money. Bumper was back there too, being admitted into the safety deposit box area. She was finished before I was, emerging from the security area with a large grey satchel.

She walked past me and stopped. She ran her eyes over the green money being neatly stacked and banded on the desk top next to me. 'I see Nebraska did well for you.'

'Better than you did. And I wouldn't give Nebraska all the credit. There's a lot more people behind this pile than a fallen star singing nursery rhymes . . . ' But Bumper was glancing at her watch. I thought she gave me a wink, but later I decided it was a tired eyelid. I looked back at the money on the desk and felt better. When it had all been counted I put the receipt in the briefcase and headed out to the car.

Bumper was just crossing the street towards an office building with a filigree brass entrance which had recently been restored. It might have been a nice office building, but a black Porsche was sitting in front of it. I got into the Plymouth and slid down on the seat. After twenty minutes Bumper and Nebraska came out of the office building together. Bumper nodded and walked away. Nebraska got into the Porsche and waited, foot gunning the engine impatiently. When Bumper's Mustang rounded the corner Nebraska pulled the Porsche out right behind it.

I couldn't stand it. I couldn't stand watching the two women drive away; I couldn't stand the feeling that there was something complicated going on. Something that I was missing. Maya was right. I was starved for excitement. And irritated at being played by Bu Mper Lee. After a few cars lined up at the intersection I made a U-turn and took off with them when the light turned green. I followed the two cars to the freeway. They passed up the first three exits, and then the rest was easy. They were clearly heading out to Moraga City.

I pulled ahead of them at a right lane tie up where they got tangled in traffic. Then I raced as far as the Moraga exit and pulled into a Dairy Queen. Half a milkshake later I saw the Mustang, followed by the Porsche, making a beeline through the housing tract homes down to the warehouse district by the Bay. I abandoned the milkshake and made my way down to the water. I didn't have to worry about anyone noticing my car. As I pulled up a group of twenty yellow admirers were greeting the shining rock queen and she was taken in to the waiting arms of Sadhima, the Membership man. Something told me it was more than membership that was going on; the looks that passed between them seemed to have already travelled some distance in the past.

The little crowd funnelled into the building and as the door opened I could hear a bigger crowd inside making party noise. I parked in the lot beside the front door and got out, grateful that no one noticed me in the excitement. I found a very bushy palm tree inside the building and stood behind it. The large lobby had been converted into a party hall. A long table was decked out with an organic buffet and wine was being poured to the tuneless sound of three sitar players sitting cross-legged on a podium in front of the garden window. Nebraska was being greeted by yellow folk, and Sadhima was answering the questions of enthusiastic followers as they clustered around the pair. Delphy, the mistreated reception-ist, stood glumly by in a corner. Nebraska was looking pale and nervous. She was responding too quickly to Sadhima's attention for a rock and roll queen. Was he the key to getting Vishnu? What lengths would she go to to conquer abandonment anxiety? Wasn't Vishnu supposed to fix that kind of thing?

I caught sight of Bumper, and moved from behind the palm to a small alcove. There was no traffic there, and I hoped I wouldn't be recognised as an intruder by the partying folk. I looked obviously other worldly in blue jeans and a white T-shirt, but nobody seemed to be noticing anything but the stage. Bumper walked up to the podium. The sitar players stopped with a twang and left the stage with their instruments. Somebody put a microphone on the stage but before Bumper could claim it from the stand, Sadhima had it in his hand. She smiled wanly, the big white triangles of her teeth hiding inside her reddened lips. Her eyes perused the crowd and I ducked back into the alcove to listen to the speech.

'*This*,' Sadhima shouted, and then whispered, 'is not a day like any other. This is a day of *rejoicing*. This is the day . . . ' he paus-ed, waiting, 'my dear friends, this is the day that the goodness and love of one of our members has brought us to a place where we can worship with a special peace and beauty.'

I peeked around the edge of the alcove. People in the crowd were making a small space around Nebraska Storm; for her supreme moment of giving she looked a little ill, or maybe it was an aura of guilt after her drug slip at the concert party. Well, she was making amends now and she was listening, like everyone else, to the oratory of Sadhima; she had no choice.

'This is a woman of knowledge,' Sadhima looked at Nebraska who raised her face and came close to achieving a child-like expression. 'This is a woman who has seen the image of eternal love.' Only as long as Vishnu's around, I thought to myself. 'She has known freedom,' Sadhima continued. She bought it from two guys in running shoes that rang her doorbell last week. 'And ultimate release.' At the end of a needle. 'And in bequeathing us this land, by providing the funds to buy and convert it from an empty lot and garbage dump,' there were giggles from the crowd, 'to a place where beauty and peace can be experienced, with the help of fifteen tons of white Washington state sand we will make it a meditation point and beach spot for our further seeking. And pleasure.' The crowd clapped their hands, a thunder of approval for Nebraska Storm. Would it wire her enough, these days?

Sadhima disappeared behind the curtain to the coffee shop. The sitar players did a few numbers while the people milled about expectantly. I noticed a man who had his hands behind the metal door of an electrical box set into the wall. He pushed a few buttons and the sitar music softened and something canned took over. Automatic metal curtains slid slowly across the garden window behind the stage: we were sealed in. A knot tied in my stomach. As darkness settled on the quieted bodies, breathing became slower and I ventured out of the alcove to mingle with the crowd. Two red spotlights were directed at the stage. From behind the curtain which separated us from the coffee shop, a fantastically costumed figure emerged. Suddenly I got it – a school play!

'That's Krishna,' I heard someone whisper, as a beautiful blue man, his skin an incandescent azure glided into the room and with a hop balanced on his toes for a moment, his thin blue torso leaning towards the stage. Blue makeup was sticking to the long hairs on his arms; it was Sadhima.

'The forest is filled with moonlight,' crooned a hidden speaker

128

near by, 'and the women make their way to the forest bower, seeking their lord.' Krishna pirouetted onstage, where he then reclined
upon a satin pillow and fiddled with a plastic flute. A group of
highly made-up characters emerged from the coffee shop in a kind
of flight pattern and balanced on their toes. Under black, green
and red wigs their faces had been painted. Foreheads were circled
with mandalas, paisleys travelled up their necks and clustered
around their ears. Bells tinkled from every ankle and wrist. Together they moved in a procession towards the stage, a jangling,
raucous centipede. My nostrils were gathering patchouli oil from
a tanned woman in an iridescent nylon duster coat who stood,
enthralled, next to me. I gave her the eye slide with lowered eyelashes and she did a similar return. I looked down. The red stage
lighting had turned me amber. I directed my attention back to the
play at hand.

The wigged women, having jingled up to the forest, were eventually greeted by a recalcitrant Krishna who asked them, 'What
brought you to the dangerous darkness? Your husbands and
parents will be missing you, your cows need milking, your children need feeding.' 'Give me a break,' I mumbled and got a shocked look from the woman next to me. It seemed like old-time
religion always spelled bad news for women. The paisley faces,
framed in synthetic hair, went on about worshipping the dust
under Krishna's feet. I looked around at the metal-shuttered windows. There was no easy way out.

Krishna gave in and they did a sort of Bangkok square dance, the
blue flame of the young man's chest weaving in and out among the
robed and painted women. 'He dances with them,' droned a voice
through the sound system, 'stroking and kneading their bodies,
leaving the marks of his nails on their flesh.' I looked up onstage
and he did seem to be doing that, except his nails couldn't get
through all their robes. The tempo had picked up and the curved
wrists were snaking in the dimming red stage lights, hips pumping
under robes, displacing yards of fabric, wigs askew, while the
blue torso turned around and around. With tablas thumping to a
crescendo the lights were suddenly cut and in the darkness a voice
boomed, 'He suddenly vanishes so that the women can return to
calmness.'

That was it? I thought. From what I'd experienced, the Vishnus specialised in coitus interruptus.

But the crowd cheered and the lights came up and Sadhima took a bow, flashing his pearly grey eyes at everybody. And at Nebraska Storm, who seemed to be waiting just for him. He climbed off the stage and went to her. He pressed his blue body against hers and gave her a big dry-cleaning bill. 'Is there somewhere we can talk? Where we can get away?' I heard Nebraska ask. So maybe it wasn't Vishnu she was after. I was confused. Was Nebraska settling for second best with Pretty Boy? But it was not a day to figure out enlightened junkies. Especially since they were walking towards the alcove to which I had retreated. I was just about to try and find an exit when Nebraska and Sadhima were stopped by the unhappy Delphy.

'You need more volunteers for the International Membership, I hear.'

'Delphy, this is not the time. I think you need to let go of the whole question.'

'Oh, I have. I just wanted to tell you, Bumper's made the selection for you.'

'Bumper?'

'Sure, she's gotten permission from Vishnu.'

'Don't make me laugh,' Sadhima said, and then, glancing at Nebraska, 'I mean, Vishnu has never really concerned himself with how the work load is divided – '

'Bumper wants Lana to assist you,' Delphy said, almost triumphantly.

'Yes, well, I see. Thank you for the news, and now if you'll excuse us, we're going downstairs.' Sadhima pressed his hand on Nebraska's shoulder, and, thankfully, they turned in the other direction, walking away from the alcove. I saw them enter into another hallway and descend a staircase. The place was rife with basements. Vishnu had his basement in Ananda House, and Sadhima had his in the main headquarters. And Bumper and Lana lived in the dormitories above Vishnu. It was quite a set-up.

I wondered where Delphy lived. She stood looking after Nebraska and Sadhima. I could feel the heat from her glowering face. I saw the yellow character by the switchbox press some buttons, turning up the room lights. Metal curtains slowly rolled back to reveal the garden and flood the flagstone lobby with daylight. Wine was passed around and somebody turned up the metaphysical muzak. The bodies began to sway slowly. I started to think seriously about leaving and ventured out of the alcove.

The tablas adopted a faster tempo and the yellow crowd became a jiggling barrier. I made my way through bodies spilling wine in their frenetic action, and met an advancing wave of yellow people who were making their way out into the garden. From behind me the costumed characters were bounding into the room to the shrieks of congratulations. I looked back and saw the residue of monster make-up still attached to their faces. 'Let the party last all day!' Bumper's voice declared from somewhere in the room and the crowd cheered. So Bumper must have been the benevolent dictator, the holiday giver. Before they started their unpaid manual labour down at the beach?

I tried to make my way nonchalantly to the door. A young man did a sudden hop in front of me and I got his elbow in my eye. I kept aiming for the door. I discovered that I could make my way through the crowd by putting my hands firmly on the hips in front of me and moving them to one side or the other. I had researched a lot of iliac crests, glutei maximi and saddle bags by the time I got to the door. I opened it against the steaming bodies and walked into the vestibule, when I heard two voices just outside.

'I don't see why I have to help him.' It was Lana. She was whining about being demoted from tantric toenail clipper to welcome wagon.

'But you could be useful to the group in having a hand in the International Membership.' I heard Bumper say. I thought about Sadhima and Nebraska in the basement.

'What do you mean?'

'Our world-wide contacts are very important. As a most trusted family member, Vishnu has asked me to ask you to become involved in this most important work.'

'Vishnu?'

'He mentioned this to me some time ago. But first your detachment was being tested. Now it's time to let go of your sadness. Think of all he has done.' Her tone was persuasive.

'And I am failing him, aren't I?'

'This may be the biggest test of your detachment ever.'

'I don't want to fail him. Not now!'

'You won't. Just report to me on the International Membership. Find out what Sadhima is doing. Exactly. Starting at this moment.'

I risked a look round the door and saw Bumper take Lana's hand and put a key into it.

'Yes,' said the young recruit obediently. I found myself boiling mad. Lana's cardboard character mouthing Vishnu platitudes was more irritating than a bad TV script. I wanted to shake her, put her in some other world, prop toothpicks under her eyelids. I looked out again in time to see Lana's back making towards the wing which housed Sadhima's basement quarters. I wasn't so lucky with Bumper. I met her head on in the vestibule. It wasn't a pleasant surprise for either of us.

'What the hell are you doing here?'

'Just wanted to see how things are going. Looks like you've got everything squared away for yourself,' I said.

'The benefits of wisdom. You could use a little yourself. Now if you don't mind, Emma – '

'I've met better gurus at bars.'

'I asked you what you are doing here.'

'I just wanted to see what kind of price Nebraska Storm was paying.'

'All churches survive on the donations of their members.'

'You mean the assets of their suckers.'

'Have it your own way. I'm not really interested in your opinion.'

'I'll bet. And I'll bet no self-respecting Hindu would set foot in this place. Much less kneel down to scrub your floor.'

'So why are you hanging around, Emma Victor? Don't tell me you're such a satisfied soul. It looks to me like you're frustrated on several levels. I think you're interested, Emma. Why don't you admit it?'

'I don't have so much trouble with seekers, Bumper, just with people who are totally convinced that they've found it.'

'Now who's jealous?'

'That's ripe coming from the queen bee of this hive of humility.

132

Everybody else is working overtime while you get your herbal nightcap served from the dumb waiter in your private quarters. I don't like your set-up, Bumper. And I don't like you.'

'Nobody ever asked you if you did.'

'You're wrong. You just passed out before you got my answer.'

We glowered at each other a minute and then I stomped out. I went and sat in the Plymouth, sulking because I knew what my answer would have been that night with Bumper.

I was tired of being around people who were so satisfied with themselves. Even Nebraska Storm could afford her drug slip, get wired and give it away. I wasn't getting wired or giving anything away these days, but maybe all the yellow people weren't so content after all. I discovered a long red hair on my jacket and plucked it off.

A side door opened and I saw Nebraska Storm leave hurriedly, wiping blue paint off her hands with a tissue and throwing it down on the street with a disgusted look. I hadn't gone for the Vishnu sexual preludes either, if that's what I was witnessing. I saw Nebraska fumble with her blouse, adjusting a bra strap, looking nervously around.

And there was something to see. Lana Flax had emerged from the basement just behind Nebraska. Nebraska turned and looked at her and Lana looked back. There was a silent conversation going on, and the way it looked to me, Nebraska wasn't calling Lana a black slut any more.

Lana stood there, and it was the first time I had seen her expression so strong. She wasn't angry at Nebraska and Nebraska wasn't angry with her either. They were like two lionesses, meeting at the boundary of two territories. Nebraska fumbled again with her bra strap. Lana fingered the portrait of Vishnu which hung around her neck. This caused a visible change of expression on Nebraska's face. She opened the door of the Porsche and slid in. Then she gunned the engine and roared away.

Lana stood there a while, watching the dust settle behind Nebraska's car. Then she turned towards the building. I wondered if she was going to report to Bumper. Bumper had given Lana the key to the basement. And what had Lana seen there? Her look with Nebraska had been almost conspiratorial. I had the feeling Lana wasn't going to report everything to Bumper. But maybe

Lana had just walked in on a grope scene featuring Nebraska and Pretty Boy. And I thought the Vishnus were pretty used to walking in on each other.

Drama, beedies, blue paint; I was ready to enjoy life, but I wasn't going to enjoy it Vishnu style. I started the Plymouth and drove out of the parking lot. Shoreline land lease, that was what it had been about. I wondered if the Vishnus would really party all day.

I went home and ironed a black corduroy blouse which ended up shiny and linty. Then I went out on the deck and found three irises that had bloomed that same day. I took out my tennis racket and bounced the ball against the newly strung face. I turned my wrist every time the ball hit the ground and after a while I got a nice burning sensation in my lower arm. Then I stopped. I got out my old tennis outfit and found that it still fitted. I put on jogging shoes and did a few blocks. I tired myself out so I could eat well and sleep decently that night. But I went to bed with the cloying atmosphere of Krishna in my head. I felt propagandised, and I thought about my own idea of peace and how I didn't have much of it. I went to sleep, falling through layers of consciousness that wore yellow clothes and put elbows in my eye.

Tuesday morning and I had trouble waking up. After my lids decided to stay open I went to the door to find the newspaper, hoping that there would be some extended coverage of the concert. It would be hidden on a back page, I supposed. I unfolded it and glanced over the banner headline, the smaller heads, the readout dashes on the front. A half inch head was in italic at the bottom of the page but it still said the loudest words to me. 'JOGGING MURDERER STRIKES AGAIN! BODY DISCOVERED IN BAY. CULT MEMBER FOUND DEAD.' And I wasn't sleepy any more.

Twenty-one

MORAGA CITY. Police were called early this morning to investigate the brutal murder of a young woman who was a member of the Vishnu Divine Inspiration movement. The body of the victim, Lana Flax, was found washed up on the shore-front at 5 a.m. this morning with the tide. Police said that the cause of death was a blow to the head with a blunt object and that the body had been weighted down.

'I don't think it was a carefully planned crime,' said Officer Downy, a member of the Moraga City Police Force special detail. 'The tide goes so far out it would beach a mack truck.'

'See page twelve,' said the jump line and I turned the pages of the newspaper. Lana was dead. That was all I could think of, as if turning each newspaper page might make it become real. I kept turning, all the way to page sixteen, and went back to twelve and folded. 'CULT MEMBER MURDERED' said the continuation headline.

'We aren't making any further statements at this time; of course the so-called jogging murderer has been operating in this area for a while and we're hoping that this new development will unearth new clues that may not only point in his direction, but lead to his possible arrest.'

The victim, Miss Lana Flax, a former resident of Boston, Massachusetts, was living with her aunt, Miss Ida Flax, in New Mexico when she first came in touch with members of the group. She had attended the Vishnu Inspiration Therapy Center in New Mexico.

The end. Two sentences about Lana. Nothing about a promising young physicist. Young woman trying to break away from her past and needing an Indian guru to do it. No, the papers were more interested in jogging murderers than middle-class black schol-ars. And Lana had washed up on the beach. I put down the

135

newspaper. The Flaxes, Jonell and her mother. I dialled the Boston number. I dialled it several times and I kept trying; it was busy for over an hour. I stood paralysed, seeing a thousand memory snapshots of Lana the whizz kid, Lana the problem child, the gawky girlscout, the cult convert, Lana dedicated to the skinny Santa Claus, Lana murdered in a dozen different ways. The tape that played along with all the stills in my head, was a recording of phone calls, in which I was telling Mrs Flax how beautiful Lana looked. How contented. How dead. Finally the phone rang, but it wasn't the Flaxes.

'Is this Emma Victor?' demanded a male voice.

'Maybe, who's this?'

'Am I speaking to Emma Victor?' The voice went up a pitch. 'Get her on the line for me.'

'Emma Victor likes to know who she's talking to.'

'Tell her Willie Rossini's office is calling.'

'Forgive me if I'm not suffering the shock waves of recognition. This is Emma Victor. What can I do for you? And who's Willie Rossini?'

'She's counsel to Nebraska Storm. She'd like to talk to you down in her office.' He stopped and waited. 'Are you there?'

'I'm busy in my own office talking to myself today. I'm all booked up.'

'That's too bad,' his voice burned.

'Not for me.'

There was a click and a second voice came on the line.

'Miss Victor, if you would be so kind as to honour me with your presence this afternoon?' I thought about Nebraska Storm. I decided that I'd been thinking much too much about Nebraska Storm these days.

'Right now I'm not so sure I'm in the mood. On behalf of your client.'

'I would really appreciate it.'

'I'd really rather not. Not this morning.'

'At the end of the day? Four thirty?' said the female voice pushing menopause. Curiosity and menopausal voices that worked in my subconscious made me want to say yes.

'You're going to have to talk to somebody, sometime, Miss

136

Victor. And you won't like it any better if you get served a summons. They don't say please either.'

'They don't have to.'

'Okay. Please. The address is thirty-nine, Eleventh Street. I'll validate your parking.'

'All right. I'll be there.' I hung up. I tried calling the Flaxes a few more times and got a few more busy signals. I stood out in the little garden for a while, until my blood started to boil and curiosity got the best of me. I climbed into the Plymouth and headed out along the freeway to Moraga City.

The Vishnu Inspiration scene didn't look divine any more. Cops were roaming around aimlessly; yellow folk were walking in and out of the building, glancing nervously towards the beach. I could see two people talking. One was a cop. I parked the car across the street to try and eavesdrop. It wasn't hard. The other one of them had a loud, boisterous voice. And he had a nervous Dobermann pinscher tensed up on a chain next to him. 'I was walking my dog, Tandy,' the man was explaining to a black cop. 'Just like I do every night. When I saw this Porsche. Black. Black as a spook, and – oh, sorry officer – '

'Go on.' The officer hid away a reaction with practised ease.

'Well, then I saw this woman. Her hair was all shiny and – '

'Where was she?'

'She was walking up and down in front of the fence, see?'

'There?' The officer pointed at a stretch of fence that led down to the beach.

'She seemed to be waiting for someone, 'cause she kept looking at that building over there,' he pointed, indicating the Commune. 'I was thinking, gee, a woman like that shouldn't be alone in such a deserted area, all by herself. In the dark.' He grinned up at the policeman, tilting back his hat. Mr Witness was full of sympathy. Watching a woman in the dark. A real pity for her to be all alone. And I didn't like Dobermanns either.

'Hey, officer. She comes from that place, right? She's one of them, you know, Hare Krishna types, right?' He jabbed the policeman in the arm with his elbow. The policeman sighed.

'And then what happened?'

'Well, like I say, I was walkin' with Tandy here.' Tandy pricked up his ears and raised himself higher on his skinny forelegs.

'So I couldn't go up to her. Tandy is an attack dog, see? I mean, if somebody says the secret word, I just never know what will happen with him – '

'Oh, yeah?' asked the officer.

'Oh, not you. I mean, you wouldn't have no problem, no.'

'Go on. What happened next?'

'She went back to her car after ten, twelve minutes. Something like that. And then she sat on the passenger side of the seat, with the door open, and one leg kind of sliding out on to the pavement. Then she opened up the glove compartment and took something out. After a minute or two she started playing with matches. Lit a couple. Waved them around. Maybe it was a signal, I don't know.'

'And then?'

'Well, then Tandy was ready for another spot. So I left.'

'Is that all?'

'Yeah.' He leaned forward and said in a stage whisper, 'It was that rock and roll dame wasn't it? I was down here with the first cherries; I heard 'em say it was her that was here. And she was gonna meet the black chick – the one that got – '

'I think that's all, Mr Trybridge,' the cop said. 'The detective will get back to you if he needs anything,' and he dismissed the man, who walked off reluctantly. That's when I knew why Willie Rossini was so anxious to talk to me.

'I knew the deceased. I'm a close friend of the family,' I said to the officer.

'Yeah?' He smiled. 'Okay, ask Officer Downy over there if he'll take you down to the beach to Lieutenant Youtoga.'

I repeated my request to an even bigger man, with pink, shiny skin.

That's when I got the grand tour of the beach and the colourless men, busy sifting and plucking things out of the dirt. I looked about for Lana, half expecting to find her there, searching the sand for some memory of her body. But the string boys were busying themselves in a different way, measuring everything in sight.

Lieutenant Youtoga wanted me out of the area and I was promenaded past rows of men, busy with ropes and tweezers, entertaining each other with stories of putrified flesh.

I turned on the radio in the car and sat there for what seemed like a long time. I breathed the same air Lana had breathed. And who was Lana anyway? A parrot, a puppet, always doing everything that was expected of her? Did she ever fight back? Did she have that much of a mind left? Is that why she'd been killed? I realised the radio was blaring disco music at me. I had to remember to reset the radio dials so it wouldn't happen again. I reminded myself of a lot of mindless chores I needed to do and wished I could have done something to alter the outcome of events.

I wanted to call Maya, spend the night at her place. Wake up with chickens and cow manure. Instead I drove home and took a ten minute shower. I put on black pants with a front pleat and polished my brown leather riding boots. I put on a matt silk blouse with woven stripes, a classic from the second hand store. I looked at myself in the mirror. Somewhere in my head I was going to the funeral.

I was also going to see Willie Rossini. I wanted Willie Rossini to appreciate my effort, in addition to validating my parking. But no matter how I tried to entertain myself with trivia I was feeling every moment that Lana Flax was dead. Murdered. 'That black slut', Nebraska had called her. I wondered how the defence diva would go for the punk queen's famous last line before the concert.

Twenty-two

The office of Willie Rossini was located in a concrete jungle of sharp sunlight and shadows and quick winds that whistled through the skyscraper corridors. But the interior was hypersealed in smoked glass and recycled fluorescent air. I needed to take the express elevator to the twenty-third floor. Willie Rossini had climbed high on the skyscraper totem pole.

I made my way to a glass door that said Rossini, Richmond and Kasawaki, Attorneys at Law. A blond receptionist with a moustache asked me to take a seat. I sat on a hard couch in indirect lighting with no magazines. I sat for twenty minutes while the receptionist did about a hundred and twenty per minute on a big electronic typewriter. Finally a buzzer sounded.

'She's waiting for you. Inside.' The receptionist waved me towards the first oak door at the beginning of a hallway behind him. I went over and opened it and walked in.

A dark room had been lined with avocado linen wallpaper and crammed with heavy furniture. On the left wall two large bookshelves housed the standard leather legal tomes and stood guard on either side of a grotesque mahogany breakfront with turnipball feet. To the right, on a walnut table a layer of newspapers had been carefully spread out and taped down at the edges with masking tape. A heavy chain lay there, its links contributing to a grease stain that spread on to a full page bathing suit advertisement from the Sunday supplement. I approached the leather-topped desk in front of me, big enough to shame a cabin cruiser. In between two pillars of paper capped by chunky paperweights of black obsidian I saw a hulking silhouette with a view of twentieth-century San Francisco behind her.

I coughed, but the steely grey-haired head didn't move. The lips pursed and eventually six blue irises looked up into mine, a series of little eyes refracted through trifocals. The glasses rested on a graceful, curving nose. Her cheeks were beginning to get jowly. At something like sixty, the profile of Willie Rossini would have improved any Italian coin.

She flopped the papers down on her desk where they slid across the blotter, and looked up at me. A pink silk blouse was stretched slightly across her ample bosom. 'Well, sit down.' She pushed her glasses up her nose. I sat down in a leather armchair facing her.

'So. You're Emma Victor,' she said and I waited for her to top that one. She leaned back and looked at me. The light from the window was full in my face.

'You wanted to see me,' I reminded her.

'Yes.' She sat up and looked down at her papers, gathering them together and putting them in the file. I started nervously tapping my fingers on the armrest of the hard chair.

'You took Nebraska to the concert the other night.'

'Yes.'

'And you are also a member of this Commune?'

'No.'

'Oh. And what is your involvement with the Divine Vishnus exactly?' Her lips smiled at the end of the sentence. No lipstick.

'I've gone to a few of their functions out of curiosity, a favour to a friend.'

'Oh. A friend. You subscribe to their teachings?'

'Ms Rossini, my time is valuable and I've been waiting twenty minutes already, sampling your hard couch and lack of reading material. I wish you would come to the point. I assumed you wanted me to come because you're afraid your client is going to be charged with murder and you hope I have some information pertaining to the case. And maybe you want that information before the District Attorney gets to me. You want to know what I know. So ask.'

'Listen, I'm going to be straight with you here . . . ' the lawyer began, leaning forward, but I was still pissed about waiting twenty minutes with no magazines.

'Am I supposed to be grateful?'

'No, but you're interested, of course, so am I. Miss Storm dismissed her criminal lawyer when she didn't need him any more. And I want to look after her.'

'I think you're looking out for yourself too.'

'That's only common sense, Ms Victor. But would you be so kind as to tell me anything you have seen or heard that relates to Nebraska's involvement with this Commune and Lana Flax?'

I looked at the Italian woman and made up my mind.

'All right. I'll tell you. I heard Nebraska say denigrating things about Lana. That includes a racial slur.'

'And what exactly did she say about the victim?'

'Don't call Lana "the victim". She was a brilliant young physicist. She was my best friend's sister. I wish you wouldn't use legalese to anaesthetise the situation.'

'I'm sorry. You're right,' said Willie Rossini. 'It must be a difficult time for you.'

'And you've got a client with a rap sheet. She was accused of manslaughter in the overdosing of Edward Anvil last year, right? This can't be fun for you either.'

'I have a feeling we're coming to understand each other, Ms Victor. Please tell me what you know.' She sat up straight and opened a cigarette box in my direction, flashing a few rows of long slim cigarettes. I refused, but she took one for herself. The big black pearl on her finger rested in a modern setting.

'When I went to pick up Nebraska for the concert I understood she was upset about Vishnu not being there. I heard her say, "I'll bet he's with that black slut" to her agent, Portia Fronday.'

'And where were you when you heard this?'

'I was walking up the driveway.'

'She couldn't have possibly been saying, "Sneeze with your mouth shut"?'

'No, I heard her say, "He's with that black slut." '

'I see. I appreciate your straightforwardness. I'm sorry if I've underestimated you. You are a woman who can clearly come to the point. And what, if I may ask, is your opinion of this whole thing? Since, let's say,' she smiled with big yellow teeth, 'you've been around.'

I smiled back and hoped my teeth were whiter. I was starting to get the hang of Willie Rossini and it wasn't a bad place to be.

'I don't think a lot of the Vishnu Divine Inspiration Commune. I'm not sure how dangerous they are. There's a lot of territory between Jonestown and your neighbourhood Buddhist Baking Collective. But a group that cuts itself off from the world could easily see the world as its enemy. It becomes a stressful situation.'

'Do you think the murder of Lana Flax has to do with this . . . stressful situation?'

'I think that what I think isn't so important. But I *know* there are unhealthy tensions in the Vishnu organisation.'

'And these unhealthy tensions, did you directly experience – ?'

'It's none of your business.' I smiled, thinking of Lailieka's beedie. But I also remembered Lana coming out of the basement after Nebraska. She had obviously heard or seen something that made them look at each other with new eyes – well, that wasn't really a fact.

'Okay,' a slow grin, 'that's clear. So, you've visited Nebraska at home, you drove her to the concert, you've been to the Commune on a number of occasions, you knew Lana Flax.' She peered down at some papers, looked back up at me and took off her glasses.

'And I've heard Lana called her that night. It would explain her little trip to the beach.'

'You know a lot, Ms Victor. So, do you think she did it?'

'No.'

'Tell me why, Ms Victor. Do tell me why.'

'Nebraska is a woman of addictions. She replaced drugs with Vishnu after what must have been the traumatic death of Edwin Anvil. But Nebraska's not that simple.' I looked at Willie Rossini and saw her mouth suddenly tighten. It couldn't have been big news to her.

'Nebraska got through the concert without Vishnu. But she took a nose dive. And that's not the only dive she took. If I've ever seen anybody get high, I saw Nebraska get high the night after the concert. I think that's becoming her escape mechanism of choice. It doesn't leave a lot of emotional energy over for murder.'

'Oh no? Why not?'

'Because heroin doesn't leave enough emotions over to make you want to pet your cat.'

'You put two and two together with surprising accuracy, Ms Victor.'

'Don't smooth me over. I just see a lot of pieces and they don't fit together so good.'

'What doesn't fit together?'

'That the cops are making a lot of noises about the jogging murderer and Nebraska hasn't even been named as a suspect.'

'All in good time, Ms Victor, all in good time.' Willie lit one of the long cigarettes with an onyx desktop lighter. Her hands were graceful, splashed with brown age spots.

'No, I don't think Nebraska did it. But when I last saw her she didn't look too happy. She sure needs some kind of help from somebody or something.'

'She needs a good lawyer,' Willie frowned. 'So you think Nebraska wasn't jealous after the night of the concert?'

'There goes motive.'

'I wish a jury would go for your analysis. But I'm afraid that Nebraska's record and current activities will not endear her to a jury,' grumbled the large woman. 'Well, thank you very much Ms Victor.' Willie Rossini stood up and walked me to the door. Her silk suit blouse was collarless, with tucks running down the front, and I could see competing edges of white lace underneath. I looked up into her eyes before taking her hand.

'Do you think she did it?' I asked.

'You're impertinent as hell but I like you, Ms Victor,' she sighed. 'No, I don't think Nebraska did it. But that doesn't cut any ice with a jury.'

'Nebraska Storm must be a difficult client.'

'Like I say, Ms Victor, I'm Ms Storm's corporate lawyer.'

'But you're worried.'

'I just try and keep everybody's best interests at heart.'

'And hope they don't conflict.'

'Something like that. May I call you again if I have any questions?'

'Yes.'

She gave me a big handshake and a smile that had it well over any smile of Bumper Lee and sighed. 'Thank you, Ms Victor. I guess that's all we need to know.'

A sighing lawyer didn't bode well for Nebraska Storm. I wondered if Willie Rossini would be calling me again. I wondered if I might ever call her. I just didn't see Nebraska doing it.

I went home and called Jonell. I got through the busy signal and Jonell's voice came on the phone, small and unhappy. We spent an hour talking. I told her about how Lana had looked in her kimono, how happy she had seemed. I lied. Then Jonell began about the murderer. She indulged in lusty revenge for a while. I didn't tell her about Nebraska Storm or Willie Rossini.

She cried for a few minutes and I listened to that. And after a while she told me that there wasn't going to be a further autopsy and the funeral would be four days from today in Boston. I didn't have the funds to go. And I didn't want to go. We kissed the plastic mouthpieces and I unglued the telephone horn from my tingling ear, which had become a brilliant pink. Lana Flax was really starting to feel dead.

Twenty-three

Lana Flax was still dead first thing in the morning. It wasn't time to drink another cup of coffee, it was time to move, clear up dishes, iron, anything. But the thoughts kept breaking through anyway. Even ironing a fitted sheet didn't keep the demons away, including the guilt ones. Why hadn't I pushed Lana to leave that place? Because she wouldn't have left of her own free will. But could I have said more, more convincingly? Perhaps Roseanna had been right. Perhaps I shouldn't have expected to have an effect on the outcome of events. I couldn't have made any difference short of forcibly kidnapping the woman. I wondered what kind of questioning Nebraska Storm was going through, how much more evidence they needed to arrest her. So I could feel exonerated from a role in Lana's death? What a wonderful thought.

I tried ironing the ends of the fitted sheet, pushing the point of the iron into each of the elastic-bordered corners. Mr Witness had seen Nebraska's car at the scene of the crime. But I still didn't get it. What was the hook that got Nebraska there? Vishnu? Her career? And why would Lana want to hook her anyway?

The sheet snapped over the rounded end of the ironing board and curled around the iron. Bumper said Lana had chakra problems. Did Lana get the gallows for unenlightenment? Not likely. Was Lana the bearer of bad news and therefore dead? I thought these guru girls knew how to play hardball, and were subject to a kind of paranoia, but murder?

Lana had given Vishnu English lessons, assisted him with his foul expulsions, known all the cleansing rituals, the inside outs. Could Nebraska Storm really be jealous of that? Could anyone? But Nebraska's car had been at the scene of the crime. And it was Lana's voice that got Nebraska Storm down there. I stuffed the sheet into the plastic basket and called Willie Rossini.

'What can I do for you, Miss Victor?'

'I have an idea I would like to check out. Would it be possible for me to talk to Portia Fronday? With your permission?'

'It's about the case?'

'Yes.'

'And what exactly are you after?'

'I'll know when I find it.'

'And do you think this information could possibly help my client?'

'You mean your corporate client?'

'You don't need to remind me of that, Miss Victor.'

'May I interview Portia Fronday?'

There was silence on the line. Then, 'Yes. In my office. In my presence. Two o'clock.'

Two o'clock rolled around and the Plymouth squeezed into another compact parking space. I took the elevator to the twenty-third floor. This time I was shown right in. Willie Rossini let me into her office herself. It hadn't changed, only the desk seemed to bear higher stacks of papers, and the dark oil which had flowed off the bolts and screws resting on top of the spread-out sheets of newspaper was beginning to dry.

Willie Rossini walked to a door on a side wall and opened it. Portia Fronday was sitting in a side reception room, looking tired and pale. She stood up and walked into the office.

'Portia,' said Willie, 'You've met Miss Victor?'

'Emma,' I said.

Portia grimaced and nodded. We both sat down in the leather chairs in front of Willie's desk. 'But I don't know if I should really be telling – '

'Telling what? What's there to tell?' Willie asked softly, but the questions came on hard to Portia Fronday. The nervous manager pushed two cuticles down, scraping the tan pearl polish off her curved fingernails. 'I've told the police everything,' she said finally, looking up.

'Then you won't mind telling it again,' suggested Willie. Portia's cuticles were saying yes but her mouth said, 'No, but I didn't think Nebraska needed legal counsel.'

'Why don't you let me determine that,' the lawyer said, putting an end to her objections. Portia smirked at her hands and sighed.

'What exactly did Lana say on the phone the night she called Nebraska?' I began.

Portia looked at Willie. Willie nodded, her glasses moving slowly up and down on their elastic string.

'Take it from the top. From when you answered the phone.'

'You think I haven't told this story about a million times already? Okay. It was about a quarter after two. I was in bed, but I wasn't asleep. I have trouble sleeping and I was reading, so I picked up the phone, which is next to my bed, on the first ring. I said, "Hello, hello" a few times.'

'Why did you say it a few timse?'

'There wasn't an answer at first. And I was impatient, I thought, Christ, calling after two a.m., it better be good.'

'And then?'

'I heard a voice say, very slowly, "Hello, I want to see Nebraska." "Nebraska's in bed," I said.

'"I want to see Nebraska," the voice said again. And then very clearly, "Lana Flax." And I said, "I don't care who you are. Nebraska's asleep."

'"I want to see Nebraska," she repeated. Then I muttered something, I don't know, like "Jesus Christ, where's the fire?"'

'Lana said, "It's important." So I switched her over to Nebraska's phone, but I didn't put the phone on the hook. I – I well, I've been a bit of a leash holder for a while. It doesn't do a lot for Nebraska's privacy, but on the other hand, she hasn't really earned the right to privacy.'

'I thought that concept was incontestable after puberty,' I said.

'You haven't lived with a junkie for five years.'

'Go on. The phone call.'

'Nebraska picked up the other line and said, "What the hell are you calling me for at this hour?" and Lana just said, "I want to see you. It's important."'

'Did she sound disturbed? Threatening?'

'No. She sounded totally calm and controlled. She spoke very slowly. Then she said, "You must meet me at the beach. You must come to my house," and then it was kind of funny. She sort of barked, and then she said "Now." Then Nebraska said, "Huh?"

147

and Lana said, "I will meet you at the beach. It's very important."

'And she said, "I will meet you at the beach." '

'You're sure she said, "I will meet" and not "I'll meet you at the beach"?'

'She was talking very slowly. I kept wondering what she was on.'

'On?'

'Yeah, if she was on drugs, or drunk. You know, the way drunks can start to articulate every syllable.'

'And what did Nebraska say?'

'Not much. She said, "Huh?" "What?" I think. And finally she said, "Does he want to see me?" And then Lana said, "You are needed." And then Lana hung up.'

'That was it?'

'Yes. I heard Nebraska get up, put the phone on the hook and after a few minutes I heard her come downstairs and then her car left the driveway.'

'You didn't try and stop her?'

'It wasn't a dope connection. I can't say as I'm wild about this cock-eyed excuse of a religion she's into, but, until now, it's kept her clean and gotten her into the studio.'

'And gotten her out of some land and cash.'

'She can use it as a tax break. As long as I get my ten per cent.'

'I see.'

'I know my business, Ms Victor, I've been personal manager for a lot of difficult people. I have to know where to draw the line in being her keeper.'

'And to hell with her soul?'

'She's rented it out before, to worse things.'

'What happened when she came back?'

Portia looked at Willie Rossini who nodded to her.

'I must have been asleep. But I went down to her car the next morning and, well, it was a mess.' She looked at Rossini who nodded at her again. 'After the concert the other night, Nebraska scored and I guess she had a little stash in the dashboard. I guess she was in a kind of mood when she didn't find anybody there, and she reached into the glove compartment and hit up.'

'That's what she says?'

'I believe her when she says she didn't see Lana Flax anywhere around. And I believe her that she passed out in the parking lot that night and didn't make it home until dawn. I believe her because I saw her car.'

'What'd you find?'

'Seaweed, sand and puke. I had the car cleaned the next day.'

'The cops must have loved that.'

'That's all you wanted to ask, Ms Victor?'

'That's it,' I said.

'And this is probably it for Nebraska,' I heard Portia mutter.

Willie stood up and escorted Portia back into the reception room and Portia mumbled something like, 'I should have stayed with journalism.'

When Willie Rossini came back she closed the door and leaned her big frame on it. The trifocals slid off her nose and she let them fall on to her blouse.

'What do you think you're up to?' she asked me.

'Like I said; I don't know. I just have a hunch.'

'Want to talk about it?'

'No. Not yet. But I might want to after I talk to a friend of mine. I'm hoping she's ready for a hyperventilation meditation, and I hope she doesn't fall out of her wheelchair.'

'Well, you let me know if you find anything. I'd appreciate it.'

I didn't promise. I wasn't sure if Roseanna would really go for it. One thing was, my cover at the Commune was blown. I looked back at the big woman with the hard glitter in her eye that was somehow friendly.

'I have to warn you, Ms Victor. I'm concerned about my client, and any information that you can dig up will be useful to her. I'm damned worried she's going to get hanged for a murder rap.'

She offered me the brown-spotted hand with the black pearl ring on it to shake. Then she opened the door to let me know it was my time to leave. I looked back over at the walnut table with the paper and screws and bolts.

'What is that anyway?' I pointed to the parts.

'Some pieces of a chain saw,' she said. 'Goodbye, Ms Victor.'

Twenty-four

It was quarter to twelve in the parking lot of the Vishnu Divine Inspiration Commune and I was sitting on the original plaid highlander upholstery of Roseanna Baynetta's souped-up woodie. The walk from the Plymouth, parked three blocks away in front of a warehouse, had left me cold, and thinking about my new friend inside going through therapeutic trauma didn't make me feel any better.

Roseanna had volunteered with a glee that could have only been perverse. She had called me back at once to tell me that she'd been through her closet and had decked herself out in sunny yellow colours. She'd even changed her wheelchair armrests to orange. I wished her luck and told her I'd meet her at the edge of the parking lot at midnight. But instead Roseanna had given me a seven digit code for the lock which automatically set the lift into action. So I rode up on the back and crawled through a maze of Roseanna's father's devices to sit in a bucket seat and wait.

Crouching down and peering over the bakelite dashboard in the darkness, I saw a door open. The sound of laughter and music, and Roseanna Baynetta came out into the night. I saw her turn and put something in the door jamb to keep the door from closing. She got the Rolls All-Terrain down a small step and then she pushed the joystick, making tracks for the van. Suddenly I saw Sadhima.

He appeared from the back of the building with a flashlight which he shone on Roseanna and turned quickly off. She stopped her chair, and when he came close they exchanged a few words. He pointed to the door and she nodded. Then he walked off.

As Roseanna came up on the lift I saw that she'd really outdone herself with a daffodil buckskin miniskirt.

'Something Dad picked up from the runway?'

'And the crocodile slingbacks and glitzy glasses.' Roseanna's violet eyes were framed by golden-winged frames filled with yellow glitter.

'How's it going in there?'

'Everything's jake, Emma. The food was delicious, the people are friendly, it's great!' She put her chair in a reclining position and leaned back. 'Of course the therapy things aren't exactly a comfort, and they keep you busy every minute. Do this, children, do that. Never a comment out of turn, never an individual remark. Busy, busy, busy. At eleven thirty Lailieka left us and somebody else came in to read us the uplifting words of Vishnu for an hour. Since dinner we haven't had a single break.'

'What did guru guard just say to you?'

'He warned me to be careful of the jogging rapist.' She laughed. 'I told him that's just who I was looking for. And I complimented him on his hair-care regime.'

'How'd you get out of the workshop?'

'Oh, that's easy. I just announce loudly that I have to go and empty my bag. Never a question. Works every time. Hey, your basic guru security type will probably be back here soon. You'd better get in now before he completes his round.'

I jumped out of the back of the van and peered around the corner of it. No one in sight. I ran to the front door where Roseanna had put a cheap paperback novel between the door and the frame and went in. I heard Roseanna working the lift out in the van and I turned and looked the portrait of Vishnu in the face. 'You going to be keeping me company in here, old man?' I asked the picture. 'Then don't let the cat out of the bag, please.' I could hear the sounds of too happy laughter in the distance. It made me nervous, and the big expensive room made me feel isolated and exposed. The hippie muzak seemed strange in the deserted area.

The coffee shop was the source of life, light shining through two sets of glass doors. But I would hardly be welcomed there. I tip-toed across the flagstone floor and went behind the big fancy reception desk. I heard a noise and ducked underneath it. Whirr, click, whirr, bump. It was Roseanna. Tap, tap, tap. Someone else. Five minutes to twelve. My heart was making more noise than Roseanna's chair.

'Oh, hello.' It was Lailieka. Surprised, then remembering. Roseanna's bag. 'Everything, uh . . . ?'

'Emptied. Yes, just like my own sweet soul, hunn-ah.' My heart sank. Roseanna was doing a totally affected Southern accent.

'Whay, I think it's the most wonderful cotton pickin' notion owah mahster has conjured up. Jus, deevine, whay, I was tellin my friend . . . ' Cut it Roseanna, I'm not inside yet, I thought. Lailieka cleared her thin throat and patiently, patronisingly, suggested that Roseanna return to the group. Then she made a big mistake. She must have put her hands on the grips of Roseanna's chair and tried to turn the heavy vehicle, because I saw the yellow slingback shoes in the footplates move and the chair jolted backwards.

'Aaarghh!' Roseanna yelled. 'Don't evah, evah, do that!'

I laughed inwardly. Even the Vishnus couldn't push Roseanna around in her wheelchair.

'Why, I'm sorry, I didn't mean – '

'You can get yoself one helluva shock, hunnay!'

'Oh. Well, I've got to go now. You, uh, you know where the group room is from here?'

'Ah sure do.'

Tap, tap, tap. It was almost midnight. Lailieka walked towards the desk, hesitated and then kept walking towards the door behind me. I crouched down further and caught sight of her Achilles' heels in yellow anklets. I heard Roseanna put the chair into gear and go through the revelling coffee shop.

Lailieka's feet stopped behind the smoked glass door. A pair of yellow socks came to meet them. I heard a tinkling laugh that I didn't think Lailieka had in her. Then I heard a husky powerful voice that must have been Bumper Lee responding with affection. A whispered conference took place, punctuated with a sense of urgency, then giggles. It sounded like they had something close, very close, going on together. I watched the ankles intermingle for a while, then they walked off in the same direction.

The noise picked up from the coffee shop. What was making the Vishnus so goddamn happy today? I looked at my watch. One minute after twelve. Then I heard it, the clear strains of the mezzo soprano of Lailieka, the divine diva, floating out from the Meditation Room. If my theory was correct she had a good grip on more than her vocal chords. Still, she had a clarity in her voice that was hard to square with murder. And she sang a prettier tune than Nebraska Storm could ever dream of.

I stood up and looked at the desk with its black liquid-crystal screen. Holes had been bored, naked wires peered out. The elaborate system was still being installed. No lights burning, none of the telephones was in use. But an interior directory of in-house phones. They couldn't have everything on liquid crystal, could they? Paper. A sheet of paper taped on to a piece of cardboard jutted out from one of the slots. Dog-eared, dirty. That was it. *Dining Room*, *Coffee Shop*, and in new type, Sadhima's *International Headquarters*, right in the main building. But I wanted Ananda House. Underneath that was *Service Area*, their own servants' quarters. Bu Mper, so this was the right place. Lana, and yes, our playmate Lailieka. All of them in one building. With the meditation cave. It was a dream come true. Living together in the dormitory with the undisturbed man in the disturbing world. All in the same crib.

Lailieka's voice went into a higher register. Out, how to get out of this wing and into Ananda House. Not through the coffee shop. My burglar ensemble of black turtleneck, black jeans and black sneakers would not fit in with the coffee shop crowd. The thought of the reactions my black crow appearance would cause wasn't comforting. And the prospect of meeting any of the meditational management types was terrifying. I looked out of the window and I saw that next to the plate glass was a double hung window which opened up near the ground. So I turned the handle, didn't set off any alarms and crawled out to kiss violets.

Lailieka's voice was louder outside. It was a cool night, and even the garden was being visited by breezes, rustling through dried diacondra, stirring up what little debris the Vishnus created. There was nobody out there and there were no garden floodlights, just footlights along the pathway to Ananda House.

I crawled along the shrubbery to the coffee shop window. I discovered I was wearing the right clothes after all. In the midst of the happy crowd, caressing each other, laughing hysterically, smiling whimsically, was a silver-framed portrait of Lana Flax. Occasionally someone would come by and blow a kiss and smile; one man even picked up her portrait and whirled around the room with it. That's one way to say goodbye. Black had more to do with my feelings, but maybe they had the right idea after all.

I crawled through some more shrubs and quickly out into the

open towards Ananda House. The door was ajar and I slipped into the lobby, a black shadow in the house of happiness. I scurried into a side hallway. I could still hear Lailieka singing, and it seemed that Bumper had chosen to be with the singer rather than with the rousing funeral crew in the coffee shop. I looked down the hallway that led to Vishnu's basement. It was empty, silent. Hello Vishnu, I thought. You going to give me away old man? But it was all beyond him. Lana's death, Lailieka's song.

What I was looking for would be upstairs. I raced through the lobby and ran up the stairs, taking two at a time. I listened at Bumper's door and quickly slipped inside. I closed the door and took a deep breath. My heart was pounding.

I looked around me. The white curtains were still drawn against the darkened garden. The big oak table and the tall ladderback chairs were waiting for Bumper's next dinner guest. The dumb waiter that brought us vegetarian food and French wine.

I walked into Bumper's bedroom and saw her bed, which hadn't waited for anyone. Had the bed been slept in, the covers thrown aside when police investigators made their call in the deep hours of the night? The rest of the room was in apple-pie order, with that freshly cleaned feeling, as if everything had been dusted, polished and put in a slightly more proper place than before. Books had been straightened and the desk was empty of papers. Even the woodwork on the windowsill around the curtain pull anchor had been dusted. The brass doorknob was shining, free of fingerprints. The Vishnu cleaning fairy had been here real recently; I wondered if she came up on the dumb waiter.

I looked on the shelves for the little copulating figurines I had dropped on the bed but didn't see them. I got on my knees and raised up the corner of the coverlet and saw my two friends, completing their act over by the wall where they had fallen between a cardboard box and a round ice cream container. I got down flat on the floor, reached back towards the statue and found their two waistlines; I pulled them towards me. On the way my hand bumped into something resting on the bottom of the built-in bookshelf that backed the head of the bed. I pulled out a black high-impact plastic box and snapped it open.

Inside a nest of moulded plastic, sprayed with a cover of forest green felt, a snub nose .38 said hello. I took it out carefully and smelled the barrel just like the detectives did in movies. It smelled like fresh oil does, before the tempura is cooked. I guess that meant that it hadn't been fired; but then I didn't know too much about Japanese cooking either. I crawled out from under the bed and on my way I found a beedie butt. I flicked it into the wastebasket. I replaced the two copulating figures on the bookshelf.

'Don't tell anyone I paid a call,' I said to them, but they were in seventh heaven with joined pelvises and happy smiles. And I didn't expect to find anything in Bumper's room anyway. I stuck my head out into the quiet hallway and made my way to Lana's room. I could hear the swelling noises of the swilling crowd in the coffee shop. They did know how to have a good time, they were just doing it at an odd moment. But maybe I had a strange way of looking at things.

One thing that wasn't strange was the District Attorney's seal that had been taped all over Lana's door. I wasn't going to fuck with that. But then, maybe I didn't need to. There was only one more doorway to go, and it had to be Lailieka's. I put my ear to the door and listened hard. I didn't want to wake anybody up in my spook costume, and I didn't want to disturb an impending orgasm or a vow of silence. I turned the knob. It was locked.

I pulled a plastic credit card out of my pocket and stuck it between the door jamb and the door, and when I felt the sliding latch bolt I gave the card a shove. The door opened. The room was dark. I didn't turn on the light. Lailieka had chosen a little cell which looked away from the garden world of the Commune out over the factories to the sky. I could still hear her singing in the distance, her voice transcending the noisy wake that was taking place in the coffee shop.

A big long window showed a horizon band of shimmering lights riding on heat waves from the city, and then a stretch of sky. The happy grin of the god of the universe. A large telescope was silhouetted against the window, peering blindly into the darkness. I found a table in the middle of the room, but I still didn't dare turn on a lamp. I got out my penlight and waved it around.

Neat, orderly. The bareness of the room was too modest for a monk. Scrubbed wooden floor, a table whose unfinished bleached top had only been scrubbed and scrubbed again. A bottle of ink stood next to a pen which rested in a porcelain holder. I shuddered. Naked, cold plaster walls. A cot stood against one wall and my heart skipped a beat when I noticed a bookshelf with hundreds of books in it. I started to look at the titles: Medieval music, and astronomy from Galileo to Mission Space Control. Lailieka had it all, and she had it alphabetised. I looked around the room and could picture the intense, brittle young woman, clutching her knowledge of the stars to guide her along her chosen path. But what I was praying for was that the organised bibliophile couldn't throw away a book. I pored over the titles. Then I got tired and looked under the bed. The table had no drawers. Suddenly thoughts of Lana came rushing back. Jonell's kid sister, dead; I'm so sorry, Jonell, my dear friend, that your sister is dead.

I went back to the titles in the bookshelf. Nothing. A big stack of yellow dog-eared papers was piled up on the far side of the bookshelf. I peered at it and turned up a few covers of musical scores. A lot of music had passed through Lailieka's throat. A lot of music was still passing through her throat. I could hear the clear tones soaring into the night. In a few places the stack had been separated, a pile pushed slightly backwards on replacement. I looked at the biggest separations, and didn't reap any fruit, so I gave up and sat on my heels and started looking quickly through all the titles. I peered at covers of Ambrose's antiphonal hits, and Pope Greg's greatest themes. Somewhere amongst the plainsong and the Golden Years of Polyphony I found it. *Improve Your English*. I slipped it so quickly under my sweater I nearly amputated my nipples.

Then the singing stopped. I listened again at the door and peered out. I raced down the stairway and out into the garden. The hysterical mourning party had taken to the garden and were dancing. There was no escape. I had to walk right through them. I just hoped that I wouldn't meet with hall monitors, high-quality singers or Bumper Lee.

Perhaps it was the darkness, perhaps it was the champagne. But the commune members seemed to be colour blind and I was offered two glasses of bubbles. And a quick feel that went with them.

I refused the champagne, and pushed the asking hands away from my body. They would only have found *Improve Your English*, anyway. Just make it out of the garden, I thought. And hope that the lobby is free of any bad traffic. I was as inconspicuous as Satan himself rushing to get out of heaven. I made it to the flagstone lobby and finally to the outside door, mercifully not locked from within. Almost outside. I peered into the parking lot and listened. No crunches of gravel that belied guru guarding.

I walked swiftly across the lit asphalt and past Roseanna's van. Safe. I got across the street and behind another warehouse before I started running. I hadn't dared to park my car closer; it was likely someone would have noticed its distinctive East Coast plates. Not to mention its charming old world character from the days when gasoline went for a quarter a gallon. And Bumper knew what kind of wheels I was spinning. I started a little jog, feeling pleased with myself. Another corner, the Plymouth was in sight. I stopped at the door and took a quick look around. Nobody was following me: behind were just the big shapes of square warehouses and cones of insufficient street lighting.

I got into the Plymouth, closed the door and pulled *Improve Your English* out from under my sweater. I turned quickly to the contents.

It was better than I ever could have thought. Vishnu was working on his diphthong techniques, and Lana had probably been coaching him on vowel displacement. The chapters that interested me were 'A Day at the Beach' and 'Business English'. I turned to the first lesson and found that Lailieka had even helped me along a little bit. She'd underlined all the sentences that Lana Flax had supposedly spoken to Nebraska Storm on the telephone on the night of her death.

I felt the glow of success, a theory proved correct by a woman who couldn't throw away a book! It was fantastic. I reminded myself of the wonderful properties of evidence. That every move we make and every act more involved than tying your shoelaces spews evidence in its wake, from sand to threads, to a pattern of blood, to *Improve Your English*.

Thanks, Lailieka. Thanks for helping me out, I thought. But I could have just told her out loud. She and Sadhima were peering right into my face from behind the windshield.

Twenty-five

C'mon, C'mon, C'mon honey, do dah dance to da disco BEAT, do dah DANCE, do dah DANCE, do dah dance to dah disco BEAT, YEAH! Wooow, woow, woow, woow – disco BEAT!'

I remembered Lailieka opening the door and grabbing *Improve Your English* out of my hands, her eyes wide and frightened, her expression snapping open to the possible complications of murder. She jerked the book from my hands while I held tight to the cardboard cover, two of my fingernails were torn off just beyond the quick. I heard Sadhima laugh.

'Is it getting a little complicated covering up, Lailieka?'

'Shut up,' Lailieka screamed at him, clutching the book to her chest, but he was leaning into the car and trying to drag me out. When that didn't work he landed a right hook near my eye as I reached towards his face with nails that weren't much use as weapons. I saw the flash of blood on my fingers, and a glint of pleasure in Sadhima's eyes before I saw the birdies which meant he'd scored a direct hit. Lailieka cried, 'What are you doing?' I tried to figure out a way to get him in the balls as I saw him hesitate and reach into his pocket and pull out a long flat box.

In the short seconds I struggled to get my feet on the car seat so I could lunge at him, but he was coming at me fast with a hypodermic needle that landed in my arm. I twisted away from it and the tip broke, but not until I saw that it had done its job, filling my bloodstream with bubble gum.

'What are we gonna do *now*?' cried Lailieka, in a voice that was getting farther away.

'That's your problem. You can't solve this with a PBX and a tape recorder,' I thought I heard a male voice saying and a funny ironic sort of laugh that echoed in my head for a long time, and eventually turned into *'Wanna do that thang, wanna do that thang, do the thang, do the thang – to da disco BEAT!'*

Head tapes, telephone tapes, disco tapes. It had certainly been days. Every now and then somebody threw water in, but only when all the lights were out. I was forced to find the water on my hands and knees. I was licking up puddles from the foam rubber mats. Bodily functions had become a big problem.

I thought about Vishnu Commune having turned to the dark side of the force. I thought about Bumper's nunnery comparisons and the thought didn't cheer me up. It was the age of science and technology and the yellow people had taken advantage of modern-day methods. Somebody had done some homework whose end result had never been nirvana before. Perhaps it had begun with the best of intentions. But that certainly didn't matter any more. At first glance the yellow people hadn't wanted much more than most of my friends. And Vishnu had something. I had a sudden memory of red roses, and remembered my nightmare meditation. His words flashed before me: 'The seasons plant and ripen. It is all the parts and no parts at all.'

Open eyes. No difference in total darkness. Close again. Upstairs was an upholstered sofa, down here a white chair bolted to the floor. Was this the logical end, the same kind of cell where Ulrike Meinhof hanged herself? Would they try and dress me in yellow clothes when it was over? Cold. Hungry, thirsty. Above me happy people were eating from a vegetarian gourmet cuisine. How long could they keep me?

Turn the mind away from their control of you. I wanted to sleep and tried out old sleep fantasies, putting myself to bed, tucking myself in. Okay. Nebraska Storm. No. Willie Rossini, there's a good focus. I could imagine her standing before the judge, her figure solid as a marble column, her curved nose lending grace to her weighty stature. And her weighty delivery. She probably went over great with juries. I imagined her objections being sustained again and again to the chagrin of nervous lawyers in three-piece suits. But even that fantasy wouldn't work.

'To da DISCO BEAT!' I was thinking about murder again. My murder. My bladder hurt. So I went and peed in one corner of the room, squatting down, holding the crotch of my pants up so I wouldn't get them wet. Warm pee. Warm. From my own body. Wet.

I cried. I tried not to. Something was happening to me in that cell. Something that was propelling me into a fear that had nothing

159

to do with lack of light or water. And that fear had kept my mind stiff as a hospital patient who'd been lying in bed for months. Or at least as long as I'd been residing in the state of California.

Why didn't I just order the bittersweet cocktail of life and drink it? Because I was too busy gazing into the face of the cocktail waitress who was serving it. She would look into my eyes with a gaze of permanent affection. We would go home. At least that's what I used to think. But now I knew that even if I found her it wouldn't matter. I knew I would have to pick up the crystal glass off the polished tray, open my mouth and put the sharp edge between my lips. I would drink. It wouldn't be milk and honey. It would be young vinegar from good grapes, or a wine of character hiding behind a discount label. It would be complicated and not quite what it seemed. I would gag at first and then swallow. And after that nothing would hurt so much. I would have an educated palate. But the waitress would never look the same.

That was the moment I really arrived in California. And I wasn't crying any more.

The disco music suddenly bleeped. *'Dahhh Dis-c – '*

Glurp! It went off with a disco hiccup. A huge light split the darkness. I felt as if someone had clubbed me with an anvil.

'Hey!' said a voice through a speaker. 'Who's in there?'

'Emma Victor.'

'Who?'

'Jack Benny. What difference does it make who I am? Let me out of here!'

I heard a few toggle switches snap, the light went off again, and then on, finally the cracks around the door became wider and outside was a scared and yellow Delphy, with two trembling peacock-feather earrings brushing her shoulders.

'What are you doing in there?' she asked. She looked closely at my face. I remembered the pain around my eye.

'I'm exploring the meditation possibilities of death rattles. How do I get out of here?'

'Well – '

'You've got to help me get out of here.'

'Out?'

160

'Your group here is involved in swindling, kidnapping and murder.'

'Kidnapping?' her voice trembled. 'Murder?'

'You think I was in there for my health? Now get me out of here.'

'Murder. So you know. I knew I should've – ' she pulled in her chin and looked down, flashing her three-tone eyeshadow at me.

'*Out!*' I hissed at her. 'Is there a back way *out*?'

Her mouth set. 'Yeah. This way. This is a back entrance – it comes out in a tunnel on the other side of the parking lot . . . ' She pointed to a door on the right and I started for it when I heard her behind me.

'Go on,' she said. She was coming with me. 'Shhh!' My wet socks slapped against the tiled floor of a long, narrow corridor.

'What are you . . . ?' She panted behind me, but I'd come to the end of the corridor and found a blank wall and a wooden fruit crate on the floor. 'Here, above the box. The ceiling – ' she said.

I stood on the crate and pushed my hands against the low ceiling. A piece of it gave way, and I stuck my head out into late daylight, a variety of sounds at varying levels. Diffuse light, a few rays of sunshine streaming through the pine needles and cones before my eyes. What a wonderful world it can be. I put my hands on the ground and heaved myself out of the tunnel. I emerged into a small grove of newly planted long-needled pines.

'Oh.' I heard a moan and looked down. Delphy was standing in the hallway beneath me, looking at the fruit crate and thinking about what a step it would be to get on it. She shook her head.

'What do you want? You want to get out of here? Come on, then,' I said.

She got on the crate and reached for my hand. I pulled her and she came up with a face that was emerging into a lot more than a wooded lot on the border of a parking area. She looked confused.

I just wanted to get away. Most immediately I wanted to get away from the possibility of being in that cell again. They certainly had done their homework. I looked over at Delphy; she was shaking and sucking on her upper lip. It was time to make a quick run for it. But now we were two.

161

'Let's duck behind a bush here for a second,' I took her by the shoulders, led her behind a juniper and pulled her down into a crouch. 'I'm looking into the murder of Lana Flax. If you know anything about it you'd better get out of here. Lailieka's already committed one murder.'

'What? Lailieka kill – no. No, you're wrong. Lailieka is a deeply spiritual soul, she – '

'Tell me another one.'

'But I saw it. I saw it.'

'Oh, great. Let's just get out of here first.'

'Okay.' Her eyes were staring at me. She wasn't blinking.

'We may have to run. So get ready.' I pulled the unfortunate Delphy with me out from behind the bushes and on to the street.

'Emma!' I heard a voice that didn't need a Southern accent any more. It was Roseanna in her Royal four-door station wagon, leaning out of the window. 'What's happening? Where the hell have you been, girl? I'm just about ready to call the police.'

'What stopped you?'

'I thought maybe you were playing spin the bottle with some of the local talent.'

'I'd rather play post office with a pit bull.'

'I've been calling Maya, but her line is out of order. But I had faith in you, Emma. I knew you'd get yourself out of this.'

'I wish you'd been less of a true believer.'

'I've been watching your Plymouth for the last two days! I was just about ready to try and get a search warrant . . . ' she was saying as I dragged Delphy towards the van. As we got closer I saw Roseanna's thin eyebrows pull together.

'Emma, what's happened?'

'Just tell me one thing,' I went around to Roseanna's door and reached up for her hand. 'What day is it?'

'Jesus Christ, Emma, it's Friday.'

'Friday? And I only peed once!'

'What?'

'Do you have some water? Please?'

Roseanna leaned over and got a sweating can of carbonated lemon-flavoured water out of the tiny fridge behind her chair. She handed it out of the window. I grabbed the can, flipped the top off

162

and poured the contents into my mouth. Then I ran with Delphy to the other side of the wagon. I opened the door, pushed the young woman's hesitant hips into the revolving bucket seat and got in next to her. 'Let's make tracks, Roseanna. This is no longer the divine neighbourhood it once was. Is my car still there?'

'Yes.' Roseanna was still staring at my face.

'Cruise me over there.'

Roseanna popped the woodie into gear and laid rubber in the direction of the Plymouth. Every now and then she would look over at me, like I'd turned into somebody else. The double decked grille-pattern smile of the Plymouth came into sight. I let out a deep breath.

'Boy, am I glad to see you, my friend,' I said. My wits were finally coming together, but natural light and sound were still a new experience. 'Our friends have a brainwash cycle that goes beyond dry-cleaning.'

Roseanna looked over at me quickly, her straight brown hair flicking her cheek. 'You got quite a shiner, pal,' she said. 'It's gonna take a lot of Helena Rubinstein to get you out on the street without people staring.'

I put my hand to my eye. 'I'm not so worried about that.' We pulled up to the Plymouth. 'Roseanna, follow me home, okay? I don't want any more vacations with the Vishnus for twenty-four hours.'

'Think I would let you go now, Emma Victor? I think we both have some interesting stories to tell.'

'Right now I'd settle for bread and water. And knowing I'll never have to see a yellow person again.' Delphy shuddered next to me. 'Present company excepted,' I apologised, giving her a squeeze on the shoulder, but she was lost in the beginning of a new life.

Roseanna put the wagon in neutral and I guided Delphy out.

'You're coming with me,' I said to her. She nodded. 'I need company,' I said. But what I really wanted was a story. I opened the door of the Plymouth and she slid in. A woman used to taking orders.

I walked round and got into the driver's seat, when I heard Roseanna's final comment.

'Well Emma, you might want to change your tune after we get back to your place, my dear.'

'Why's that?'

'You'll know what I mean when you hear the tapes.'

I turned the key and started the engine. I did a U-turn and tore down to the freeway, with the shiny black van of Roseanna Baynetta following in my wake. Tapes? When I'd gotten off the ramp on to the freeway I felt a little freer, a little farther away from what had happened. The world was passing by me with an arbitrary mixture of colours, sights, smells. I felt good.

I turned to Delphy. I thought I could handle anything. I even thought I could handle the story she was going to tell.

Twenty-six

Delphy was fiddling with one of her peacock earrings. She was gazing out of the window at high rise condominiums and shopping centres, and chewing her lip.

'So, Delphy. How long have you been with the Vishnus?'

'Seven years now.'

'How old are you?'

'Twenty-three.'

Jesus, Mary and Joseph. A recruit at sixteen.

'Did you know there was a special room in the basement?'

'Yes. Of course. It was used for some of the meditations for a while. Then the therapies took a different direction. We didn't need a sound-proofed room.'

'Or white furniture.'

'I don't know where that came from. That's new. Emma, what did she do to you?'

'She who? I think Sadhima has a very esoteric taste in interior design.'

164

'Sadhima? That must have been one of *her* projects.'

'Whose?'

'Bumper's.'

'Bumper? Bumper didn't do anything to me. Maybe if she had I wouldn't be here. It looks to me like Sadhima and Lailieka are busy covering up Lana's murder. It looks to me like they did it.'

'But it wasn't Lailieka that killed Lana. I know it.' Delphy took in a breath. 'I was with Lailieka when – when – it happened. It was Bumper. I saw her.'

'Are you sure?'

'Of course I'm sure. I saw it with my own eyes. It . . . it feels good to tell it.'

'Keep going then.'

'It was at the midnight meditation.'

'What did you see?'

'The entire family had gone to bed after the party for Nebraska Storm. Usually there are only seven or eight that come to the midnights anyway. But Lailieka always goes. It's her initiative, it's her music. And I always try to go too. It's not just for the meditative aspects of the music, I love to hear Lailieka sing.'

'Okay, okay. Go on.'

'Well, there were just two of us that night. We sat on two of the round cushions looking out of the window at the water. Lailieka started to sing, those beautiful tones ringing out over the water. And then suddenly she stopped and told me to go and get the candles. We have candles by the stairway, in a fireproof box. She'd never stopped in the middle of her singing, but I did what I was asked.'

'Of course.'

'As I went to get the candles I passed in front of a mirror on the opposite wall. Lailieka's head made a silhouette against the moon-lit dunes and then I saw it move as she followed the progress of a figure struggling on the beach. I could see it too, a figure with bright red hair and a yellow jumpsuit, dragging something heavy and limp. I saw two dark legs.'

'Are you sure about this?'

'It was Bumper Lee dragging the body of Lana Flax down to the beach.'

'You're sure it was her?' My mouth managed to go drier than it was. I had to hold tight to the steering wheel.

'I'm sure. There's no mistaking Bumper. And she and Lana had big, well, some problems. Vishnu took Lana totally into his trust in New Mexico. And Bumper . . . she was jealous I think.'

'You're sure?'

'I know what I saw,' she said. So Bumper had tied the concrete blocks on to Lana's feet. My stomach turned. And Lailieka saw it and made the tapes to put the blame on Nebraska Storm. To cover Bumper. Love was grand, after all.

'What – what should I do?' Delphy asked.

'What do you mean?'

'Well, where should I go? I mean – '

I looked at Delphy and saw a woman confused about every longitude and latitude that might direct her. For seven years she'd been a product of guru destiny. And she was used to taking orders.

'You come home with me,' I said, conveniently responding to the signal which had gotten me in trouble so often, and compounding many errors I had made in the last several days – and the last several years of my life. I saw the freeway exit sign that meant home, and pulled off the freeway. Roseanna was right behind me.

I apologised to Roseanna again for my inhospitable stairs when we arrived in the driveway. We stared again at the winding concrete stairway leading up to my house. After unloading her story Delphy was reading a comic book in the Plymouth. She probably had an IQ around the level of room temperature.

'I bring my living room with me.' Roseanna swivelled her captain's chair around so fast her brown fringe flew out at the edges. With a flip of the ballerina wrist a synthetic zebra-stripe upholstered bench emerged from the floor. I got in the wagon after a quick eyeball to Delphy who was still regressing with Donald Duck. I was still reeling from Delphy's revelations. I climbed in and sat back on the bench. Something inside my brain was still dancing to the tune of a disco beat. I looked at Roseanna without seeing her, but she looked at me and saw everything.

'You okay, pal?' She reached out to me and I sat on the floor and leaned my head against her leg. She petted my hair and after a while I took deep breaths and began to feel her foot rest biting into my back. I leaned forward.

'Just gotta catch my breath.' I opened up the little refrigerator and pulled out another can of sparkling water. I sat back on the zebra-skin couch and drank it. 'Thirsty.'

'I see.'

'So how'd it go for you at the Commune?' I asked Roseanna when I had finished the second can. I wasn't ready to tell my story yet. It was still happening inside my head, complete with white lights and changing temperatures.

'Except that somebody tried to hump my wheelchair in the middle of the night, fine. I tried to talk to a couple of the janitorial types. Seems the place gets a good going-over every day. Seems like your friend Lailieka personally cleaned the room of Bumper Lee soon after the murder, causing some comments among the scullery maids.'

'Very interesting.'

'Other than that, I couldn't get out of the group except to empty my bag and I didn't want to fake an attack, so I was stuck there, spending the night.'

'Sleep well?'

'There was a lot of moving of blankets around, rising and falling of bed lumps in rhythmical patterns. It was kind of cute, a bumping bliss slumber party.'

'And somebody tried to hump your wheelchair? You didn't sleep in your chair, did you?'

'Ah sure didn't, hunnah,' said the Alabama Roseanna. 'But somebuddah sure knew how to do ah smooth transfer from chair to mattress.'

'Oh yeah? So what happened?'

'Mind your own business, Emma Victor. Didn't you hear what I said back at the ranch? I got tapes, girl. Long play.'

Roseanna switched a latch on the birch panelling of the wagon and a flap fell open revealing a double-reeled tape recorder with clear plastic spindles wound with brown tape.

'Not exactly state of the art,' she apologised, leaning over to fiddle with the knobs. 'Cassettes have been the thing for some years now.' Roseanna picked up a headphone set and put it on her ears. She engaged the play handle and slowly the tapes started to turn and the counter numbers to move. 'Check this out,' she said, switching the sound into the speakers. I heard a fart and a flush.

'What is this?'

'Tapes of the bathroom. At the Vishnu place. I put a recorder behind a john.'

A terrible whoosh of water like a flood coming through the speakers filled the wagon, followed by the sound of a tank ball fitting into a valve seat and the flow shutting off.

'Not such a good place to put it, I guess. Let's do a little fast forward.' She pushed a button and squinted at the unit meter. A frantic chipmunk sound leaked out of her earphones. 'Ah! Voices!' she cried, doing a quick rewind, and turning on the speakers.

'It's the mechanism of your problem situation,' said the tape recorder. 'Don't forget, he is telling us to help us create our own happiness – '

'Skip it. On to the next one.' Roseanna pushed fast forward and stopped the reel again.

'He broke his date with me; I just don't know what's wrong,' whined a tinny voice.

'Maybe you need to work on your personal resistance. I think you have a lot of hostility – '

'Let's fast-forward this one,' I started to say when I heard, 'No! I think Sadhima's putting his foreign girlfriends to work because – because he's up to something. There's no other reason why my job is getting changed.' It was Delphy.

'I know what Sadhima was doing,' I said to Roseanna. 'He was doing me over in a little white cell. And that's the voice of our friend in the car. Somewhere along the line she started thinking for herself.'

'I have the feeling something's going on,' Delphy said, her voice echoing hollowly against the tiles and hard surfaces of the bathroom, sounding lost and alone. The other voice replied angrily, 'I'm sure whatever Sadhima is doing is for the good of the Commune. His devotion is . . . ' and the woman began to extol the breadth and depth of Sadhima's vocation until she was mercifully drowned out by a flush. Roseanna pushed fast forward. Stopped, rewound a second, and pressed play.

'Bumper, this isn't the time to be worrying about the bank accounts!'

'I want my grandmother's trust money back. I want it all back. And then we'll see what the future is – '

'Bumper, let's get out of here.' It was Lailieka. She was crying.

'Oh, why are you always in such a hurry?'

'But Lana – '

'Oh that's all sewn up. Nebraska Storm bumped her off. Right?'

There was a dead silence that echoed off the tiles.

'I'm sorry.' I heard Bumper's voice soften, and the rustle of fabric. 'That sounded a little hard.'

'And Vishnu – '

'Oh, there are a number of scenarios,' said my former seducer, the confident killer. 'Maybe we'll just make a press announcement and ride it out and keep the family together. Or maybe we'll make our press announcement and move to Brazil. In another few weeks we should be on a beach, watching a cucaracha band. I just have to get my trust money back.'

'But Bumper, there are people snooping around. You don't know – '

'What can they find, Lailieka dear?' I listened for the tones of a murderer in Bumper's voice. She was either going for an Academy Award or she was psychotic. And I had almost gone to bed with her. Lailieka didn't answer Bumper's question and I just heard the sounds of sniffles and a low voice saying, 'Don't worry, don't worry,' and the sound of a tap turning on and off a few times. Roseanna pushed the tape on fast forward for quite a while, but the sound I kept hearing was Bumper's voice.

'Forty flushes and that's all she wrote,' said Roseanna, and turned the tape off, replacing the earphones to one side of the set and closing the compartment door. I leaned out of the window and saw that Delphy had finished the Donald Duck comic book. She was sitting bolt upright in the front car seat and chewing the side of her mouth hungrily.

'What are we going to do with our guru deserter?'

'Invite her over here. I want to meet her,' Roseanna said.

Delphy stepped into the wagon and sat on the edge of the couch

169

next to me. She twiddled a piece of hair and extended her hand out to touch a crystal that was hanging from the upholstered wagon ceiling. It spun and sent lights spinning into her eyes. Her chin trembled.

'That's beautiful,' Delphy said, looking at the crystal. It was a touching moment but I couldn't smile yet. The Vishnu white room still had possession of my soul. 'Your wagon really has good vibes,' Delphy confirmed. Suddenly Roseanna and Delphy were talking about being grounded and West Coast volcanic vibrations.

Then the phone rang from deep inside the house. House. Keys. Phone. Sunlight. I was still shaking somewhere deep inside. Even entering my own dwelling didn't quite still the chattering of my senses. Nor did the voice of Willie Rossini's blond receptionist, asking me to come downtown.

I went back down to the wagon. I stood outside and Delphy's voice drifted out. 'For some time now I have felt that my reasons for returning to this plane are to bring more to the average life most people here seem to lead,' her voice was earnestly explaining.

'I know what you mean. I know what you mean,' said Roseanna.

'I am quite an astral being and, well, the point is that I felt there was something I'd come here to do. So when I heard Vishnu – ' the young Commune member went on.

'I hate to interrupt this conversation, but I have to get myself downtown.'

'Actually, I was just going to invite Delphy here home with me for lunch,' Roseanna said to me, and turned back to Delphy. 'Maybe you could regroup your head a little bit more over at my place.'

'Yeah, sure. Swell.' Delphy perked up a little. 'I'll just get my sweater out of the car – ' She hopped out of the wagon and walked towards the Plymouth.

'Willie Rossini just called me,' I said to Roseanna quietly.

'Go for it, Emma,' said Roseanna. 'But don't be such a girl scout. If you've got any fantasies about helping Nebraska Storm, keep Emma Victor in mind too.'

I knew what she meant. I couldn't afford to be altruistic or curious with my spare time. I needed a job when all this was over. But I couldn't think about that now. I was thinking about what it would be like sending Bumper Lee to the cooler.

'Take good care of the commune kiddie,' I said to Roseanna. 'She may end up a star witness in a murder trial.'

'Jesus Christ, you mean this kid is hot?'

'She doesn't know it. I don't think she's putting too much together right now. But someone won't like it when she doesn't show up for bedtime prayers. Just keep a low profile. I'll call you later on.' I leaned in to the wagon and Roseanna leaned forward and the sides of our lips brushed.

I turned and saw Delphy waltzing cheerfully towards us. There was somebody new to take care of her. 'And Roseanna, don't scare her with all your James Bond equipment.' I moved aside to let Delphy climb into the passenger seat.

'Why Emma,' Roseanna raised her thin eyebrows at me. 'Equipment, frightening? That says more about you than it does about me.' She put the wagon in gear. I walked back up to the house. I wasn't really ready to go downtown. My body was shaking and my eyelids fluttered uncontrollably every few minutes. So I took a hot bath. Very hot. Then I looked in the mirror. That was a mistake.

I tried taking a nap, but little noises around the house kept waking me up. Was Bumper coming after me with ropes? Was Sadhima going to appear with a ghetto blaster? Surely he'd discovered my escape by now. And Lailieka would notice Delphy's absence, and she'd know what that meant. My name and address weren't in the phone book yet. But I hardly felt safe.

The disco beat was still there. I tried to turn down the volume. I tried taking deep breaths. I started pacing around my house. It was a wonderful home. It had flickering green shadows in the dining room in the daytime, and an old-fashioned kitchen. But I couldn't rest. And I couldn't feel safe.

Finally, I decided to get in the Plymouth and drive downtown.

'So where have you been? I've been trying to reach you for over forty-eight hours.' Rossini looked me carefully up and down. She was wearing an ashes of roses sweater set and a matching A-line

171

skirt. She'd been chain-smoking the long thin cigarettes – the onyx ashtray on her desk was full.

'Somebody organised a Hallowe'en party with only tricks out at the Vishnu place.'

Willie squinted and took a closer look. 'You don't look so good.'

'And this is five hours and a bath later. But I did find out one interesting thing. Lana Flax didn't call Nebraska. Someone doctored a tape from some language lessons that Lana was giving Vishnu.'

'What?'

'Portia Fronday received a call from an edited tape. Remember how Portia and Nebraska both asked Lana questions and Lana just kept repeating her message like the time at the tone? But,' I sighed, 'no evidence. I'm sure the tape is destroyed. I had an English book in my hands which would probably stand up in court as proof that someone took sections out of it and spliced tapes to make a phoney phone call. Portia Fronday's testimony would corroborate it. But I don't have the book any more. You just have my word.'

Willie Rossini gave me a look that said my word wouldn't be worth a lot in court. 'They've got a hell of a lot of circumstantial against Nebraska. She was under the influence that night and we've got a judge who locks up dopers and throws away the key on them no matter how much state's evidence they've turned. I'm worried about Nebraska. Really worried. That bit about Portia having Nebraska's car cleaned didn't help.'

'Something nice about a murder where all women are involved.'

'Huh?' A long ash fell off her cigarette.

'They're all cleaning up. Even after each other.'

'Listen, Miss Victor – ' Willie turned to me. 'You've got a hell of a lot of chutzpah – you want to get paid for it?'

'It's probably the only thing I've got to sell. You wouldn't want my car.'

'How does three hundred dollars sound, for digging into this thing and coming up with hard evidence?'

'Against who or what?'

'I don't know yet.'

'And I don't know who I'm working for. You or Nebraska.'

172

'Let's say you're working for me.' She smiled and the black pearl ring glinted on her hand.

'Three hundred dollars?' I was thinking about how it would feel to be a bounty hunter, with the price on the red head of Bumper Lee. I wasn't thinking about the three hundred dollars.

'Five hundred then.'

'I've got a shiner and a complicated psychological hangover. I'm not sure I'm willing to risk another night like last night.'

'Seven hundred and that's my top offer,' Willie Rossini said, and pressed her mouth shut. No extra hundreds were going to fall out of it.

'I just have to think about it.'

'The money?'

'The idea.'

'Think about this. My client is innocent and has a manslaughter record. But she's innocent. That's the bottom line. You can do the footwork to see that justice is done.'

'Or I'll be subpoenaed as a witness anyway.'

'I'd rather see you do the footwork.'

'Me too. But I'll let you know. Keep your five, I mean, seven hundred dollars and I'll get back to you.' I walked towards the door and had a sudden inspiration. 'Ms Rossini, if I found some evidence that cleared Nebraska, would you consider free representation for one of the parties involved – not the one accused of murder?'

'How guilty is he?'

'She. Only of being hopelessly in love.'

'That can be pretty guilty. I might consider it. Why?'

'I have a soft spot for women with protective instincts.'

'I would try and avoid those kind of soft spots, Ms Victor. They usually end up in hard places. But I'll consider it.'

'You'll hear from me.'

It was time to go home and kiss the pillows. If I could sleep. Maybe later I would feel more human, but now I was just hearing voices. Sometimes the voices went to a disco beat. Then they would melt into Lailieka's antiphonal singing. And all the notes were becoming a funeral march for Bumper Lee, who kept repeating the same thing over and over again in sweetened honey-ripe tones, the gentlest of outrages. 'But what can they find, dear?' She was clearly mad.

I hoped I wouldn't have any unexpected yellow visitors and that I could rest in peace the rest of the day. As I fell asleep I realised it was the first time I had forgotten to check the mailbox.

Twenty-seven

I woke up after a nine hour half-nap without anyone breaking into my house, trying to kidnap me or murder me in my bed. I slept without dreams, without yellowness and without death stains. But as soon as I woke up little sounds around the house began to bother me.

My eyelids had stopped fluttering convulsively, but my head was still buzzing. What would Bumper do when she discovered Delphy missing? Lailieka would know right away that Delphy had seen too much. What was going on at the crazy commune, and why weren't the cops more evident than the District Attorney's taped seal on Lana's door? It didn't make sense. I lay on my bed and tried not to think these thoughts.

I walked to the phone, marvelling at my ability to turn lights off and on at will. I tried to call Roseanna but only got her answering machine. I called Maya but she had unplugged her telephone. She had probably unplugged the phone because she wanted to make undisturbed love to her new girlfriend. I brooded, trying to feel happy for Maya, and failed. I called Roseanna back. Answering machine again; on hearing it a second time, the command to leave a message sounding like something a friendly interrogator might ask.

I turned on the tap and thought of the wonder of being able to find and drink water whenever I felt like it. I felt a frightened restlessness come over me. The sun had set and in the silence of the house a panic was crawling up from my stomach and travelling along the light brown hairs on my arms. What had happened to me in that cell was not as bad as murder. But even my home started to feel like another kind of prison. Sensory deprivation had done a job on me. It was time for a think and a drink. I took my second shower of the day, put on a T-shirt with alternating blue, purple and white stripes. I pulled out a powder eyeshadow palette and with the right combination of green, purple and blue I matched my healthy eye to the one suffering contusions. The effect was ghoulish but symmetrical, and under the dim lights it wouldn't matter anyway.

I walked to the car like a frightened rabbit. What was wrong with me, anyway? I sat trembling with the motor on for a moment. Then, with it still running, I got out and quickly checked the mailbox at the end of the path. It was empty. I got back into the car and turning on the headlights, I headed down to Caroline's, the best women's bar the Bay Area had to offer at the moment.

I tried not to think about Bumper and failed. Risking a first degree to get back Granny's trust fund money. Big deal. Her father was a shrink in Beverly Hills, and she was on top of another kind of weird heap. Whatever. My nerves were jangling. I needed a night off.

I found a roomy parking place across from the wooden front of the bar. Suddenly I had no idea why I was there. Only because I didn't want to sit at home. How could Bumper have killed Lana? The question ought to be: for what reason? Something deep in my gut turned but nothing in my head clicked. Lana must have had big goods on Bumper.

I got out of the car and walked to the door. I'd failed at meditation, I'd failed the padded cell test and I hoped I wouldn't fail the dyke bar test. I had the same needs that got all those yellow people lumped together, but they would meditate and profess true happiness in convincing tones and I would, if I was lucky, meet a barroom guru and stay up till three in the morning talking. Or feel sexual tension, or share a joke with more than three people and drink Perrier all night long. Nothing ultimate, just satisfying. And something to put a little mental distance between me and the white interrogation cell.

I opened the arched door to smoke haze and darkness. I swept my eyes over women sitting in groups of twos and threes at little round tables. I earned a few glances. I looked at the long row of women at the bar. They looked back at me. It was that kind of night and those kind of looks. Your eyeballs got tired and you kept your mouth shut. The music was too loud anyway.

I drank a beer and looked at myself in the mirror between the liquor bottles. The eye makeup was downright attractive. Character lines were showing around my mouth, which had once used to smile too much. I'd lost the smile and didn't have much small talk to replace it. I was stuck with the lines for ever. Settling into the darkness, the white lines in my T-shirt glowing across my chest, I stopped looking in the mirror. I must have looked better than I felt because a woman with a lot of gold earring and too much to drink came wobbling up towards me.

'I like stripes,' she burbled.

'I don't even know where to go with that one.'

'Well, we could talk about it.'

'Stripes seems a little limited to me.'

'No, silly,' she laughed. 'About where to go.'

'You're just a little too drunk, I think.'

'Okay, be that way.'

'I don't have any choice, but I'll let you know if I catch up.' I gave her the kind of smile that gave me those wrinkles around the sides of my mouth.

I sat looking at the stripe woman some more in the mirror. I watched her walk over to a group at one of the round tables. The group seemed to be busy walking out of the place and coming back again in five or ten minutes in different combinations. I recognised the stretch jean woman from the concert party come in and go out – it seemed to be one of her habits at gatherings and the woman who liked stripes went out with her and didn't come back. Pity. After a year of using whatever it was that kept taking Stretch Jeans outside the bar, her conversation openers would probably be even more limited.

I sensed a movement behind me and looked in the mirror to see a woman in a black leather jacket and dark curls go into the disco.

I watched an aquarium behind the bartender's back. An angel

fish swam back and forth. The door opened wide to the disco and the funky bass beat leapt out, mingling with the pop music of the bar area, and causing panic waves deep in my bowels and an imaginary thirst in my throat. Would disco music remain my Pavlovian bell for the rest of my life? This development clearly wouldn't increase my chances for romance. The water in the tank jiggled to the bass beat that leaked from back where the dance floor was. The cop had said it was an amateur job. So you blew it when it counted, Bumper Lee. And you even had a tide table on your desk. Back to the mirror and two blue eyes. I missed my friends in Boston, I missed my old doctor girlfriend Frances, even though she wasn't so playful in bed. Sometimes I thought she only required a pulse. I missed Maya, who had deserted me for her new flame. I missed everybody and nobody. Vishnu would say I missed myself.

A new tune started up from the back room. Maybe it was time to just give up and give in to the disco beat. Maybe I wouldn't lose my wits, maybe I would triumph over behaviourist conditioning. If I was lucky maybe the pounding would stop me from thinking. If that didn't work I could hyperventilate. I walked past the other folks at the bar into the strobe lights and the synthesised disco sound. Hyperventilation was clearly out. There was only one kind of attention I wanted that night.

I opened the swing door to where a lot of women were doing their best to shorten the life of a parquet floor. The one person I didn't expect to see there was Nebraska Storm. There she was, twelve feet high, writhing on a video screen like a snake with gas pains, suspended high above the dancers. Nebraska Storm lit by a black light, in a former incarnation video clip, this time with fluorescent pink hair standing straight out from her skull. Her mouth opened and emitted a wail that could have been a musical disembowelment.

The stagelights cut to magenta, the camera to a close up and Nebraska's face became soft. Her voice played with a melody as sweet and haunting as Mozart. 'I can't give you, I can't give you, I can't give you . . . ' she sang. 'The tiger charged, the money lied, a poet died, a knife in the heart of, a knife in the heart of, a knife in the heart of love.'

Well, she was a better singer than writer even then. The camera zoomed in to show tears in her eyes. They didn't look planned. Edwin Anvil, her drummer, had died just a few months after this video was made, before she cleaned up her act and turned yellow and sickly sweet instead of just sick. I looked back at the old Nebraska Storm and liked what I saw.

'Talk to me, baby,' she crooned. 'Talk to me,' she demanded, 'talk to me in tongues.' Her Cleopatra eyes widened, a pink tongue waggled out towards the camera. She knew what she was doing. She hit a high C.

The women in front of the screen, the real ones, were slam dancing, rock and rolling, self-conscious and sometimes cruising. They were wearing organdie blouses, neckties, leather stud bracelets, T-shirts with political and commercial messages. Underneath it all were a million stories of failure, success and survival. The expressions were concentrated, cool. A message flashed across the screen. 'Nebraska Storm will be appearing at the Women's Benefit Concert. Don't miss her exciting comeback and help your community!' The message was out of date, very out of date and I laughed for the first time all night and felt better.

The music picked up again and I dropped a whiskey down. I watched the woman with the dark curls frisk around the floor. She had dropped off the black leather for a brick red sweatshirt. The music stopped, someone asked her to dance and she refused, but she wasn't sweating that I could see. She'd cut off the neck of the sweatshirt and it kept slipping very slowly off her shoulder. Every now and then she would pull it up over the smooth skin. Silver gymshoes sparkled under the split hem of black toreador pants. The music picked up and she refused another partner, leaning back on the bar. I waited another number and when I walked up to her she didn't refuse me.

The music changed into something slow and heavy. We raised all four of our eyebrows. I led her on to the floor.

She put her arms up around my neck and then we were dancing slow. Her sweatshirt began to slip off her shoulder. She pulled back, laughing, and hiked it back up. She had a small gold pendant necklace and the freshest complexion this side of bottled water.

I put my hands above her hips and guided her towards me. It was a good way to keep the panic feelings away. She smelled like

178

flowers and couldn't have been more than twenty. She liked me too and kept looking up and laughing when I said silly things like, 'I bet you do this with all the girls.' We had two whiskeys and were both getting there fast. Once she pulled me to one side of the dance floor and ducked slightly behind me. She could have stayed there all night, but she explained that her girlfriend's roommate had walked in. Her girlfriend was busy that night, she said.

'There's nothing wrong with revenge,' I lied, taking advantage of her drunken condition. By this time the lights were lower, the music faster and our breasts were nestling against each other like four friendly teddy bears. It was all about comforting wasn't it? Bumper was right, but I was getting woozy, not wired. 'Let me take you home,' I said.

She giggled and that said a lot. 'You really are a fast one.' That said even more. I took her to my car instead. The cold night air barely touched me as we swayed down the street to the Plymouth. I got in and she jumped into my lap, her fingers circling around the buttons of my blouse which were stubborn, and my nipples which weren't. I was rediscovering side zippers on her toreador pants and sliding my hands slowly along her small buttocks, lifting her towards me. It wasn't so difficult to hold her but she wasn't exactly dead weight. How did Bumper do it with Lana? We went on like this for some time. We got hotter and wetter and the windows started to steam up.

'Nostalgia is fine,' I said to her sweet freckled face and her mouth bruised maroon red with kisses, 'but I graduated to beds a while ago. Let's just call it a very nice hot night in the front seat and go our separate ways home.'

'No, come to my house, please. It's not far.' I thought about Bumper, disappearing star witnesses and all the noises I kept hearing at my house. So far the bar had seemed like a safe place. And nobody seemed to be lurking around the Plymouth. I realised that a nice hot half hour in the front seat had been all I'd really wanted, but I didn't want to go home. Home didn't feel so safe any more.

I walked us back to the bar to call a cab. I was too tipsy to drive and the Plymouth had served its purpose already. We didn't cool off until just before the taxi came. By that time I was cold. She told the driver her address and snuggled up to me in the back seat. I

179

stroked her hair and felt suddenly motherly. Going home with the woman may have been a big mistake, but nobody seemed to be following the taxi as it made its way through the city streets.

'I'll be back in just a minute,' she sang out when we got to her house, leaving me in the living room and disappearing behind a bedroom door. 'I'm glad my roommate's out. He had a hot date tonight,' she said in between the rustlings and sounds of closet doors opening and closing. It was taking her a while. The pause was too long, the high had worn off. She was a nice woman who smelled like flowers and wore silver gymshoes, but I wasn't sure I really wanted to go all the way on a first date.

'Come on in,' she called finally. I was looking forward more to lying on the bed than on her. I took a tentative step across the hall and a floorboard squeaked under my foot.

That was when I heard the deadbolt in the front door rattle violently, as someone jammed the key into the lock and turned it. I looked down the narrow hallway. The door burst open and a huge figure loomed in the doorway in a golden taffeta evening gown. The figure was topped with massive amounts of red hair and had a build like a linebacker.

Twenty-eight

'You got another stocking for me, Erin?' called a beautiful panic-stricken creature that was probably male. He aimed his voice over me towards the back bedroom and pulled a mink stole around his shoulders. His wig was shedding long strands on the expensive fur piece.

'You borrowed my last pair two weeks ago!' I heard my companion call from her bedroom. Disappointed, the attractive drag queen frowned.

'Hey, what have we *here*?' He lifted his eyes up and down

180

across me. 'She's cute but she's got a problem with her eye shadow,' he called out to Erin.

'Hi, I'm Emma,' I said.

'Hey, but I think the kind of problems she's got don't have to do with eyeshadow,' he said softly, leaning closer inspecting the swelling under my eye.

'Not to worry. I'm a bottom,' I said to him.

'Maybe you ought to stick together. Erin could use a little wimp solidarity.'

'Thanks,' I said. 'I needed that.'

'Have it your own way,' he shrugged, raising his two creamy powdered shoulders from within a stiff taffeta bodice. 'I'm going out to ruin my other stocking,' he called out. 'Bye girls! Don't do anything I wouldn't do.'

'We can't,' I said for the second time to a faggot in one week. Sometimes I wondered if safe sex wasn't making them jealous.

They needn't have been. I got into bed with Erin and we slept like children holding hands. I woke up to a fading dream image of Bumper drowning in the rhythmic undulations of a jiggling fish tank and a hungover taste in my mouth. My stomach was going to town and I couldn't escape how drunk I'd been.

And I couldn't escape the smiling young face next to mine, ready to make coffee, ready to have sex and ready to go to Mexico. She wasn't hungover, that was what being twenty was like.

'You do this all the time?' asked Erin, turning over in bed putting her face close to mine. 'Every weekend?'

'Only since I've lived in California. Holding hands is about the farthest I've gotten,' I said.

'I can't believe that. You're too much the looker. Come on, what happened last weekend?'

'If you really want to know, it started with a Friday lunch.'

'And did you go home with her?'

'No, she threw me out of her house before we got down to anything. She didn't like me hanging around her neighbourhood and then she got a heavy phone call and shoved me out the door.'

'The bitch!' Erin kissed me on the shoulder, slowly working her way to my clavicle. 'But, well,' she reconsidered, on the way to my armpit, 'things can happen. Last month I was doing it with my girlfriend when she answered the phone and her grandmother had died. Just died! Can you imagine? We were probably doing it when she had a stroke!'

'Well, this phone call didn't call for sympathy. I just got shoved out,' I said. But I was remembering my nightmare meditation flash and something was ringing a bell.

'Aww, did she call you back to apologise?'

'No, but she called me back to try and indoctrinate me.'

'Indoctrinate?'

'She showed me her guru, fed me and passed out before we got to the good stuff.'

'Gees, you really had a bad one last weekend. Did you ever see her again?'

'Only at the bank,' I shrugged. 'She's that kind of woman. Big on banks.'

'So she can only play on the weekends, right? I had a girlfriend who was rich once.'

'This one was rich once too. But she made a mistake and now she's trying to pull something really difficult off.'

'What's that?'

'She's trying to get rich twice.'

My hangover was fading and I was ready to go home. My descriptions of last weekend and Bumper's banking activities were making sense. I had a sudden feeling about that phone call that Bumper had got before she threw me out. And then I knew why Bumper had invited me over for dinner. It was because I had been Nebraska Storm's chauffeur while the banks were closed. And the thought of linebackers with phoney red hair and women who knew tide tables like the backs of their hands started to add up in my head. And it didn't add up to murder.

'I'm going home now,' I said. Erin protested and used all the tricks a twenty-year-old person could have learned to get me to stay. It was a big bag of tricks, but it didn't work. I looked at her bookshelf. 'Your Way to Jesus', I read on a spine. 'You into religion?' I heard myself asking in Californese.

'Oh, I go on Sundays, you know. I've met a few people who are real Christians at All City Methodist.' Then she showed me a hat she'd worn once, a black cloche with a few feathers.

182

'It's a nice hat,' I said, and it was. I refused her hands for a while. 'You're a nice woman,' I said, 'but this isn't going to work. I'm sorry. I made a mistake.' I finally got out of the door under a protest of kisses and walked north to my car. I was sorry I'd made the mistake with the young woman with black curls. But I'd make a lot worse mistakes. And I started to have a damn good idea about who killed Lana Flax. And why.

It was time to call Willie Rossini, pass go and collect seven hundred dollars.

Twenty-nine

I went to the nearest pay phone and found out that Willie Rossini and her blond receptionist were out for the day, leaving only their answering machine behind. What a day for the courtroom Callas to play golf. I decided to assume the seven hundred was mine. Meanwhile there was a star witness loose and Roseanna Baynetta was babysitting her. I tried them out at the alfalfa farm home. They weren't answering the phone either. It was a strange stillness. I was waiting for something to break it, and that something could be another murder.

I climbed into the Plymouth and drove out to Moraga City, my sweating hands making it hard to get a grip on the wheel, the fear in my stomach making it hard to get a grip on myself. A fog bank was moving in from the ocean and would soon hover over the hot freeway asphalt, cooling us all off. But images of ropes tied around swollen ankles were dancing to the disco beat in my head and a liquid panic started to take hold of me.

The Vishnu place looked the same as it always did. Kept up. The grass strips lining the swept sidewalks were trimmed and edged and the entry doors were all closed, keeping in the secrets of padded cells, enlightenment lifestyle and several ways of dying. I was just foolish enough to go in one more time to taste it again.

I parked in the lot. I decided to try the front door. I walked into the lobby and smelled trouble. But it wasn't any kind of trouble that was going to affect me. The same crowd was by the phones, but they were quietly standing in line and not lounging around any more. One talker had a hand cupped over her mouth as she spoke into the mouthpiece. Maybe the Vishnus weren't all thinking alike, or using the same vocabulary any more. They clustered in small groups and whispered nervously. Nobody had noticed that a stranger was amongst them.

Delphy's coveted receptionist job had been handed over to Juna, who was pushing buttons, shouting 'Hello' frantically into the receiver and then hanging up while buzzers sounded from the complex machinery. She didn't notice me either. I walked out into the garden. Assorted cult creatures were bustling in and out of the coffee shop. I felt totally invisible. It wasn't exactly comforting. Maybe sensory deprivation on Vishnu ground had disassembled my molecules. My commonsense was gone, and I no longer felt afraid. I felt like looking for trouble. And I knew where to find it. I headed towards Ananda House.

I walked past Vishnu's portrait and into the big lobby with the light filtering through the mandala stained glass windows, little winks of god falling across the spiral staircase. I walked across the pink synthetic carpet, hearing little muffled hiccups from the top of the stairway. I touched the brass railing and got a static shock. Vishnu was everywhere and nowhere today. I looked up. Lailieka looked back at me too. The last time I had seen that face was behind a windshield, before a hypodermic had hit my arm.

'I thought you'd come back,' she hissed. She composed her mouth and tried to smooth out the white skin that stretched across her wide forehead. But her eyes were red and long streams of black hair clung to the sweat on her thin neck.

'I always seem to make it back here, one way or the other. It's not my idea of a good time either. Ever tried living with a lot of white furniture, none of it a toilet?' I said, but I was scared.

Lailieka looked at my eye and her face became even whiter, the patches of freckles standing out against her skin. I hadn't had that kind of effect on a woman in a long time. 'I don't know, I didn't know. I'm sorry for anything that's happened to you. But it

184

doesn't really matter now.'

'It matters to me. I hope I'm not left with purple coloured crow's feet in my old age. But I suppose you have bigger things to worry about, now your set-up is about to fall down.'

Lailieka's jaw set, sharpening the contours of her face but her chin started to wobble. Her chin won and then Lailieka was crying. 'Until you came snooping around, I thought – ' she gulped, 'I thought, well maybe we could just keep it within the family – '

'I'll bet you'd like to blame this on me, wouldn't you? That would suit your way of thinking.'

'I don't know what's happening – what's been happening. Don't you see it's all, it's all – ' and a sob burst out of her mouth. 'It's all gone wrong. It was supposed to be good. It *was* good.'

'Just tell me where Bumper is.'

'You've got Delphy, haven't you?' Lailieka's lips twitched. 'She saw it in the mirror, didn't she? It's all over, right?'

'Yes. Delphy saw it in the mirror. You were hoping, after engineering the tapes, that it could all be blamed on Nebraska? Well, it's time for truth therapy.'

Lailieka didn't say anything.

'Did you tell Bumper you saw her with Lana on the bluff that night?'

'Yes. I told her just a few minutes ago. I – I didn't want to know – that she was a murderer. I didn't want her to know that I would do anything, anything, to save her. Why did I have to see it?'

'Maybe it was arranged as a test of your feelings.'

'You mean Bumper *wanted* me to see her carrying Lana down to the beach?'

'Something like that. What did she say when you confronted her?'

'Nothing. She just stood still for a moment and then said she had to straighten something out.' Lailieka started gasping; the truth therapy was making her hyperventilate. 'I didn't know – I didn't know, that she hit it off so bad with Lana – ' the woman wheezed.

'I'll bet she didn't either. When she left, which direction did she go in?'

'I don't know. Outside. She was wearing her jogging clothes.'

The door opened at the bottom of the stairs and a thin voice

185

mewed, 'Lailieka, telephone. In the lobby.'

'Yes, yes. I'm coming. No. Tell them to call back,' she called
from the top of the stairs, her voice straining for the old authority
and giving up at the end.

'It's all over, Emma,' she sighed, wiping her eyes with her
freckled hands, leaving grey streaks on either side of her nose.
'We have to dissolve the leadership, dissolve the commune. I've
already started. I told Sadhima. He suspected all along. He seemed
to understand, especially when I said that Bumper just wanted to
be alone. To think things over.'

'And you may have cooked Bumper's goose,' I said, the information reaching my plaid tennis shoes and making them run down
the staircase.

'Oh my God, Emma, did I do something – this doesn't mean that
she's going to kill herself?' Laileika's words faded after my feet.

'No, I think somebody else may arrange that for her,' I yelled,
and ran out of the garden and through the lobby.

It was getting cold outside. The mist had swiftly reached this
side of the Bay. I turned to the right and I ran to the fence that
guarded the back lot. The gate had been padlocked shut.

I slipped my fingers through the cold wire, put a foot on a tension bar and pulled myself up. I was glad that the Vishnus hadn't
gotten as far as barbed wire yet. I hoisted myself over and my feet
landed in the thin coastal grass. I sprinted down the path at the top
of the bluff and headed down towards the water.

Thirty

I sprinted over aluminium beer cans, and the heaps of
rags and garbage that the sea and the salt and the sand had moulded
into lumps of colourless debris. Little flags of plastic whipped

in the wind that was tearing up from the Bay.

I ran around a big truck tyre which someone had tried to burn for fun one day and past an area staked off with string, with a sign from the District Attorney's office warning everyone to keep out. I didn't see why they bothered, since they'd abandoned the scene of the crime so quickly. The little murder beach was deserted.

I tripped over a bundle of matted quillwort and the thin slimy strands got tangled up in my shoelace. I pulled at my foot and the grass gave way, leaving green scum entwined in my laces. I could hear voices on the wind, somebody laughing further down the beach. It had a hollow, nasty sound, not like someone who was enjoying a stroll by the water. The sound seemed to come from the bluff, and I made my way towards it, ducking behind rocks along the base of the cliff. Above me the Meditation Room looked out on to the beach. But no one would be able to see what I saw. I came closer, my tennis shoes squishing succulent bulbs and bursting the air bladders of brown kelp that had washed up by the cliff. Flat against the wall, I approached a big rock. Crouching down I crawled behind it, and looked over the edge.

Beyond it the water had carved out a shallow cave in the surface of the rock. I saw a flash of yellow nylon, the edge of Bumper Lee's running shorts, and the rubber nubbed sole of her running shoe, slowly lifting itself up and down like a cobra ready to strike. Bumper's foot was still curving back when I heard the irregular rhythm of Sadhima's nasty laugh. I drew up behind a clump of pampas grass and garbage and inched closer until I could see his pearl-grey eyes.

'I want the wig,' Bumper said in a desperate tone. That wouldn't have been so important except that her right hand held a gun.

But Sadhima wasn't buying. 'The wig! The wig! She wants the wig!' he sneered. 'What's the matter, tired of the natural look?'

'You framed me.'

'Come on, the cops think it's the jogging murderer, so what's the big deal? Let's wait a few days, you and me.'

'Give me the wig.' I could imagine Bumper's big teeth flashing on and off as she mouthed the words.

'Why should I? You going to shoot me? You don't have the guts,' said the man who built interrogation chambers. 'No, Bumper, I'm afraid it's all over for you. Shooting me will just turn the key on your gaol cell for a few more years. Lailieka is my big security, if I talked she would too.'

'You won't get away with it.'

'Oh no? After what you've got hidden in the basement? Is anybody going to believe you after that? No way. And wasn't your Lailieka helpful in engineering those tapes. Oh, it's just perfect. All you ladies, so busy, so ready to take over. But I certainly got you all to sign your own death warrants. And it was so easy.' The man from Harvard laughed softly.

'You hate us, don't you? You just hate women,' Bumper took a tentative step towards him. 'And you hate the idea that we want to do something good. I don't know what you're up to with the International Membership but you're not going to ruin – '

'Come on, Bumper baby. It's everybody for themselves now.'

The snub-nosed .38 trembled in her hand and I saw her lower the gun slightly and hesitate a moment before sealing her fate. The gun came up again and I felt the sickness of an impending tragedy.

I stood up and cried out at her. I didn't really know what I was doing. I didn't know who I was saving, but I didn't want Bumper to shoot Sadhima and for once in my life I was a complete success.

Bumper turned her head towards me for a split second. Sadhima lunged forward and tried to chop the gun out of Bumper's wrist with the side of his hand. But he didn't gather the glory I was after.

Bumper's big paw held the weapon firmly in her hand, although her wrist swung round. I saw the inside of the barrel and her finger jerk. I was a big success all right. Bumper didn't shoot Sadhima. She shot me instead.

Thirty-one

There was a crack and the smell of gunsmoke and something in me burned and exploded and I fell. There was black in front of my eyes for a while then I looked down and saw a dark hole six inches above my knee. Something red and thick that was my blood bubbled from it and spread out from the charred hole in my blue jeans.

I looked away and tried to clear the blackness. I rolled over on my side to see what was happening with the two cult members. Bumper had dropped the gun and was looking at me like I'd just landed from Mars. But Sadhima had found a stick in the sand and quickly threaded it through the ring of the trigger guard. He held the gun aloft, and it swung back and forth, upside down. He took a quick side glance in my direction. Through a constellation of little white stars I saw Bumper turn away to look back at him. She took a step forward and Sadhima held the gun up higher out of her reach. Then he whipped a handkerchief out of his pocket and covered his hand with it. He took hold of the gun and aimed it at Bumper.

'Just another piece of evidence,' he said. 'It will make a nice story. Lailieka confronts you. She's witnessed Lana's murder, or at least she's seen you on the beach with the body. Then she tells me. You figure you can keep Lailieka quiet, but I'm one too many.

'You come looking for me down at the beach, with your own personal registered sidearm. It's perfect. You threaten me. Shoot our innocent bystander here as I try and disarm you, and in the ensuing struggle the gun goes off again.' Sadhima looked at her with strange pleasure. 'And when the gun goes off, dear Bumper, it's going to shoot you.'

He took a step forward but a sudden voice cut the air. 'Freeze!' The voice came from a uniformed figure up on the cliff to the left of us and as Sadhima whirled around with the gun in his hand a sharp pinging answered his reflex movement. I forced my eyes wide open to see the pretty boy hit the sand. I looked at Bumper. It was getting easier and easier to keep my eyes open.

I followed Bumper's line of vision over the body of Sadhima where cops were swarming over the edge of the bluff. I saw the imposing form of Willie Rossini, leading the men and women in blue. She ran towards where I was lying on my dying bed of kelp, quillwort and plastic disposable bottles. Suddenly I was tasting starlight.

'Hold on, pal,' Willie looked at my leg. She pulled a scarf from around her neck and tied it high up around my leg. 'I got your message on my answering machine about coming down, called the cops, and got wind of big action here.'

'Yeah, well, I've seen all the action I need.' The prickly sensations had just turned into a cauldron of burning lead above my knee. Even that was getting farther away. A young white cop came over and asked me if I was okay. I said yes, for want of anything better to say, and she said she'd called an ambulance. I looked at Willie.

'You'll be all right,' she said. I started thinking about how seven hundred dollars weren't going to cover my hospital bills. I looked over towards the cave where Sadhima was being cuffed.

'The sedative dart should be good for another twenty minutes at least,' a female cop was instructing a rookie. Together they dragged him off the beach.

Bumper watched as the figures hauled Sadhima away. Then she drew closer. 'Emma!' she cried, and knelt over me. Willie Rossini got up and walked over to the white cop. They moved away, leaving us alone.

'You bitch! You shot me,' I grumbled.

'What were you doing here?' she asked, with a shocked mouth that made her big teeth bigger than ever. 'How did you get here?'

'You know, a little sympathy might go a long way right now.'

'I'm sorry, I'll make it up to you, I'll – '

'You'll pay my hospital bill, that's what you'll do. I don't need any more dinners.' I looked up at Bumper and she was looking back at the Commune.

'Sadhima has set me up, Emma.'

'He's an idiot.'

'He's framed me for murder. I'm going to go to gaol for the rest of my life.'

'You should know better than that. Or are you just trained to believe everything the top men say? Was that Vishnu's final lesson?'

'What are you talking about?'

'Sadhima's not so smart. I was down here on the beach when the cops were gathering evidence. What sheds more than a Persian cat in the summertime? A wig. Do you think he could carry off dragging Lana down to the beach and anchoring her down without leaving a trail of synthetic red hairs all over the place? I saw dicks with tweezers putting long, thin strands in plastic envelopes. And unless the hair matches yours you'll be in the clear.'

'Oh my God – could that be right?' She started to cry but something stopped her. 'But that's not all – ' her voice broke. My throbbing leg was asking for attention. I looked down at it and saw Willie Rossini's scarf. It had brown horses on it. Black saddles and silver stirrups floated in a pattern in between the animals. I looked back at Bumper.

'I thought maybe I wasn't so good a dinner partner any more. I should have more confidence in myself.'

'What do you mean?' She leaned over me and pushed some hair out of my eyes.

'I mean the whole set-up of having me to dinner,' I said, but my voice was losing strength. 'And why Sadhima's so sure he's going to pull off this frame. Because you have another dead body in the basement. You've had him there all weekend. Under lock and key. Vishnu. The guru god himself.'

Thirty-two

'About Vishnu – '

'Still trying to save your ass?'

'How did you know?'

'I figured it out from a woman in silver gymshoes. She had a rich girlfriend once. And her girlfriend only played on the weekends because during the week she was busy with the bank.'

'What do you mean?'

'You really think I don't know? I know just how the whole thing happened. Do I have to tell you?'

'Yes.' Bumper looked curious, scared and she started slowly stroking my forehead.

'It all started with lunch. You were on the way to your bank, to the safety deposit boxes, stopping briefly at the Palace for lunch, carrying the fruits of your cash flow, when I told you I was taking

Nebraska Storm to the concert on Sunday.

'But you didn't expect to see me at the Commune later, checking up on Lana. Then you got a phone call while I was in the lobby. The phone call that changed your future.

'The message that panicked you on that night was that Vishnu was dying or had died. He was sick and frail anyway. And God only knows what effect the cleansing rituals had on him.

'That put you in enough of a panic to shove me out the door. I figured later Vishnu had had a stroke or a heart attack. That really screwed things for your plans. What would happen to the whole set-up? The money was in the safety deposit boxes in the bank, stuck there for the weekend. And Vishnu had promised Nebraska he'd be there for her concert on Sunday. She could have made a big stink and demanded to see him. And she probably wouldn't have been satisfied at viewing him through a plexiglass box.

'No, you couldn't let news of Vishnu's death leak out. Not until Monday, when you could get all the cash out of the Commune's safety deposit box and into yours. And Tuesday Nebraska Storm would even be upping the ante one hundred thousand grand and a waterfront title. You had to wait to let the world know Vishnu was dead. Ordinarily that would be no problem. Vishnu had kept a vow of silence before. The scene was practically gift-wrapped for you down there in the nice cool basement with climate control, with blasts from air conditioners to keep him on ice and keep all the candles flickering in a sealed-in chamber. He was sitting there in voluntary rigor mortis for you even when he was alive.

'And I could just come calling on Nebraska the day of the concert and give her the news that Vishnu was okay. It was a great set-up for you, Bumper. And I fell for it, just like all the other suckers you've pulled in with your paradise line. You just worked a different kind of string with me.'

'I'm sorry – I just – '

'You just wanted to switch the money over and get Nebraska's contribution to boot. It was too big to pass up. But I don't think you'll get canned for Vishnu. The boys you're underestimating are the pathologists, the lab men that are going to find a natural cause of death.'

'When he died I didn't know what to do.'

192

'Bullshit.'

'I saw the Commune collapsing.'

'You saw your deflated bank statement quickly enough after that. And you used me to try to keep it safe.'

I looked up and saw Lieutenant Youtoga looking down at me. He looked about as happy with me as I was with Bumper, and I hadn't even shot him in the leg. I wasn't getting much sympathy from anyone these days. But maybe I didn't need so much sympathy any more.

'You think you're pretty smart, don't you?' he asked.

'No. Otherwise I wouldn't be lying here with a bullet in my leg.'

'Be that as it may, Miss Victor, you just bungled one of our biggest drug busts ever.'

'What?'

'This guy has set up a pretty elaborate international operation here. He was expecting a major hash delivery tomorrow.'

'Afghan black or red Lebanese? You mean this whole thing was about soft drugs?' I asked, but my voice had lost its delivery.

'It's not nice to have met you,' grumbled the detective, walking away.

Bumper's hand stopped stroking my head as we watched the detective's retreating figure stride angrily across the beach. I was beginning to realise why Sadhima had killed Lana Flax.

I suddenly saw Nebraska adjusting her bra strap after talking to Sadhima. Nebraska who'd been let off a manslaughter charge a year ago. Nebraska who had set up a conversation. And Lana who had been an unwitting eavesdropper. What she had heard had sealed her fate. And Lana, instead of reporting to Bumper, like a good trooper, had apparently confronted Sadhima himself. And who was the joker in all this? I was. Because I'd misunderstood Nebraska's conversation with Portia. And I certainly had the two guys in dress Levis pegged wrong. The only thing they'd been pushing was Nebraska Storm's doorbell. Nebraska hadn't been *getting* wired, she'd been *wearing* a wire.

All this was crowding into my head, and the pieces came together at last. Bumper's red hair was making a tent around my face and I could make out the figures of cops on the beach through the strands. I even heard a helicopter in the sky above me. I scanned the bluff and found just the folks I was looking for. Little white figures against the grey sky, carrying a stretcher. A stretcher for me. The white sparks had stopped flashing in front of my eyes. They were replaced by black circles which were growing ever wider. It was time to pass out.

Thirty-three

I was coming, coming up. Emerging into light and pain. The pain was still down the block, maybe even around a corner or two. Mostly women inhabited the neighbourhood, under little white clouds. Their smiling faces would say hello, and ask after me, as they passed me by on the street. Eventually I was better and the neighbourhood became clearer. And the smiling faces didn't smile so much. Nurses in white uniforms were saving it for an invisible roommate who groaned and half lived behind a curtain next to my bed. Soon people came in other colours. Pink tweed skirts, silver gymshoes, violet eyes, brown folksinger's hair. One of the faces even coalesced into Nebraska Storm.

She entered the room with Portia Fronday, and they were both wearing flowing gowns appropriate to a Greek chorus. And they looked just about as happy.

'Hello,' Nebraska said and bit her lip as she followed a tube that went from under the bed to under my bedclothes. Portia mumbled the same thing behind her.

But I was looking at Nebraska. A bright yellow flash of sunlight across her face made her features seem pale. She looked terrible. Lines had gathered around her eyes, and there were bags beneath them.

'We brought you some flowers,' Portia said, waving a bunch of purple freesias at my bed linen.

'Thank you. There's an empty vase under the sink.' I reflected that purple freesias hadn't brought me luck. The last time I had

194

received such flowers I'd also had a phone call from Bumper Lee.

'I hope you are feeling better,' Portia said.

'Actually I'm feeling worse. I think the angels of mercy have started me on withdrawal.'

'Time to bite the bullet,' Portia smiled.

'And I thought I'd just gotten rid of it.'

'You'll be okay.' Portia reassured me, in a way that made me think she'd been shot before too. She turned towards Nebraska who was studying the hospital linoleum.

'I've got to go check the meter. I'll wait for you in the car,' Portia said. 'Goodbye, Miss Victor. I hope you have a speedy recovery.' Not speedy enough to come into my neighbourhood again, she was thinking. Then she left the room in a swirl of white rayon and the slap of sandals against the hospital floor, and I was alone with the fallen star.

'Emma, I wanted to talk to you,' Nebraska came closer and put a hand on mine. She was wearing dotted organdie gloves. The little dots were flocked and black; I could feel the texture on my hand. I wasn't wearing gloves. I'd opted for an intravenous line that season.

'I'm not sure my stars are in alignment for this. You should have come two days ago. I was stoned to the gills and not feeling much of anything.'

'I need to let go of everything that's happened,' she whined. Her purple cellophaned hairdo moved as she shook her head.

'I'll bet.'

'Don't you see how difficult this has all been for me?'

'Then why am I lying in a hospital bed and you're swinging your pageboy around?'

Nebraska's hand clenched the freesias. She wasn't doing any of us much good.

'I like your gloves. Did you wear them to Vishnu's funeral?' I asked. 'Or was Vishnu's funeral another party like the one they threw for Lana? Doesn't anything get too complicated for you people?'

'I'm afraid I'm not exactly welcome within the ranks of their family any more.' Nebraska dropped her head and expensive hair hid her pinched face.

'I'm not surprised. I'm not so happy to see you in my hospital room either.'

'Let me explain it to you, Emma,' Nebraska bit her lip. 'Please.'

'Okay. I could do with a good story. Go on and pull up a chair.'

Nebraska threw the freesias in the sink and got a moulded plastic chair. She dragged it over the linoleum to my bed. My roommate behind the curtain groaned. I could tell that Nebraska wasn't used to pulling up chairs for herself, but she didn't have any trouble sitting on them. She sighed. She fiddled with her gloves, pulling at the fingers slightly and then smoothing them back on. When she'd finally finished with her digitals she began.

'You have no idea what life used to be like for me years ago, when I was finally, really making it. No more hauling amplifiers, worrying about the rent. I was there. I was giving everything I had on stage and I was getting it all back in spades.' She leaned back and a sparkle came into her eyes. 'It was marvellous. A love affair with the public. Imagine, my songs, my clothes, even my earrings were making headlines.'

'Sounds awful,' I mumbled, but she wasn't listening.

'The whole world was watching me. And I knew there were millions of people who loved me.'

'And Edwin Anvil?'

'What do you want me to say? That I killed him?' she spluttered.

'Say anything you want to. But you can hold the steam that's coming out under your collar. I can't have been the first person who's asked you that question.'

'Who kills anybody when you're part of a drug tribe, Emma? You follow the same ritual over and over again. You do it with each other. You do it for yourself. You get the same results every time. Well,' she conceded, 'almost every time.'

'You mean some people overdose.'

'Yes, Edwin overdosed. And I was holding the needle. It's like it happened yesterday. I can see it all in front of me.' She hung her head and started fixating on the linoleum again.

'That must have been tough,' I said. 'You must have been scared. So you made a deal with the DA to infiltrate the Vishnus.'

'The DA? We had the Feds and Interpol in on it too.'

'Yow,' I let out a breath. 'That is impressive.' I looked at the rock star with the only respect I'd ever felt for her.

'It was after the indictment. And yes, my main ambition was to beat the rap. That was all I could think about. That and trying to stay out of prison. And I did have to get clean. At least for a while. So it seemed a good idea to pretend to be part of the Vishnu family.' She shrugged.

'Did the DA pay the bills?' I said, imagining the house calls from Interpol.

'Sure.'

'Our tax dollars at work. Don't they have anything better to do? Didn't you have anything better to do?'

'Well, I had to save my neck, didn't I?' she spluttered. 'It was about all I had left. So, okay, I went into the deal with a bad attitude. I was just waiting to clean up and get high afterwards. I enjoyed myself there. The fresh air and the good food worked wonders for me. And eventually I stopped missing dope. That was after I met Vishnu. And he was giving me darshan.'

'I hear he gives great darshan. Go on.'

'It was like coming home, Emma. I can't explain it. I can't put it into words. Vishnu made everything clear to me. He brought me above the mere struggle of kicking drugs, above common existence. He took my music up to a higher plane too.'

I wasn't going to say anything about the audience response to her musical metamorphosis. I didn't mention the disappointment that had led her behind the tent after the show either.

'So you went into the Commune for the DA. And you came out a disciple.'

'It's happened before. Undercover agents sympathising with the world they're trying to infiltrate. I may have just been looking out to save my own neck, but I'm human too,' she said defensively.

'And so was Vishnu, living the life of royalty. So it was the case of the counterfeit convert.' My leg throbbed as Nebraska shot me a nasty look. It was like all the other nasty looks I'd gotten from Vishnus for being sacrilegious. It didn't scare me a lot. 'And you were still making reports to the DA?'

'They knew about Sadhima from the start. I was supposed to hang out until he'd set up his operation in the States. After a while it didn't seem like that would interfere with my spiritual path.

197

After all, Vishnu wouldn't have approved either. He was totally against drug use.'

'How clean of him. So you saved your neck.'

'And I lost Vishnu.'

'He died of natural causes. Lana Flax didn't.'

'It's not my fault that she didn't cover her own bases. She wasn't just blindly devoted to Vishnu, she was just blind. I didn't ask her to come snooping around. She was always so possessive of Vishnu, so parochial and pure about what went on at the commune. The whole thing would have worked out fine if she hadn't interfered.'

'What do you mean?'

'Mean? The whole thing was in the bag that day. There I was, alone in the basement with Sadhima. I was sure I could turn Sadhima over and remain at the commune. After I'd donated the beachfront property, I thought I would win the eternal gratitude of the family. I thought I would never be turned away after that. So I was almost home safe.'

'And the taping was set up for the day of the party?'

'It was the perfect moment. I'd made my big donation, Sadhima was feeling solid after his performance as the potent Krishna.'

'And you knew he'd want to consolidate his power with yours?'

'Right. He wasn't into Bumper or Lailieka. Not to mention a Goody Two-Shoes like Lana. He invited me down to his basement quarters. It was just a matter of saying that I was a little tired. A certain tone when you ask for a little pick-me-up gets you just the right offer.'

'So he brought out some coke.'

'Sure. And after that we were buddies. Common communion. I had my microphone ready and I got what I needed to get me free from the DA and the Anvil rap for ever. Sadhima told me about his drug routes, different ways he had of smuggling. He seemed proud of it, he was laughing, smiling at how perfect it all was. He almost seemed to enjoy thinking he could put something over on Vishnu too. That made me really want to nail him.'

'And Lana got caught in the crossfire.'

'I had just finished with Sadhima. I could feel the miniature tape recorder tucked in my bra and I couldn't wait to go home and take it out and put it somewhere safe. Portia knew I'd been doing all this and she couldn't wait for it to be over either.

'I opened the door to leave Sadhima's room,' Nebraska went on, 'and I saw Lana standing there. I took one look at her face and I knew she'd heard it all. She just stood there, accusing me with her eyes. She didn't know I'd been taping the whole thing.'

'You didn't try and warn her?'

'No. Listen, it wasn't my fault that that idiot was peeping through keyholes. I remembered thinking, "Sadhima is behind me; maybe he hasn't seen her and I can just get out of here." I closed the door quickly. I left Lana standing there with the information contorting her face. Talk about naive! She even followed me up the stairs and tried to scare me with those accusing self-righteous eyes. I hoped she had the good sense not to confront Sadhima or rat on him. It was going to spoil all the plans for the bust.'

'You've got a big heart, Nebraska. But apparently he did see her, or she did confront him?'

'Yes, that would be her style. She was long on righteousness and short on common sense.'

'I'm sick of your complaining about Lana, Nebraska. You saved your own neck and she died for it. And everything's turned out just fine for you, hasn't it? No, self-sacrifice isn't your style. But negligent manslaughter is. And you fault Lana for lack of common sense? I don't see a lot of common sense or humanity in your actions. Or anywhere in Vishnu territory.'

'I feel sorry that you're here in the hospital.'

'Don't waste your sympathy. I arranged this for myself, thank you. And Lana didn't screw up your bust, I did.'

'I forgive you,' Nebraska said earnestly. I almost laughed. A hard knotty pain was starting to develop in my thigh.

'I'll pick you up and drive you home, when you're ready to leave here,' she offered. I shuddered. She was the kind of woman I'd like to hold a cross up to.

'No thanks.' The pain in my leg was increasing.

'Have it your own way,' Nebraska said, almost huffily. But then she reached over and patted my hand with the flocked spotted gloves. I couldn't put my hand away without dislodging the IV line. Her eyes melted with tears. Her relationship with herself had touched her deeply. I closed my eyes. I was getting a clear image of what a bullet hole could do to muscle.

'Visiting hours are over,' said a nurse who popped into the room. He gave us an exaggerated wink, misjudging the level of intimacy I had with Nebraska. Usually it was swell being in the homo-erotic atmosphere of Northern California. I started to do a warm fade.

Nebraska stood up and dragged the plastic chair back over the floor. My invisible roommate groaned again from the other side of his or her curtain.

'Good luck to you, Emma.' She smiled in a way that seemed to tie up the whole package for her. I didn't bother to reply. Apparently even shallow confession was good for the soul. But what else could I expect? Nebraska Storm had the integrity of a Presto log.

But she turned to look at me one last time. It was a long moment. Then she floated out of the door and I floated away.

Thirty-four

Three days later I went home from the hospital. They released me late in the day, not being able to decide earlier if I needed another blood test, or another sleepless night in the perpetually wakeful institution. I was glad when Roseanna Baynetta picked me up and took me home with her.

It was late by the time we got to the alfalfa farm. Roseanna turned on the lights as we entered the small wooden bungalow with the plasterboard walls. I could see a field of alfalfa stretching out into the darkness outside a picture window that took up a wall in the living room. We rolled and limped across the room together, three out of four legs useless between us, and got into the big bed in her bedroom.

'I'm not sexually attracted to you, Emma Victor,' Roseanna warned me with a possible wink. We undressed, removing clothes from our limp limbs with the ones that still moved and functioned. We got on the bed and put our assorted legs under the covers.

'I know,' I said, lying. I had no idea, any more, if Roseanna was sexually attracted to me. I had no idea if I was sexually attracted to her. I had the feeling we were beyond all that, but maybe it was just another workable illusion I was entertaining. I got up again and took a plastic bag that said Emergency Room from the cradle of Roseanna's leather wheelchair seat and limped to the bathroom. I brushed my teeth and washed my face. When I returned I put the bag next to the bed. I carefully put my bandaged leg under the covers again. Roseanna reached up, switched off the overhead light and turned on a small aluminium-capped bedside lamp that was clamped on to the headboard. I saw that I had one too.

Roseanna opened a book and I reached into the bag to pick up yesterday's paper. It held no surprises.

CULT LEADER TO HAVE FUNERAL 'CELEBRATION'

Bu Mper Lee, spokeswoman for the Divine Inspiration Commune, revealed that Vishnu, the cult leader, had died of natural causes earlier this week. The county coroner has confirmed a heart attack to be the cause of death and has released his body to the members of the group who plan a massive funeral celebration.

'It's going to be an unforgettable send-off,' the red-headed spokeswoman promised.

But would Vishnu remember, I wondered. He was immutably dead, only good for pushing up ikebana flower arrangements and inspiring an overflow of haiku poetry among the faithful. A lot of disgruntled commune members wouldn't be thrilled with Nebraska Storm, but I supposed they wouldn't care for long. Many of the yellow folk would be busy trying to rejoin the fragmented world they had left to join Vishnu. Or maybe they would just try to invent another god as quickly as possible.

I heard Roseanna's breathing become heavier and I reached over and turned off the light above her head, looking down at the face unguarded in sleep. I kissed her. I reached back into the plastic bag, pulling the gauze bandage on my leg and causing myself to grunt in pain. My leg kept on throbbing as I took out the mail that Roseanna had so thoughtfully picked up from my house and brought with her to the hospital.

I tried to open the envelopes quietly, looking over to see if I was disturbing Roseanna. Her breathing didn't change. The mail contained mixed blessings. I found my first California phone bill which included installation charges, a cheque for fifteen hundred dollars and a note that said, 'Best Wishes,' from Willie Rossini and finally, a letter from Boston. Frances had written to say that she had found a new girlfriend. Suddenly my leg didn't hurt any more. I turned out the light and lay alone with myself in the darkness. Eventually I fell asleep. Much later I woke up with a start, feeling that many things had changed. I read four in the morning on the face of a digital clock and I was right, things had changed and I was alone in the bed. Roseanna was gone.

I got up and limped past the place where her chair had been parked. I dragged my leg into the living room. Silhouetted in the picture window I saw the outline of a wheelchair and a woman sitting in it, head thrown back. The alfalfa, pale gold in the darkened field, shone like an abstract painting behind her. I coughed and slowly the head turned towards me.

'Yes?' she said quietly.

'Are you okay?'

'I was having some pain,' she explained, and then she answered my unasked question. 'I'm meditating,' she said.

'Okay.' I went back to the bedroom and sat on the edge of Roseanna's bed. I glanced over at the letters I had opened before taking so long to fall asleep. I stood back up and drew on a terry cloth bathrobe that was hanging on a peg on the back of the door. The bathrobe came about four inches above my knee to the bandage with the round yellow spot in the middle. I limped into the hallway and opened the screen door. I sat on the wooden ramp in front of Roseanna's house and thought about all the reasons why a person could move to California. The doctor had promised me that I could play tennis in three months. There was a waning moon and the night air was soft and kind. I looked up at the stars and saw two of them fall. The rest of them just sat there.